# THE BREAK-UP ARTIST

# THE BREAK-UP ARTIST

Philip Siegel

Recycling programs for this product may not exist in your area.

ISBN-13: 978-0-373-21115-9

THE BREAK-UP ARTIST



This edition published by arrangement with Harlequin Books S.A.

For questions and comments about the quality of this book, please contact us at CustomerService@Harlequin.com.

**Printed in U.S.A.**

For Mom, Dad, and Steph—
my first fan club.

# A WARNING TO ALL WHO READ THIS

Couples are made to be broken.

That's what my sister, Diane, told me when I started my business, and she knows better than anyone. "Don't get duped like I did, Becca," she said almost a year ago, as she shoved her wedding dress into a garbage bag. She'd had it designed to look like Kate Middleton's, lace sleeves and everything. It's a shame nobody saw her wear it.

We all like to think that there's one person out there who will rescue us from the tower, slide the glass slipper onto our foot, brush away our one falling tear and tell us if there's six more weeks of winter. Or something like that. But that's not how the real world works. Just ask the cheating boyfriends and girlfriends I have to deal with on a far-too-regular basis.

Back in olden times, people were up front about why they took the plunge. For land, for money, for children. Marriage was a business contract. That's how it started, anyway. Farmers would marry off their sons and daughters in order to double their acreage. Society's first corporate merger. Next were dowries, where brides came with a down payment. But history, as it always happens, was rewritten. The truth was washed away like a house in a flood, and in its place sprouted one vague excuse: love.

People use that word to go around and do what they please. They don't have to worry about who gets hurt because it's all in the name of love. Love has no rules, no boundaries. It's gone all these years unchecked. That doesn't make it whimsical; that makes it a tyrant.

I may not be an angel in all this, but I'm certainly not the bad guy either. If you can't handle my line of work, then go read the latest bodice ripper. I'll leave you with this: How many lives have been ruined because of love?

Who's really the bad guy here?

# 1

Calista McTiernan looks away from the screen. Tears form in her eyes. The levee's about to break. I wish I could reach through my computer monitor and give her a hug. I hear these stories too often.

"Ever since they started dating, Bari's become a totally different person. Derek's favorite band is U2, and now magically it's hers, too. Derek is into politics, and now Bari is watching CNN religiously. I laughed it off because she acted this way with her last boyfriend. But then..." Calista shakes her head.

"But then what?" I ask in my best British accent, looking directly into my webcam.

"Then she dyed her hair brown, she started dressing like some J. Crew mannequin, and this week she quit cheerleading." Her blond locks fan around her pea-sized head. Her hair's the same shade as mine, but hers is real.

"People change. It happens."

"Yeah, but this isn't the same. Derek's making her do this. He told her he thinks blondes are trashy, and he didn't want some slutty cheerleader girlfriend visiting him at Princeton next year. He said that. To her face!"

"He did?" Derek Kelley has been student council president for three years, and what little power the Student Government Association—aka the SGA—holds has gone to his head. He seems friendly in the halls, but guys are just as capable of being fake nice as girls.

"Bari said he was joking around, but I'm not laughing."

"Have you tried talking to her about it?" I can already guess the answer.

"She says she isn't into cheerleading anymore and she's never felt like a blonde." Calista rubs her forehead, and I can feel her concern through the screen. "Everything that made her Bari is disappearing."

I lean closer in my chair, all business, and hold Calista's attention. "So, you want me to do this?"

Calista squeezes a fresh set of tears from her eyes. I instinctively reach for the Kleenex box on my desk, forgetting we're on Skype. "My best friend is pushing me away. You don't know what that's like."

*I do,* I want to tell her. My eyes wander to the floor and the pair of golden ballet slippers next to my desk. *It's like a hole through your heart that can never be filled.* A part of you that is missing forever. I should throw the slippers out like I've done with the rest of my memories from that train wreck of a friendship, but I won't. I never do. I keep them here, in plain sight, a perpetual reminder of why I do this.

I force my attention back to the screen. I can never get

personal. One misspoken word, one accidental truth, and I give myself away.

"I told her I didn't think Derek was treating her well," Calista says.

"And what did she say?"

Calista stares at the screen, her bottom lip quivering. Only the hissing of her radiator fills my speaker.

"She said, 'You just don't understand because you're single.'" Tears stream down Calista's cheeks. She buries her face in her knee to compose herself.

I clench my lips together. I have to remind myself to stay strong for my client. She can fall apart, but I have to make things right. Blood rushes to my face in frustration, coloring me the same shade as this shapeless graduation robe I'm wearing.

Calista continues, "I feel like if Derek had his way, she'd never talk to any of her friends again. Especially me."

My raccoon mask conceals my raised eyebrows. I've seen Bari and Calista joined at the hip since elementary school. They once tried convincing our classmates that they were cousins. (I fell for it.) They seemed to have one of those über-tight friendship bonds that I thought would survive the dating world. Then again, I'd thought I had that, too. But now I know that once people get into relationships, friends—and rational thought—get tossed aside.

"It's a good thing you came to me," I say.

"You seriously can break them up?"

"I have a perfect track record."

"How?"

"My methods are proprietary and confidential."

"What does that mean?"

"It means I'm really, really good, and you'll just have to trust me." I catch my reflection in the screen. I'm shocked anyone's been able to take me seriously in this disguise. I look like an escaped mental patient, but that's better than looking like myself. Luckily, my work speaks for itself.

"It's not going to be easy. I think they've already said 'I love you' to each other."

"I'll take my chances," I say. Why do my classmates believe that saying those three words automatically protects a couple? They're not relationship insurance. They're just words, and if people actually meant them, then I would be out of a job. Bari and Derek are a couple destined for flame out. I'm just speeding up the inevitable. And if I can save Bari before she's permanently under Derek's thumb, so much the better.

"Before we go forward, I want you to be certain about this."

She gets so quiet I can hear the static crackling in the background. "I—I don't know."

"A minute ago you were devastated."

"I know. But..." Calista hugs her chopstick legs into her chest. I wonder if she's one of those girls who stays skinny no matter how much she eats. "This seems kind of severe. I don't know, and maybe a little petty, too?"

I clench my jaw. "When was the last time she called or texted you just to say hi?"

Calista ponders this. She shrugs her shoulder.

"So you think it's fair that she's cutting you out of her life? Just because she has a boyfriend?" I ask calmly.

“No. But Derek—”

“Derek hasn’t mastered the art of mind control. She’s choosing all of this. To disappear. To change. To stop being friends with you. It’d be nice if Bari suddenly came to her senses, but that’s not going to happen, and you know it,” I say. Blunt, but not untrue. “So now here’s where *you* choose—are you going to let her continue on this path uninterrupted or are you going to do something about it?”

“So you really will break them up?” she asks between sniffles.

“For a hundred dollars via PayPal I can.” The wheels begin turning in my head. I flash Calista a warm smile, telling her I got this. Maybe I can salvage this friendship. No girl should have to live through a best friend cutting her out of her life.

Her face brightens among the red splotches, and she smiles for the first time tonight. “Let’s do it.”

# 2

My mom still makes me a peanut-butter-and-jelly sandwich every morning. It was the only thing I ate for breakfast when I was in elementary school, and she stuck with it. Now that I'm older, I found my ideal get-up-and-get-'em meal: a large cup of coffee. Black, no sugar.

Sharp rays of morning sun pierce through the kitchen windows. My dad sits at the table with his coffee and oatmeal, watching a guy shout on TV. Apparently, the fluctuation of Chinese currency can make some people quite flustered. My mom hands me a cup of coffee, and I push aside the sandwich with my mug. She picks it up and takes a bite. And so goes our morning routine.

"Busy day today?" my mom asks.

"Kinda." I have a new couple to break up. Oh, and I have a math quiz. "Where's Diane?"

My mom heaves a sigh, then gives me a look like I should know better. "Still sleeping."

Which I should've known, but I hold out hope that one day the answer will be better. My dad shakes his head and mutters to himself.

"Hey," my mom says to my dad after taking another bite of my former breakfast. "Why did you get one-ply toilet paper last night?"

"It was on sale," he says, his focus returning to Chinese currency.

"You couldn't spring for two-ply?"

"Not if it's not on sale."

"We don't live in a tenement."

"More like a Turkish prison," he says with a half smile.

She rolls her eyes and takes a bite of the sandwich. My dad eats a few more spoonfuls of oatmeal then gets up. He puts on his suit jacket, then his winter coat. He kisses me goodbye, and gives my mom a pat on the shoulder while she wipes down the counter. It's like this every day, every year, the same motions. Way to keep the romance alive, guys. If it was ever even there to begin with.

My dad pauses at the door, and for a second I wonder if he's going to pick my mom up in a hug and plant one on her, like lovey-dovey parents in a cheesy sitcom.

"I'll be on the 5:57 train tonight. I'll just pick up a roast-beef sandwich at the station for dinner," he says.

"Okay," my mom says, washing out his oatmeal bowl in the sink.

Yep. So much for love.

Before I break up a couple, I have to do my research and examine their dating history. I have to know their past if I want to understand their present. Having a significant other will put any student at Ashland High School on the social radar, and chances are if you're in a relationship, someone else is talking about it.

In history class, I use the middle section of my three-subject notebook to build a dating dossier on Bari and Derek, tucked in between U.S. history and trig. I don't like to build dossiers when one of my targets is two rows over from me, but she's so engrossed in texting someone (let's be real: Derek), she won't even notice. Nothing our teacher Mr. Harrison says elicits a reaction from her. Bari clutches her phone against her stomach, as if waiting for the next message to inject her with another ounce of life.

Usually, I'm able to list off a person's past relationships from memory.

Bari Mandell

Dating History:

- Joey Pollaro: fall freshman–spring freshman.[1]
  - Joey—JV basketball. Bari—freshman cheerleading. Equivalent caste. Presumably met through games and parties.
  - PDA Level = HIGH[2]
    - Regularly held hands in hall.
    - Ample kissing and petting in public.

---

1 I only have rough time periods of when two people began dating. Not exact dates. That would be weird. It's not like I know them personally.

2 Based on a scale from LOW–SEVERE that I copied from the Department of Homeland Security website.

    - Rumors of having sex in the bathroom at Matt Wachtel's party.
  - The dumper = Joey
    - Break-up occurred over Spring Break. He "just wasn't feeling it anymore," according to Nneka Jeffries.
    - He began dating Courtney Liu over the summer.

Derek Kelley

Dating History:

- Tessa Colletti: summer junior–fall senior
  - Tessa—volleyball jock, so-so student. Derek—cross-country, in all AP classes. Began dating while life-guarding at Munsee Lake.
  - PDA Level = ELEVATED
    - Kept a low profile in school, but were all over each other at games and parties and at the lake.[3]
  - The dumper = Derek
    - He wanted to focus on college applications, according to Bryn Levin.
- Bethann Mancuso: winter sophomore–spring junior
  - AP power couple. Ran against each other for student council president.
  - PDA Level = GUARDED
    - Some quick kisses before/after class.
    - He always ate lunch with his arm around her.
  - The dumper = Derek
    - Broke up because of natural causes?

3 Derek looks really cute without a shirt on.

Bari's dating history is straightforward. When a guy on the basketball team asks out a lowly freshman, it's hard to turn him down. That was almost two years ago, though. I find it surprising that Bari went boyfriendless for that long. She's what every guy wants: petite, skinny but curvy (the good kind). But amid the fierce competition for coupledom, that doesn't always cut it.

Ashland High has an overabundance of girls. It's a sixty-five, thirty-five split, the biggest gap of any school in New Jersey. Something must've been in the water fifteen years ago, give or take. This gives guys a huge advantage. They can be fat, lazy and pimply and still get to be choosy. Finding a suitable guy to date is a study in Darwinism. Survival of the hottest. The options dwindle with each year. Upperclassman girls don't date freshman guys in some unspoken, outdated and totally gender-biased rule. Lelaina Ryder went out with Troy Hawke for two months last year and received an endless barrage of cougar jokes until she graduated. No wonder Bari jumped at the chance to be with Derek. He's a definite catch. He's one of the few guys at Ashland who is both smart *and* cute. He has ins with most cliques in school. Half the auditorium swoons at his sparkly smile and wavy hair during student government assemblies.

Spend five minutes talking to him, though, and you'll notice how many times he manages to slip "Princeton early decision" into conversation and how hard he worked to scrub his voice of his New Jersey accent in favor of some affected, faux-aristocratic inflection.

His break-up with Bethann was felt throughout the AP hallway, where they had a mini fan club. They told their classmates that their relationship had run its course, but I'll never forget overhearing Bethann talking to her friends a few weeks before the break-up. She'd done better than she thought on her SATs and had decided to apply to Princeton. The girls, and even some guys, swooned at the prospect of Derek and Bethann going to the same Ivy League college, getting married and then popping out smart babies a few years later. I glanced at Derek, who was smiling like the rest of them. But he had this despondent look in his eyes, almost like dread. I was the only one who wasn't that surprised about their split. I guess Derek couldn't stomach Bethann being as smart as him. Tessa was a step down in that department, but at least she was off to University of California, San Diego, in the fall.

I wonder if he likes Bari because he knows he's smarter than her. I wonder if she minds.

I glance over at my target, who has taken a brief rest from her phone. She smushes together two paper hole reinforcements and slides the result onto her left ring finger. She gazes at her fake ring with stars in her eyes, clearly forgetting for a moment that it's a piece of plastic worth three cents. It's never too early to start planning your wedding, I guess, though I hope she hasn't booked a band yet.

Mr. Harrison ends class a few minutes early. As I shove

my notebook in my backpack, a paper football falls out of the trig section. I unfold the football and instantly roll my eyes when I see what it says: I NEED A BOY!!

# 3

I wait for the note writer outside her locker. I hear her cheerful voice booming from down the hall. Val—never Valerie—is midconversation with a classmate; her green eyes light up when she sees me. She has bright blond hair and a smile on her face even when she's upset, which is rare. Her childhood pudginess is slowly morphing into a more mature figure, but she dresses herself well to hide any trouble spots. Right now, she's all about blazers.

I hold up the note and raise my eyebrows; she hangs her head. We both bust out laughing. Yet more proof that I have a really weird best friend.

I crumple the note up and toss it into the trash. "You love cutting to the chase, don't you?"

"If I can't say that to you, then who can I say it to?" she says.

"Nobody else, I hope." More classmates funnel into the hall, pushing against us. "Ready for lunch?"

Val makes her midday book exchange at her locker. She only carries two books and a notebook with her at one time. According to her unofficial research, this makes her appear studious yet willing to have fun. Carrying three books is nerdy. They are hard to hold in one arm, and she would die of embarrassment if she spilled them in the hall. Val refuses to wear a backpack. They don't suit her, she claims.

We cut through swaths of students en route to the cafeteria. "I hope you don't truly feel that way," I say.

"What way?"

"That you *need* a boy. You don't need a boy. The only things you need are oxygen, food, water and a dozen pairs of shoes."

"I know, I know." She waves her hand, cutting me off. She won't listen when I'm right, but she won't refute me either. "So PB&J was a bust. None of my prongs worked."

"Not even prong three?"

"Nope. When I invited him over to do homework, I didn't expect him to actually do homework!"

Val had a three-pronged plan to make Patrick Burroughs Jr., aka PB&J, fall for her. Prong one was to switch lab partners so that they'd work together. Prong two was to download some of his favorite music and casually listen to it during lab, piquing his interest. Prong three was to invite him over to work on the write-ups together, with the music setting the mood in the background. I tried telling her that she and he were too different. He's very serious—buzz cut, steely eyes, always talking in short, terse sentences—and she's fun and bubbly. Her opposites-attract theory did not pan out. But she was dead set on this. She even made charts.

"He smelled so good, too," she says, letting out a ginormous sigh. She checks the time on her phone. "And because of Michigan, aka Evan Lansing, I have like a hundred more captions for the stupid yearbook to write by Friday. Note to self—never join a club to meet a guy again."

I nudge her elbow. "Hey, it's his loss."

"And his yearbook's gain."

"In ten years, all he'll have in his life is that overpriced photo album, and he'll be clinging to it in an alley and whispering your name to himself."

Val gives me a strange look.

"Was that too creepy?" Some girls are highly adept at giving the cheer-up talk. Even if they know what they're saying is 100 percent well-worn cliché, it still manages to brighten their friends' moods. I am not blessed with that skill. But maybe if Val stopped making the search for "True Love" her main mission in life, she would have more luck.

A cacophony of conversation bounces off the walls in the cafeteria, a hotbed of gossip. Stories and social reputations are getting confirmed, denied or shared, information traded as if it's the floor of the New York Stock Exchange.

Val and I put down our books and my backpack at our table and head to the lunch line. A loud, perky yelp comes from the entrance, and we swivel around to watch the daily yuckfest. Steve Overland carries Huxley Mapother through the double doors, past admiring subjects and adoring lunch aides. After four years, I've gotten quite good at ignoring them, making myself forget that I ever had a past with Huxley. But Calista's tear-streaked face flashes in my mind, and suddenly I'm back in the middle-school cafeteria, watching

Huxley abandon me to sit with Steve, refusing to make eye contact. Nothing is more definitive than lunchroom seating.

"Excuse us." Addison, Huxley's friend and lieutenant colonel, shoves me aside, creating a wide path for the couple. I rub my shoulder. Just because she said it nicely doesn't mean it was a friendly push.

Steve sets Huxley down at their corner lunch table, the one bathed in natural light at which all students must crane their necks to gander. They are a sight to behold, a *Seventeen* photo shoot live in our school. Huxley hides her face in embarrassment, lightly slapping Steve on his broad shoulder. But I can detect the pure delight radiating from her olive skin as she soaks in the stares of her kingdom.

"They are so cute," Val says with an added *aww*.

"They probably rehearsed that all weekend. And why is he wearing his football jersey in March?"

Val leans against the wall and takes a breath. She's tired, and not from our walk.

"I need a boy."

"You want one. But you don't need one."

"Want, need. You say tomato, I say ketchup." We each put a premade grilled-chicken salad on our tray. Val grabs two Diet Cokes from the cooler. "I want to do couple-y things. I want someone to walk to class with, and a guy who'll be waiting for me at my locker and text me when I wake up saying he had a dream about me. And I don't care how that makes me sound because it's you, and no matter what I say, you're contractually obligated to be my friend."

"So you just want a boyfriend to show off in school? Flash him around like the new Cynthia Swann bag?"

It never bothers me when Val complains about wanting a boyfriend, which does happen often. It's my duty as a best friend to listen and bite my tongue. I want her to be happy, even if having a boyfriend ultimately won't achieve that. I know she'd never ditch me like Bari ditched Calista. She's a real friend.

"That *is* a nice bag," she says.

"They sell really nice knockoffs of them by my dad's office. I couldn't tell the difference."

"Becca Williamson, don't you dare. Do you really want to settle for a knockoff over the real thing? Don't make me wash your mouth out with off-brand soap."

"Fine. You're right. No fakes for me."

We laugh and fantasize about that Cynthia Swann bag. After I break up Bari and Derek, I'll be able to buy it. I'll just tell Val I pooled together multiple birthday and Christmas checks from my grandparents.

"Five ten," the cashier says to Val.

Val hands her a five and rummages through her bag for some change. Her face flips to a deep-hued red. Avoiding any type of humiliation in the cafeteria is essential. "Do you have a dime?" she asks me, but I'm already searching my pockets and coming up empty.

The lunch lady starts ringing me up, leaving Val to continue her frantic search. "Do you got it or not?" It's like the cashier's voice is engineered to be loud and maximize embarrassment.

"I have it," a guy says from behind me in a deep radio-deejay voice. Ezra Drummond and his puff of black hair waltz up to the register with two nickels.

"Thank you so much!" Val says.

"My pleasure. I couldn't let a fellow student starve...or go without caffeine."

"And they say chivalry is dead."

"I don't think anything under a quarter can be considered chivalry, per se."

"Uh-huh." Val's gift for gab goes missing.

I pay for my meal and step out of line, waiting for Val to join me.

"Thanks again." Val speed walks to our table. I scurry to catch up, making sure I don't spill or hit anyone.

"So I totally got a vibe from Ezra," she says. She does the 1-2-3-look as he makes his way back to his pack of theater friends.

"That was really nice of him."

"That was more than nice. You have to admit, there was definitely some kind of vibe there."

Ezra's a generally friendly guy. We randomly had a bunch of electives together sophomore year, and he still gives me a nod when we pass each other in uncrowded corridors. I shrug my shoulders. "I don't know." I don't have the energy to go this path with Val. I'm hungry.

But we can't eat just yet.

We reach our table to find it dotted with comic books and Capri Suns, and instead of empty chairs awaiting us, we have three scrawny guys.

"Hi." That's the first word I've said to Fred Teplitzky and his patch of acne in about six years. "Um, we were sitting here."

"We saved your seats." The other two guys, Quentin Yao and Howard Langman, pat the chairs next to them. Is this a date ambush?

"Can you please move your magazines?" Val asks. They grab their comic books away from Val's incoming lunch tray.

Fred jumps out of my chair. I'm face-to-face with his beaming smile and surprisingly straight teeth. Props to his orthodontist. "Listen, there were some fisticuffs at our usual table, and we need a new home. We could all squeeze and make it work here."

*"Fisticuffs?"* I ask. When was the last time somebody used *that* word?

"We went to sit at our table today, but it was taken by the D'Agostino twins and their girlfriends," Fred says, nodding his head to the table. Lucy Dorsett and Gina Janetti are snuggled in with equally ripped John and Jack. "We tried to tell them that we've been sitting there since September, but they aren't the type of guys to listen to reason. They have those arm-chain tattoos."

"Don't they usually spend their lunch period smoking in the parking lot?" I had to sit next to Lucy in sixth period last year, and I almost died of secondhand smoke.

"I guess they wanted to add more fiber to their diet," Fred says.

"There's a table by the kitchen," Val says. She firmly believes that you are who you sit with, and sharing a table with these guys—even though they're all nice guys—will not help her social profile.

"It smells like lard and grease over there," Quentin says.

"Invest in potpourri."

Val turns to me for solidarity. I can't tell the D'Agostino twins apart, but they each have their right arm around their girlfriend. I never noticed how many couples populate the cafeteria. Why do they get to dictate the seating chart? You never hear of a gaggle of girls or a group of guys evicting a twosome from their table.

"It's fine," I say. "Join us."

Val shoots me a nasty look, but before she can say anything, I whisper into her ear: "I think Ezra and Fred are friends, or friendlyish."

Val's face lights up and she reverts to her 1-2-3-look.

"Really? We had speech class together freshman year, and he was always really nice. Hmm...Ezra Drummond." Val smiles to herself. She's coming dangerously close to a neck cramp. "And the hemp choker necklace really brings out the hazel in his eyes...."

If I have to spend a lunch period listening to people talk about crushes and comic books, my head may explode.

"Whoa, they're eating each other alive!" Quentin points to Derek and Bari at a side table. His mouth swallows her tongue whole. His hands dig into her hips.

PDA = HIGH.

They stand and stroll up to the garbage cans with their trash, holding hands and keeping one eye on each other the whole time. Calista eats with other cheerleaders, but isn't engaging with them. The newly minted couple pass Calista's table, completely oblivious to the loneliness in her eyes. Bari could probably decipher Calista's exact mood with one glance, if she'd only pay her friend a speck of attention.

I glance across the cafeteria and watch my former best friend have the lunch period of her life. Huxley nestles her head against Steve's shoulder. She doesn't even notice I'm staring.

# 4

My English teacher Ms. Hardwick is one of the youngest teachers at Ashland, and as coach of the cheerleading squad, she likes to think she's one of the girls. My parents thought she was a student when they met her. They couldn't believe she taught honors English. So it's difficult to take her seriously when she discusses Shakespeare.

"Okay, guys," she says, taking a seat on her desk. "You should've all finished *Romeo and Juliet* over the weekend. So let's discuss. What did you guys think? Wasn't it super sad at the end?"

Shana Wigand raises her hand. "I found the themes of forcefulness of love and the inevitability of fate to be the most captivating."

"Now, Shana. I asked everyone to read *R and J,* not Wikipedia. C'mon, guys. Give me your honest feedback. We all know this story in one form or another."

Silence.

Ms. Hardwick smacks her lips together. They're soaked in red lipstick. "Anyone? Don't be shy."

"I thought they were so romantic," another classmate says.

I know that voice. That calm, cold voice in the center of the room weighted down with unbridled confidence.

"Huxley, care to elaborate?" Ms. Hardwick asks.

Huxley sits up straight, refusing to slouch like us common folk. There always seems to be a spotlight on her olive skin and cascading brown hair, straight out of a shampoo commercial. She'll make a perfect senator's wife one day, and she knows it.

"Their love was passionate and intense, but quiet and delicate at the same time. It was...beautiful." Huxley says her words slowly, since nobody will dare interrupt her.

"Nicely put," Ms. Hardwick says. A tidal wave of nods flows across the room. Even Greg Baylor and his jock crew in the corner agree.

"It was so amazing. Even reading the synopsis gave me chills," Shana says, not missing an opportunity to score brownie points with Huxley. And the teacher, too.

"They were the pinnacle of true love," Huxley says. Does she realize that 90 percent of what she utters is straight-up cliché? Probably, but the class eats it up anyway.

I roll my eyes. Killing yourself because you can't date someone seems a tad overdramatic.

"Care to comment?" Ms. Hardwick asks someone. Then I realize she's looking at me. Now so is the whole class.

"What?" I ask, my palms slick with sweat.

"You don't seem to agree."

"I don't know." Maybe if I give bland answers, she'll let me go back to blending in with the class. Why is everyone staring at me? Please go back to texting, writing notes, staring out the window. Anything else.

"Are you sure, Becca?"

I shake my head yes. I choose to risk my participation grade and keep my mouth shut. They don't want a second opinion. They prefer the first one.

"It's okay, Rebecca," Huxley says to me, in her friendliest tone. It's incredible how easily she turns it on. "I think it'd be interesting to hear how someone who's never had a boyfriend interprets the play."

The girls around me snicker softly. I grit my teeth into a smile. My thoughts override my nerves, and before I know it, I'm turning in my chair to face Huxley. "Romeo and Juliet were not in love. They were full-on crazy."

The class remains silent, giving me weird looks instead.

"Crazy? That seems kind of extreme," Ms. Hardwick says, tossing objectivity out the window.

"But meeting, allegedly 'falling in love' and dying for each other in less than a week isn't?"

"It only takes a few seconds to know you've found your soul mate. When you know, you know. That's how I felt with Steve," Huxley says. The class swoons, and *I'm* ready to go out the window. "That's love."

I won't let Huxley have the satisfaction. She always has the satisfaction. "That's not love. That's poor decision-making skills. Romeo and Juliet were two very repressed and unhappy people. Being forced to stay apart made them want to be together more. It's like when a parent tells their child not to go into the attic—where is the one place they want to go? It's not because they love the attic." Greg Baylor nods his bulky head. Getting through to the class makes me push harder.

"Interesting point," Ms. Hardwick says. "How much do you think their love was based on their circumstance?"

"All of it. It wasn't love," I say, like it wasn't already obvious.

"Rebecca, are you seriously comparing true love to a spare room in your house?" Huxley asks. She raises her eyebrow at me, like I'm a stray hair in her food. "Didn't you read the play? The language, the sonnets, the monologue Romeo recites to Juliet. You don't think any of that was genuine?"

"As far as pickup lines go, it was all right. But just because it sounds pretty doesn't mean it's true. And honestly, it's a little pathetic that Juliet fell for it so quickly."

"Why would Shakespeare have them say it if they didn't mean it?"

"Because he knew the public would eat it up. Obviously, people still do." I grip the edges of my desk, steadying myself. Adrenaline soars through me. My brain and mouth are in sync for once. "I mean, when we watched *Titanic* in fifth grade, you cried for like two days after. You couldn't listen to that Celine Dion song without breaking down."

The class laughs at that. *Direct hit!* Huxley clenches her jaw for a split second before turning her smile back on. I just broke her number-one rule.

"You know, *Titanic* is pretty much *Romeo and Juliet* on a sinking ship," Ms. Hardwick says. "*West Side Story* is also a modern interpretation of the play. Has anyone here watched *West Side Story*?"

Huxley ignores her. "They died for each other, for love."

"For mutual infatuation."

"Now, ladies—" Ms. Hardwick begins. Huxley holds her hand up.

Huxley maintains her friendly tone, but her eyes narrow slightly. Only I can make it out. It's a look I remember from those times when I would steal a fry off her plate or beat her at jacks. She stands up. Her long legs propel her above the class.

"Ms. Hardwick, if it's all right with you, I'd like to address the class. Plead my case, if you will. Becca can do the same."

"The best way to understand literature is to get involved in it!" Ms. Hardwick says. "After you both talk, we'll put it to a class vote."

I stand up, too, right back at her. She has a good four inches on me. I'm the munchkin to her Dorothy.

"You girls don't have to stand, though. This isn't a debate." Huxley and I flash glares at each other. Oh, it so is.

Neither of us sit down.

Huxley clasps her hands together, keeps her back straight. She is in her element. I never thought that people could change so absolutely. I used to believe that if you looked closely enough, you could see their true selves hiding behind the facade. But Huxley proved me wrong.

"Romeo and Juliet may not have had the ideal relationship. No couple is perfect. Even Steve and I have disagreements from time to time. Yes, it's true," Huxley says, though I doubt anyone believes her. I'm sure girls steal her old pen caps and gum wrappers to create homemade shrines where they pray to the relationship gods for a union as perfect as Huxley and Steve's.

She runs her fingers through her hair. It falls right back into place. "But there was love at the core. There was something spiritual, some subconscious connection that was pulling them together. It wasn't logic. You don't go through all of this for someone you think is so-so." She puts her hand over her heart and gives me a look of concern. "Now, I know you have never been in love, been pursued or had a significant other in any way, shape or form. Not even a kiss, unless you count rolling around on your bed with that poster of Leonardo DiCaprio."

The class howls over this, and I join in with them to pretend that I don't care, even though I feel like I'm about to crumble.

"Whoa, Becca. Sex animal!" Shana calls out.

"But despite your *extremely* limited experience," Huxley says, "you can't say their relationship was all a total sham, Rebecca. Can you?"

Huxley receives a smattering of applause as she takes her seat. Shana holds out her hand for a low five that never comes.

I'm sure Calista used to believe this, as did Lily, Kim and my other former clients. I remember my sister used to sound like this, right up until her heart got stomped on and beaten with a baseball bat.

"You're up," Huxley says to me.

I can't move. All my words and coherent thoughts slip

away. My face has turned shades that don't exist on the color wheel.

"Becca?" Ms. Hardwick asks. The room goes silent, waiting for my rebuttal.

"They were nuts," I say, with an apathetic shoulder shrug.

"Becca and Huxley, you both make valid points." Ms. Hardwick hops off her desk, happy to have control of her classroom again. "Let's put it to a class vote. Who thinks Romeo and Juliet were not in love?"

None of them raise their hands.

Huxley flashes me an ear-to-ear grin, that smile that cuts like a knife. You don't mess with a future senator's wife, she's telling me. Ms. Hardwick waits an extra moment to see if any students change their minds.

None do.

# 5

After school, Huxley's words still rattle around in my brain. Most kids at Ashland believe the crap that she spews. It's mass mind control, and I'm the one person who didn't drink the Kool-Aid the second my hormones began raging. It's incredible how revered she is, considering four years ago nobody would've listened to a word she uttered.

When Steve Overland moved to town in eighth grade, he instantly shot to conversation topic number one like a natural disaster on the news. Guys who played in his peewee football league were eagerly anticipating his arrival. Not because he was cool, but because he had an amazing arm, which I guess *was* cool to them. He walked into class the first day, friends with the most popular guys in school. And with his mat of brown hair and aw-shucks smile stamped on his face, he became the crush of every girl at school.

Especially Huxley.

Huxley and I didn't experience the huge explosion in social activity that happens to most girls during middle school. In sixth grade, seemingly overnight, our deck of classmates got reshuffled into tiers of popularity, and we were near the bottom. I knew we weren't popular, but we weren't losers. We got invited to a few bar mitzvahs and summer pool parties, but our social calendar wasn't exactly blowing up.

Huxley's family live in a huge house atop a hill, and she used to tell me she felt like Rapunzel up in her tower alone. Still, we made our own fun. Huxley came up with the activities for us, and I followed along for the ride. That was our dynamic, and it worked. We did our own thing, and middle school was fun for us, but a dud compared to the popular crowd. I guess I never noticed how much it frustrated Huxley.

Even though Steve was a grade ahead of us, his old school had a different curriculum, and he was forced to take seventh-grade science. Since there were no kids with an *N* last name in our grade, Steve and Huxley wound up sitting next to each other and became lab partners. Huxley seized on the opportunity. On the second Monday of school, she burst through the double doors looking like a model. No more ponytails and cardigans for her. She maneuvered her way into Steve's lunch table, then his social circle, then his heart. There was no warning. I observed this like the rest of my classmates. Huxley went from some girl to That Girl. Dating Steve catapulted her to the top of the social stratosphere.

I thought she would bring me along, but as she got invited to more parties, more outings, there wasn't a place for me in her new circle of friends.

People forgot where she came from, or who she was before Steve.

She didn't want to remind them.

I arrive home, and I can already hear the screaming as I open the garage door. After doing the stay-at-home, avidly-watching-soap-operas thing when we were young, my mom turned the spare bedroom into an alterations room. She's become known about town for her mastery with hemming, with one future client even approaching her at a funeral. In a cracked-out twist of fate, most of my mom's clientele are brides and bridal parties. I don't know how she can work in that alteration room poring over wedding dresses after what happened with her own daughter. Maybe helping others can wash away the memory for her. Whatever the reason, it's a lucrative business. Brides will spend gobs of money to ensure their special day is more perfect than everyone else's.

The shrill complaints of another bride-to-be take over the house. I pop into the alterations room to say hello and offer my mom moral support. She's working on a flowing, Disney princess–like wedding dress while the svelte, short bride yells into her cell.

"Mommy, no! We are not going with carnations. I want at least two dozen white roses in my centerpieces...they're cheaper? You want me to go with some cheap flower for my wedding? We aren't gutter trash."

I crouch down and kiss my mom on the forehead.

"Hi, honey," she says, unaffected by the shouting. She's learned to tune it out.

"How's it going?" I peer up at the bride, who's now yelling through tears.

My mom senses my sarcasm. "Planning a wedding is very stressful. But it's all worth it in the end."

*If you make it to the end,* I think. Or else it's just a waste of money. Wouldn't these funds be better spent helping the homeless?

"What?!" The bride shrieks into her phone. "I am not making Leah a bridesmaid. She'll look so ugly and fat in the dress. And her hair is a frizzy mess. She is going to ruin my wedding pictures...I don't care that she's my sister!"

"She sounds very much in love," I say.

I'm halfway out the door when I spot a thick blue binder weighing down the sewing machine. *Courtney & Matthew * May 25* is scrawled in ivory cursive across the front. Inside are dozens of tabs covering every possible detail of this bride's wedding, along with pictures and magazine cutouts and logistical facts and figures for each. You'd think she was running a multinational corporation.

"Please don't touch that," the bride says to me, the "please" just tacked on. "That's my Dream Day Scenario binder. I worked really hard on it."

For a moment, I thought she'd said Doomsday Scenario. Not that far off from the truth. "Sorry."

She squeezes together a fake smile and returns to the phone call. "No, Mommy. We aren't doing folded napkins for the table. Napkin rings...because they're freaking classy, that's why!"

It's times like these that I forget there's actually a groom involved. She probably does, too.

* * *

I lie back on Diane's bed and stare at the heartthrob posters pinned to her ceiling. It must be weird to wake up in the same room you had in high school and find nothing has moved.

"Man, these are some ugly bridesmaids dresses. Sweetie, that color is not champagne. That is crusted-over vomit." Diane clicks through pictures online from her friend Marian's wedding. Her friends dance up a storm—though at this point, I guess Diane's downgraded them to acquaintances.

I lean in and size up the dresses. They're poofed out on tulle steroids, but the soft beige color does complement their bridesmaid bouquets nicely.

"Wow. The whole gang's there," Diane continues. "Aimee and her creepy husband. And poor Erin, you will never lose that baby weight, will you?"

"Why didn't you go?" I ask.

"I would've been gawked at more than the bride. 'Oh, there's Diane...at the singles table. Whomp whomp.'"

"They wouldn't do that. They're your friends."

"They ditched me." Diane spins away from her desk and shoots me a half smile. "You know what that's like."

She sticks her thick brown hair behind her ears. It matches her eyes perfectly. Combine those with her round face and slightly bulbous nose, and she's the epitome of cute and endearing.

"I think Ted's a flamer. I give it a year, tops."

Until she opens her mouth.

"But back to Bari and Derek," I say, or else we would talk

about her friends all night. I motion to get on the keyboard. My gossip dossier sits open next to her monitor. "May I?"

"Of course." Diane wheels away and stretches her feet on her bed. I consider Diane my break-up consultant. She's the only person who knows what I do, the only person who would be supportive. Sometimes I need her advice, or a second opinion, or just someone to laugh at how ridiculous my classmates are.

"So I think Derek should be the dumper," I say. I can't imagine what this will do to Bari, but it's for the best. I'm not in the business of ruining lives. People need the most help when they think everything is fine, right before their worlds get flipped upside down.

"Should? He so is, B. He's done it twice before, so let history repeat itself. He obviously can't stand girls who are smarter than him, so do Bari's homework for a week and watch him drop her like a hot potato. You know men and their pride."

Diane scrapes some food crumbs off the *u* in her Rutgers sweatshirt. That and her flannel bottoms became her uniform as soon as she took off her wedding dress. I guess when you plan to marry a doctor, you don't prep a plan B. But watching daytime talk shows is not a viable career. Diane dabs water on the stain, and smiles with pride when it's gone.

Each morning when I wake up, a part of me hopes that I'll come downstairs and find Diane in a business suit, sipping coffee and checking her phone before racing to catch the train into Manhattan. She'd have some awesome job in a skyscraper in Midtown, followed regularly by happy-hour cocktails with coworkers. She would be someone I could look up to again.

I kick aside a heap of dirty clothes and plop back on the bed. "That doesn't seem entirely right, though. He and Bethann were together for over a year, and they seemed happy."

"Key word—*seemed*."

"It's not like she suddenly became smart overnight. Why now?"

"Maybe he wanted to clear his slate for Princeton?"

"Then why two more girlfriends? It doesn't make sense."

Diane brings up Marian's wedding pictures again. "Is Ted wearing a top hat? Are you kidding me?"

"It's not like any of it matters," I say with a huge exhale. "You break up one couple, three more grow back in their place. They're like gray hairs."

"Be positive, B!" Diane says, which is odd coming from her. "And think of it like this—most of these couples won't survive anyway. And those that do will end up overweight alcoholics who fantasize about bedding their spouse's best friend. It's win-win no matter how you look at it."

Blunt, but sincere. That's what I love about Diane. Despite the circumstances, I'm glad that she moved back home last year. We've become incredibly close, something that our eight-year age difference had always prevented.

"Come here," she says, opening her arms for a hug. I go over to her. She grabs my sleeve and wipes her nose on it.

"Gross!"

My mom knocks at the door as she opens it. The knocking was just a formality. "Hey, girls. Whatcha doing?"

Diane nudges my dossier closed with her elbow. “Just talking,” Diane says. “How was Emily Post down there?”

“She’s under a lot of stress. Her wedding’s right around the corner,” my mom says, always choosing to see the good in paying customers.

“I remember the feeling,” Diane says, and my mom and I don’t say anything for a second, until she laughs and it’s like a *Time In!*

My mom smoothes out the bed where I’d lain. She’s about to sit when she notices the wedding pictures. “Oh. Is this from Marian’s wedding? She looks beautiful. Oh, and I just love those bridesmaids dresses!”

Diane and I trade looks. Everything my mom says makes us want to laugh. We don’t know why.

“And Erin looks great, too. Diane, have you sent her a card yet?” my mom asks. I move my legs as she takes back her place on the bed.

“For what?”

“Congratulating her for having the baby.”

Diane rolls her eyes. Leave it to my mom to turn a bonding moment into a nag session. “Why am I congratulating her for giving birth? She probably had an epidural.”

“He’s about to turn one, and you haven’t even acknowledged him.”

“I don’t think it’s right to congratulate someone for having an ugly baby. It will only encourage her to have another one.”

“Owen is so cute. He’s got the chunkiest thighs.”

“He looks like Benjamin Button.”

I stifle a laugh. My hand presses against my mouth. My

mom chuckles, too, and immediately covers her head in shame.

"See! You think he's ugly, too! Maybe in a few years, I'll see him walking with a cane around the playground," Diane says.

My mom shakes her head. "You were so close to those girls in college. What happened?"

"They became a cliché, and I became a laughingstock."

"This again? Diane, it's all in your head."

"Yeah? So where are they now?" Diane sulks lower into her chair, her back hunched over like a tortoise shell, all her energy dissipating. It's a battle she can't win, so why even try. "You want me to send the card. I'll send the card," she says quietly.

"You know what, you're twenty-four years old. Do what you want." My mom looks at me for backup. I give her a half-hearted smile. I'm staying out of this, which for her means I'm taking Diane's side. But someone has to. How can she forget what happened?

My mom clicks the door shut, shaking her head at another failed breakthrough.

"She'll never understand." Diane turns off her computer.

Before bed, I pour myself a glass of milk. I don't know if it really helps put me to sleep, but I've been doing this since fifth grade, so now it's just part of my routine. The door to the alteration room hangs open, and the bride's binder reflects the outdoor lights. It latches on to my morbid curiosity and lassoes me inside. I flip through pages of immaculate wedding design. The bride's taste isn't some lacy, field-offlowers monstrosity. It's warm colors, sleek bridesmaids dresses, and I do agree with her on napkin rings. Maybe this bride has it right. She isn't factoring love into the equation. This wedding is a realization of her dream design. This marriage is an investment in her future. Plain and simple. I gain a whole new appreciation for the binder, for her honesty. I'm sure she's been planning her special day since she was my age, years before she even met the man who would be her husband.

A scheme springs into my head, and I call Diane down right away.

"What up?" Diane says. When she joins me, she comes face-to-face with the Disney-princess dress. Instead of laughing at it, she stares into every seam. Sadness washes across her face. Her caustic facade falls to the side. I wonder if she's looking past herself, into some alternate universe of what could have been. It's a quiet reflection, one of those moments we simultaneously are drawn to and try to avoid.

"I'm sorry" is all I get out. Diane remains entranced.

I wrap my arms around her and squeeze, resting my chin on her shoulder. "Those bridesmaids dresses totally looked like crusted-over vomit. You dodged a bullet."

Diane rubs my hand, forcing a smile that won't come. "So like I said, what up?"

"I know how to break up Bari and Derek."

# 6

Part of me would love to see Michigan's yearbook be a disaster as payback for taking advantage of my friend. But Val and I are good girls, so we're spending our Thursday night working on captions.

We lie on her bed, staring at pictures of our fellow students smiling and laughing, making it seem as if Ashland High is the new Disney World.

The homecoming spread takes over her computer screen. She can't take her eyes off the king and queen in the middle. Jealousy, hopefulness and sorrow mix together on her face.

"I don't think she's that pretty," I say of Huxley, whose head seems shaped for a crown. "Her lips are too big, her waist too small and she has overly angular shoulders."

"They're so perfect," Val says, clearly only thinking about her own imperfections. She can't look away. She, like the rest of Ashland, is transfixed. Her hopes and dreams sit in that frame. I could tell her how funny and amazing and beautiful she is every hour on the hour, and it would make no difference. Because to her, the only proof of that is to have a boyfriend.

"Oh, please. No couple is perfect."

"They aren't? They're so cute together. Holding hands down the hall. Cheering for each other at games. Once I actually heard them finish each other's sentences." She pulls up another picture of the power couple, one of many Michigan stuck her with. Steve "surprising" Huxley at her car with a giant teddy bear on Valentine's Day. Girls talked about that one all week.

"It's just a stuffed animal. It's probably collecting dust in her basement," I say, but it's no use.

Val holds her computer next to my face for a side-by-side comparison I want no part in. "You know, I think that sweater and skirt she's wearing would look great on you. Well, maybe not that peach color since your skin is much lighter—"

"Paler."

"—*lighter* than hers. But maybe something similar..." Val's eyes pivot between my outfit and Huxley's.

"Doubtful." I push the computer away.

"I'm serious. You're a total catch. You're so smart and pretty and all-around amazing, and it's kind of ridonkulous that you don't see that."

"Really?" I know Val's giving a stock friend speech, but she says it with so much gusto, I almost believe it.

"Yes! Maybe if you didn't cover up like some Amish housewife. Seriously, how many cardigans can one girl wear?"

"The sky's the limit."

Huxley has a figure. I have a body, and it's thin and unspectacular from all angles.

"I think if you stopped wearing three layers of clothing every day and showed yourself off a little, you would look dynamite! The guys at school would go crazy!"

"The guys can do whatever they want. I am not taking fashion tips from the homecoming queen from hell."

"Didn't you two used to be friends back in the day?"

"Moderate acquaintances."

"Whoa, sorry." She holds up her hands in surrender. "My mistake."

Val jumps on her bed; her silky blond hair flaps her in the face. She won't let this idea go quietly. "C'mon, don't you want some male attention?" I know Val doesn't mean to be insulting, but it still stings.

I stand in front of her full-length mirror. My looks are sufficient enough for my middle-of-the-road social status. Val's help wouldn't do much good. Calista is beautiful, but that isn't enough apparently. Who knows what gets guys' attention? I only play games when I know the rules.

"I'll pass for now," I tell her. "I think I'm yearbooked out, too."

"Wait! I need to ask you for one more favor."

"Seriously?" I groan and sit back down on the bed.

"I'll give you a kidney someday." She opens up her email. "Can you help me with something?"

"What?"

"I want to send Ezra an email." She pushes the computer onto my lap.

"About homework?"

She shoots me a look. We both know that's not likely. "I've been thinking about the other day in the lunchroom. He was totally flirting with me, but because I was incapable of stringing together a sentence, he probably thinks I'm not interested."

"Are you interested?"

"I think so. He's a really great guy," Val says as if she's now some kind of Ezra expert.

"Is he even your type? He's kinda artsy." I always see him reading published scripts or slipping DVDs into his backpack. He's definitely an atypical Ashland boy.

"He's such a talented filmmaker."

"Have you ever watched any of his films?"

"No, but I've heard they're very good." Val opens up a Word document on her computer. "I think he'll appreciate a really funny, thought-provoking email introduction. I don't know. You're more of a writer than I am. I need you to add some of your trademark Becca Williamson pizzazz."

"I think he just broke up with Isabelle Amabile like a week ago?" Ezra gossip isn't exactly front-page news. He's one of those boys who's just there, doing his thing in the background, not rocking the boat. Kind of like me.

"A week is a long time. The Earth was created in a week."

"Wait," I say, a memory springing to mind. "Didn't it end badly with him and Monica Washington before that? Didn't she go on some tirade?"

"The Diet Sprite incident," Val says like it's old news. "They broke up. Monica went ballistic and dumped a cup of Diet Sprite over his head during lunch."

Yeah, that's not something you want to hear about your

friend's crush. Val reads my face; she can probably sense my exact thought in some BFF ESP superpower.

"Monica is cray-cray. Remember the time in ninth grade when she went on that shoplifting binge at Home Depot, and we had to have that assembly about stealing? Ezra barely made it out alive. And Home Depot? Seriously? Set your sights a little higher." She sticks up her finger for a pinkie swear. "Look, I promise I will not make a scene if we break up."

"You two aren't even together yet."

Val fiddles with a loose string on her bedspread. "Ezra is obviously a romantic. If he's not feeling it, then he's not going to fake it just for the sake of being in a relationship. I thought you would champion someone like that."

"I'm not *not* championing Ezra..." My voice trails off. I feel like a wet blanket next to Val. Either she's too impulsive, or I'm too cautious. "I just don't want you to get hurt or get stuck in something like yearbook again."

"That's so sweet," Val gushes. "But I need to get in there quickly. And if I can't do it face-to-face, then I will do it through email. But I need to strike now."

"That sounds like a great battle plan, but do you actually like him? Or is this about having a boyfriend?" I cringe at how much of a killjoy I sound like. But it's better than having my best friend risk public embarrassment or rejection.

"Neither of us has ever had a boyfriend, and that needs to change. I am tired of being in the minority, watching other people be all couple-y while I sit in the bleachers and act supportive. This is our time, Becca. Or, at least, my time."

"Jeez, Val. Being single is not a death sentence."

"Well, I won't let it be a life sentence!" She grabs the laptop and retreats to her desk. "Are you going to help me or not?"

I can't tell if she wants Ezra, or just a boyfriend. Someone to give her an oversize, inconvenient teddy bear. Val may not know the answer either. Vulnerability and desperation flicker in her eyes. I feel it, too. The couples in our school making the single—no, unattached—people feel inferior. I can only break up one couple at a time. I'm not trying to ruin anyone's life; I just want the tide to change at our school, so that my best friend doesn't have to carry around this anxiety, this insecurity that just because a guy doesn't want to walk with her in the hallway or shove his tongue down her throat, there's something wrong with her, with us.

"Val," I say. She looks back at me. "Do you like him, honestly?"

"Yes," she says, her voice regaining composure.

"What do you like most about him?"

"He has a really cute voice. It's deeper than the guys at school, and he always sounds so smart when he talks." Val hugs the pillow under her, an image of Ezra superimposed on her mind. "My favorite is when he speaks—his head always tilts up and his eyes look up and to the left. It's awkward and adorable at the same time. If that even makes sense..."

Her cheeks redden. Although I am wary about how this all will end, nothing I say can change her mind. I just have to be ready and waiting with a box of tissues. I grab her computer. My fingers take over the keyboard. "We should include something about movies, of course. I saw him reading a biography of Martin Scorsese once."

"Who's that?" Val asks.

I hope this doesn't blow up in her face.

# 7

I realized that what Derek hates most isn't blonde cheerleaders or smart women—it's commitment, especially now. He liked that Bethann was intelligent, but not that she was going to follow him to Princeton. Tessa is going to school all the way in California, and Bari will still be in Ashland next year. Even though he's making Bari play by his rules, he doesn't view this as a serious relationship, and he'd freak out if things headed in that direction, like they did with Bethann. I'm assuming he wants to enjoy his senior year, and then go off to Princeton wild and free.

When I get home from Val's, I get to work. I print off dozens of pictures of Bari and Derek from Facebook, and using the glue and scissors I must've had since elementary school, I cut out their heads and paste them into bridezilla's doomsday wedding scenario. *There's Bari and Derek posing by a gazebo at sunset! There's Bari in a wedding dress with a burgundy-and-orange bouquet! There's Derek slipping a ring onto Bari's fin-*

*ger underneath a wicker-and-floral—but rainproof—canopy!* Bridezilla's thought of everything. I wish all arts-and-crafts projects were this enjoyable. A smile overtakes my face—a genuine, gleeful smile, not one used to cover up something else.

Even if this gets Bari and Derek to break up, I know it will just be using a squirt gun on a forest fire. Relationship zombies will still rule my school. Why can't all couples just admit to the charade? Then people would stop getting hurt, and we could all get on with our lives. The rush of frustration courses through me, just as it did last January at the Snowflake Dance.

I had spent the past month tending to Diane's broken heart and hearing my parents stress about losing wedding deposits. I was excited for a night of fun and dancing with Val. It was like a night off.

And at first it was. The cafeteria had been transformed into a winter wonderland of fake, fluffy snow. Great music, decent eats, a packed dance floor. Val loved dances because they had this anything-could-happen aura, and as the music blared, I could feel it, too.

But during the last hour of the dance, kids went from having fun to having a mission: hooking up. All school dances must be sealed with a kiss, apparently. The dance became a game of tag, but neither Val nor I were it. Nearly every song played was a ballad and the circles of dancers morphed into couples swaying to the music. And one by one, they began making out for everyone to see. I probably sound like some eighty-year-old nun, but in my experience, kissing is fun to do, but not to watch.

Val and I were relegated to the far reaches of the dance

floor, next to the stack of unused cafeteria chairs. Val's face drooped into this despondent, dejected look. It was like I'd never left the house. And to top it off, before the final song, the principal announced Huxley and Steve as the Snowbirds—the dance's version of king and queen chosen by the planning committee. (They are like the Meryl Streep of dance royalty elections. Spread the wealth, people!) We had to stand in a circle and watch them slow dance and stare into each other's emotionally vacant eyes before other pairs joined in. The night was everything my life wasn't, and I left the dance so ready for a new day.

That Monday at school, I realized I was not alone. I overheard different girls in different groups—girls who usually would never say two words to each other—complaining about the same problem: couples. One girl bitched about the friends who abandoned her at the dance to hang out with their boyfriends. Another claimed her friend turned into a demon monster whenever her boyfriend was around. I was not alone.

Hearing the discontent simmering in the halls and between desks gave me the assurance I needed that this school could use someone to level the playing field. A relationship Robin Hood. A week later, I scribbled my ad on a bathroom stall.

I had my first client forty-eight hours later.

Long story short, that's how at six forty-five in the morning, I find myself walking down the deserted halls of school, gripping the modified binder in my hand. I scan my surroundings when I reach Derek's locker. Just the hum of the heating vent and the stiff smell of the floor buffer accompany me. Diane had given me a master key for all V56 locks she received when she was a camp counselor, and it has been the greatest gift. All locks used on school grounds must be V56, in case the principal ever wants to do a locker search. I empty out Derek's folder labeled "SGA" and replace the papers with what's in the wedding binder. For the cherry on top, I pull out a crisp, white envelope from my pocket, tape it to the binder's inside sleeve and shove everything back inside.

Dear Derek,

I did some brainstorming. What can I say? I'm a planner. Why wait for tomorrow when you know what you want today ☺ I can't wait to see you at the assembly!

Love,
Bari

My footsteps echo in the hallway, and I just keep wondering if all people enjoy their jobs as much as I do.

I don't know why the principal doesn't see it. Assemblies are a waste of time. It takes the school twenty minutes to file in and sit down for a fifteen-minute assembly that only delivers three minutes' worth of useful information. Val wanders away from her class to sit next to me. She looks at her phone, trying to will an email to populate.

"No response yet?" I ask. We both know the answer, but it's an excuse to let her talk about Ezra some more.

Val shakes her head no. I want to smack Ezra for not instantly asking Val out.

"What's my percentage?" she asks.

"What?"

"What's the percentage chance of Ezra responding?"

"I don't know. Twenty-five?"

Val's face drops. "Twenty-five?"

"Or thirty-one."

Her eyes expand even farther. Two gumballs gawking at me. "That's all? Not even above fifty?"

I can't tell if she wants me to be honest. But as my friend, she deserves my moderated gut reaction. I want to cushion the blow in case Ezra doesn't pan out. "Well, it's more like twenty-one. You haven't spoken in person yet."

"Right, right," she says, uninterested in cold, hard facts.

"I'm not saying that twenty-one can't change."

She appreciates the encouragement, but she remains serious. "Beck, I think I may actually break through with this one. I think there could be something here. I feel it in my bones."

"Maybe that's just osteoporosis."

One of the French teachers shushes me. The principal takes the mic.

"Students, thank you all for coming today. We have an exciting announcement. We received some incremental funds from the school board, a nice figure. And after meetings with the SGA, we've created a plan for using these funds to benefit Ashland in the best way possible." He waits for applause that doesn't come. It's not like we're getting the money personally. "Your SGA president Derek Kelley will walk everyone through the exciting features coming your way over the next year!"

"Thank you," Derek says, all power and poise on stage. He rests his accordion folder on the podium. "My fellow students, as a result of these funds, we will be building a brand-new, state-of-the-art TV studio and launching a morning news show anchored and run entirely by students. The feed will be hooked up to all classroom TVs."

Silence. I may have just heard a pin drop one town over.

"Welcome to the nineties," I whisper to Val.

"Pretty cool, right?" Derek unwinds the cord around the accordion folder and reaches inside. "We anticipate the project will be completed by early May, so even though I'm headed for Princeton—early decision—this fall, I and my fellow seniors can experience this new step forward for Ashland High. I have all the details in this binder."

In a miracle of obedience, the auditorium remains quiet while Derek opens his binder. I watch closely as he reads the letter taped inside, then flips through the pages.

"Come on!" a kid shouts, but Derek ignores him. He keeps flipping.

Whiteness drains his face of color. By the look in his eyes, you'd think he was looking at photos of POWs—not matrimonial bliss.

"Derek?" The principal motions him to keep talking, and for probably the first time in his life, Mr. Future Politician is completely speechless. He throws the binder in his book bag and runs into the wings. Everyone goes back to talking at full level.

"Students, quiet down!" the principal says, but it's useless. When an assembly has a hitch, chaos inevitably follows.

Val nudges my elbow. "What do you think that was all about?"

"I have no idea."

Students are about to make a mass exodus, but Steve Overland jumps up to the stage. He gets much more applause than the principal.

"Hey, guys, what's up?" Steve asks with his boyish, dimpled smile, the carefree grin of someone who has no real problems in his life. The principal taps him on the shoulder and points back to Steve's seat.

"I just need one minute, sir. Sixty seconds."

The principal feigns annoyance and backs away, but we all know it's merely an act. It's no secret that he got a serious bonus when the football team won the state championship. The principal wouldn't dare anger his prized possession.

"So, let me tell you the real reason we're up in this assembly," Steve says.

Val and I trade looks—hers excited, mine confused.

"It's somebody's birthday in this room," Steve coos into the mic. "Will the real Huxley Mapother please stand up?"

Huxley complies. She hides her head in faux embarrassment, a look she seems to have down pat. I slouch back in my chair.

Steve takes a deep breath. "I'm a little nervous."

A random gaggle of girls in front cheer him on. He winks at them.

"Here goes nothing." Steve takes his sweet time, but he can, because he's Steve Overland, and who's going to tell him to get off the stage? He begins singing some Frank Sinatra song that I'm sure gets played at every wedding in America.

My classmates go wild: standing up and whooping, clapping to the nonexistent beat. There's at least one *aww* every five seconds. Steve's a decent singer, but it's just a stupid song. Huxley probably came up with this whole "spontaneous" scheme herself.

"Happy birthday, Hux," he says in between breaths.

Now *I* feel like a POW.

# 8

People don't shut up about Steve's *American Idol* audition all morning. I hope they filled their Sweeping Fauxmantic Gesture quota for the day and will spare us any theatrics during lunch. I wait for Val outside the cafeteria, farther down the hall from the rush of students so she can actually find me. We usually walk over together, and I wonder what's keeping her busy. I lean against a glass case holding Ashland High's cherished football memorabilia. Some of the players in the black-and-white photos are cute, which is creepy since they're grandpas now. I guess since the case didn't feel all-American enough, the school put a photo of Huxley and Steve being crowned at homecoming in the center of the display. He wore his muddy football uniform to the dance. Everyone thought he would continue playing football in college, but he's giving it up next year to attend Vermilion, a nearby university, to stay close to Huxley, who's only a junior. Girls think he's such a doting boyfriend; I think he's beyond whipped.

Through the clutter of scurrying underclassmen, Val approaches. She's not alone, though. An unmistakable puff of black hair peeks out over the crowd.

"Hey," Val says.

"Hi," I say back, my eyes darting between her and Ezra.

"Um, this is Ezra."

He releases his hand from hers and shakes mine. "How goes it?"

"Good," I say again, realizing that I'm being totally awkward, but not at all adorable.

I watch Val give Ezra the "hang test": How long will he let her hand hang next to his before he holds it?

Ezra passes with flying colors. When he grabs her hand, she has to work overtime to restrain the joy gushing out of her. I've never seen her so happy.

I can't believe it worked. I feel a pit of dread form in my stomach.

"When did this...?" I gesture at their hands.

"Between third and fourth period," Val and Ezra say at the same time.

"Whoa," he says. "That was kinda weird."

Kinda? I wonder if they practiced this meeting with me to make sure their coupledom was extra gagworthy.

"Ezra came up behind me at the Coke machine after third period."

"I had to meet this funny, awesome girl who loved movies as much as I do."

"And then he bought me a Diet Coke!"

"You're telling it wrong. I bought you the Diet Coke while we were talking. I didn't have champagne on me, so I had to use an alternative carbonated beverage to woo you."

Val beams with pride.

"So you guys are official. Already. After one Diet Coke."

"I don't live my life by labels," Ezra says. He brushes a strand of hair out of Val's face. "You make me want to be a better man."

"I do?"

"That was from *As Good as It Gets*."

"It's my favorite," Val says.

"You're my favorite."

I roll my eyes. Is he for real? If only Ezra knew how much romance was actually involved. How her movie knowledge was taken from the internet, condensed into a cogent outline and written by me. How he is just the closest available option who happened to have some spare change handy.

"Let's eat. I'm starving!" I signal for the cafeteria.

Neither of them move. The pit of dread expands.

"What?" I ask.

Val scrunches her eyebrows together. "I'm going to eat with Ezra today." She leans against his shoulder. Their PDA level is rapidly escalating.

"We have some catching up to do," he says. His eyes go up and to the left. Val's right. It's both awkward and adorable.

"Oh."

She gives me a look only I can read, silently pleading with me to go with it.

"Okay." I manage my best fake smile. I tell myself that this is what Val wants, and that I'm happy she's happy.

"It was good seeing you," Ezra says. They walk into the cafeteria holding hands.

And so it begins. Val's march toward the dark side.

I follow behind them, a commoner scrambling to her table. Across the cafeteria, Huxley's laughter takes over the room, all attention drawn to her corner table, just as she prefers. She giggles into Steve's broad chest, reacting to something probably not that funny. For a second, I think she's laughing at me.

Steve pulls her in close and lights a candle atop a cupcake.

"I'll talk to you later!" Val says to me, but I don't believe it.

I come home to find my mom and dad in their usual positions in the living room: she's watching TV on her overstuffed chair we call the Throne, and he's reading the newspaper on the couch. They make great roommates.

My mom waves me over to the Throne. Once she settles in, she won't leave it until dinnertime. "Can you see how Diane is doing?"

"Did something happen?"

"Open up the paper on the dining table. To the engagement section."

I scan the page of announcements. In the top right corner, I find the article in question. *Sankresh Ramamurty, 25, engaged to Priya Ghosh, 25.* I get a lump in my throat. My mom reads my next thought.

"Diane saw it this morning."

I remember Sankresh's brown skin next to Diane's pale complexion, a Williamson genetic quality. I once joked that they would have the cutest butterscotch babies. "Sounds delicious!" Sankresh had said back, and then he pretended to take a bite out of Diane's arm. They reminded me of Steve and Huxley, except they weren't showing off for anyone. They were just being themselves.

I tiptoe to Diane's room, my feet getting heavier with each step. I tap at her door with my index finger. No answer. I tap again.

"Diane, it's Becca."

The door swings open. "Hey," she says. Diane has some light makeup on, and her hair's pulled back into a tight ponytail. She's beautiful. But I can't help but notice the red puffiness around her eyes.

"How are you doing?"

"I've had better days," she says. I'm glad to see her sarcasm still intact.

"I'm sorry."

Diane shrugs. What can she say to that? "Thanks for feeling sorry for me"? She waves me to enter. Her room is spotless. I should take notes.

"I'm almost sorry for him, for having to marry that horse-faced woman." Diane checks her skin in the mirror, verifies her face is not horse-shaped. I figured the knives would be out, though I suppose it's better than a replay of when he first called off the wedding. I can still hear the screaming echoing in my ears. I just wish Diane had an in-between mode. "You know his mother set the whole thing up."

"It's an arranged marriage?"

"Obviously. He's only marrying her to make his family happy. He's a total coward. His mother will cut off his inheritance if he doesn't marry an Indian girl. I wish I had known that earlier than six hours before my wedding, but whatever."

I used to love hanging out with Sankresh and Diane. It was like having an older brother. He was teaching me how to play piano on a Casio keyboard he'd picked up at Goodwill. I threw it out the day he called Diane to break off the wedding.

He called. He didn't even have the guts to face her in person.

"You're better off." I put a tentative hand on her shoulder.

"I know. But I had to learn that lesson sometime."

My tentative hand becomes a back massager. Diane welcomes it. "I'm here if you ever want to talk about it." I sound so unconvincing and fake, worse than a guidance counselor.

"I know you are. But I'm fine."

"Don't worry. One day, you're going to find a great guy—"

"Stop it, B. Are you actually giving me the 'one day' speech? There won't be a one day. I know the silver lining to what happened is that you were able to learn from my mistake. I thought Sankresh loved me, but he just wanted a Western fling before following tradition. I was used, just like everyone else. People just use relationships to get what they want: money, power, sex, connections, self-esteem."

"Didn't you date that guy in college because he had a car?" I ask. Diane rolls her neck forward, letting me work her upper back.

"Right. But it's never about love. Did Erin, Aimee and Marian marry those cardboard-cutout snoozefests because it was true love, or because they all make a lot of money, and my friends wanted a hot husband to show off at their big parties in their McMansions?"

"Right." Aimee's and Marian's husbands are pretty cool, though. Aimee and Bill went skydiving on their honeymoon, and Ted plays drums in a band. (Okay, Erin's husband is a boring square, but two out of three isn't bad.) Diane always had a blast hanging out with the group, even before they began pairing off. But now's not the time to argue.

I run my fingernails along her shoulder blades. I saw a girl do it at a slumber party. It seems to do the trick and calm Diane down. I can't give a pep talk if my life depended on it, but at least I'm not totally useless.

"Did you see that they already set a date?"

"That's fast." I only glanced at the article; Diane has it memorized.

"June 28. That's the day Sankresh and I had our first date. Five years to the day. He took me to this Italian restaurant and we sat in the courtyard in the back. They forgot to put our order in, so they threw in free tartufo. Sankresh let me eat the cherry in the center."

Diane never talks about Sankresh, not this stuff anyway. I don't know if she's talking to me or to herself anymore, so I just give her a supportive squeeze.

She spins around and grabs my shoulders. Her eyes are wet but urgency lights up her face. She stares through my eyes directly into my mind, like she's been able to do forever. "You're the Break-Up Artist. I don't want you to get—"

"Duped. I know." A chill runs through my body. I throw the newspaper into her overflowing garbage. "Don't worry. I'll never forget."

* * *

I check my email when I get back to my room. And then I check my *other* email. LeBreakUpArtiste [at] gmail [dot] com. (I decided to be creative.)

Perched at the top of my inbox is a message from a Mr. Towne. The email has been sitting there for a day—way too long. The name doesn't ring a bell, but most people don't use their real names with me in the beginning.

To: Le Break-Up Artiste
From: Robert Towne

My wife saw your ad on a bathroom stall...it's worth a shot. I need you to break up Steve Overland and his girlfriend, Huxley Mapother. I've attached a picture. Let me know next steps.

I reread the email about five more times. The words don't change, but each time they seep in more. I deal with low-profile relationships, ones that don't cause major seismic shifts in the tectonic plates of gossip our school rests upon. Huxley and Steve are the San Andreas Fault of relationships. (Wow, I guess our current unit on geology is more fascinating than I thought.) Maybe this Towne guy is confused. I open the picture.

It's Huxley and Steve at homecoming—the same picture on display at school.

# 9

It's not until after dinner that Mr. Towne pops up online. I email him back asking to video chat. He asks for ten minutes, which gives me enough time to set up. I tape a black blanket to the mirrored sliding door behind me to eliminate all traces of personality from my surroundings. I pull out my grandfather's vintage suitcase from under my bed and remove my costume: my raccoon mask and Diane's old graduation robe. As I slip them on, I contemplate who this Mr. Towne could be. A vengeful father? A frustrated teacher or disgruntled janitor?

But it's none of the above. Mr. Towne looks exactly like a Mr. Towne would. He's an adult dressed in full dad attire—baby-blue polo buttoned all the way up and tucked into khakis with his gut protruding. Thinned hair, creased face, but a boyish smile. Despite his age, he still looks fitter than some guys in my school. He sits at his desk and doesn't say a word.

"'Ello love," I say in my British accent.

“I didn’t know you were British. I assumed French,” he says, totally calm. It’s making me nervous. He leans back in his chair. “Is that what you normally wear?”

“Um, no. It’s my work uniform.”

“You really British?”

“Why, of course!”

He stares at me, his gray eyes coalescing into a steely glare. “I get it. Gotta protect yourself.”

“Is Mr. Towne your real name?” I ask him.

“Does it matter?”

He flashes me that boyish grin, dimples caving in both cheeks. He was probably Steve Overland thirty years ago. His high-school sweetheart and three kids are probably down the hall singing Bible hymns.

“Don’t worry,” he says. “I have no idea who you are, and I don’t care to know so long as you get the job done. So let’s stop prying and get down to business.”

I exhale in relief. Most of the awkwardness has left the room. “Why does a fortysomething man want to break up some high-school couple?”

“Why do you need to know?”

I’ve never had to pry information from a potential client like this. I’m not interested in competing in a “who’s more paranoid” contest. “Do you want me to do my job or not?”

We have a stare-off. I won’t let him dictate how I run my business. He cracks first.

“I’m a family friend of the Overlands. I was there when Stevie got his first tooth and first touchdown. I’m always looking out for him. And right now, I’m worried about his relationship with his girlfriend. His family does not like her at all. They think she's snooty and controlling."

I nod. Sounds like they know Huxley well.

"I understand first love and hormones and all that nonsense, but Stevie gave up a football scholarship to a well-known university to go to some local college close to her. His parents have tried to talk to him about what a big mistake he's making. But he won't listen. That girl's got him wrapped around her finger. So..."

"You need my help?"

"Yeah. I don't know if this is just some prank you're pulling, but we're out of options. All college admissions decisions become binding May 15. That's less than three months out. I don't want the kid to throw his life away."

"Vermilion is a good school, I've heard," I say. Steve wore a pine-green Vermilion sweatshirt to school when he got accepted. I couldn't care less, but it caused murmurs in the guy corners of my classes. My mom said Vermilion was an overpriced liberal-arts school that charges an arm and a leg just to remain exclusive. It's not ranked that high in college guides, but Huxley likes telling people otherwise.

"Vermilion is Division 3, barely," Mr. Towne says. He rests his hands on his gut. "Steve should be at a D1 school like Chandler University in Texas. He has the talent. That's where the real recruiting for pro is done." Mr. Towne's cheeks flush with red.

"You think if he and Huxley are broken up, he'll go to one of those schools?"

"Definitely. That kid was born to play football, and he

knows it. The only thing stopping him is right between that girl's legs. Excuse my language."

I shake that mental image out of my head. Huxley and Steve. She has him, the whole school, wrapped around her finger. She won't give that up. Not before senior prom and graduation, the two most public events in her high-school career. Some people begin dating just so they have a boyfriend or girlfriend on hand for those occasions.

"You still there?" he asks.

I grunt in response.

"So can you do it?"

"I don't know." I bite my lip. So much for my comfortable, calm demeanor.

"What do you mean? You have done this before, right?"

"These two are different. They are like this impenetrable fortress. I don't think Huxley will let anything come between them. She would know if someone was messing with her."

"You can start a rumor or something."

"She would use her minions to squash it and then hunt down whoever started it." Lena Herman started a rumor that Huxley was using laxatives to slim down, and Huxley found out that same week. Lena transferred to Catholic school a month later...and she's Jewish!

"I was hoping you were the real deal."

"I am, but I don't know if they can be broken up." Or maybe I don't know if I can do it. If I get made, she'll be out for blood. And she's brainwashed the school, so they'd chase me out the front doors with burning pitchforks. You have to know your limits sometimes.

"I'm giving you my honest, semiprofessional opinion."

"What if I tripled your rate? Three hundred dollars?"

My eyes widen at the thought of three hundred dollars. But then Huxley's face pops into my head, and the money fades away. "If Steve's family can't sway his decision, what makes you think I can?"

He lets out an exasperated sigh. "It sounds like you're scared of her."

"Scared of her? No way!"

"You're making excuses when you know this girl is no good."

I get a short burst of pleasure hearing him say that. I'm not the only one who thinks she's awful. "She's just annoying."

"I remember there was this bully when I went to high school." Mr. Towne leans back in his chair, and it looks like he's reaching back decades for the memory. "He loved picking on anyone with a pocket calculator. No one ever fought back. Until one day, this scrawny kid walked right up to him in the lunchroom and gave him a bloody nose. No warning, no hesitation. The whole room busted out laughing at him. And you know what that bully did in return?"

"What?"

"He left me and my friends alone for the rest of high school."

I was expecting him to be the bully. But then, who knows, this could all just be made up, or stolen from some episode of *The Andy Griffith Show*.

"Listen, I need to know. Can you make this happen?" Mr. Towne doesn't mince words.

"Let me think about this."

"Think quickly. If I don't hear from you by Sunday, I'm rescinding my offer."

# 10

*Movie Tonight?* I scribble down my note, write Val's name on it and stretch my arms behind my head.

My classmates fidget in their seats, restlessly readjusting themselves in their chairs. It's Friday, eighth-period Latin class, and I can feel the excitement about the weekend pulsating through the room. Except for Bari, whose blank, drained face stares at the board as if it's Monday morning. She trudges out of class once the bell rings, avoiding all people. A pang of guilt jabs at me, but it's for the best. I'm not evil; I'm a Good Samaritan. One day, she'll thank me—or, she would if I could tell her who I was.

I walk in between desks to get to Val.

"So what time should I pick you up tonight?" I ask. "The movie starts at seven forty-five."

Val hugs her two books and notebook to her chest. "Great," she says with hesitation. "Is it okay if Ezra joins us?"

My Friday excitement dissipates. I struggle for an answer.

Should I be easygoing and fun, or honest? Val will turn into Relationship Val if he comes, and the night will be ruined.

"Is it okay?" she asks again.

"I guess, if you want to."

"Are you sure? If you don't want him around, I understand."

"Why wouldn't I want him around?" Hopefully, she doesn't ask me to list out the reasons.

Val exhales. A smile returns to her face. "Great! I wanted to ask because I wasn't sure if you liked him or not."

"What? I just don't really know him." Although I shouldn't be, I'm taken aback by Val's assumption. I can't be mad that I barely see her anymore; no, it has to be that I don't like Ezra.

"I was worried there for a second. I want you to like him. He's amazing, and I'm not just saying that because I'm his girlfriend." She blushes when she says *girlfriend*. "So what movie are we seeing?"

*"Starship Alien II."*

"Didn't we hate the first one?"

"We almost got kicked out," I say. We both burst into laughter at the memory. *Starship Alien I* was so horrible that we couldn't stop giggling and making comments. Why do horror directors think that girls love walking around topless while a killer alien is on the loose? The usher came into the theater and said we had to be quiet or leave.

"That movie was terrible! I'm kind of excited to see how bad this one will be," she says.

I'm excited she's excited. Maybe it won't be that different from old times.

I sit in the backseat of Ezra's white Toyota Camry, playing with a hole in the seat fabric. The rhythm of his windshield wipers drowns out the inside banter coming from the front. I feel like the baby in a car seat. *Single Person on Board.* Where's their decal?

Whenever the road is smooth, they hold hands on the middle console. At every stoplight, Ezra blows hot air on Val's fingertips and then kisses them.

"What?" Ezra asks Val, who won't stop looking at him.

"Nothing," she says coyly. "I guess I was just looking at you."

"Well, then, you're driving home so I can look at you."

They've done this twice already.

"So, Ezra, are you excited for the glory that is *Starship Alien II*?" I ask, reminding them that someone is in the backseat.

"What's it about?"

"These astronauts on an abandoned ship have to take down an evil race of aliens who eat human brains, and they realize that if they can kill the queen, who is giving the aliens their brain-sucking power, then they can escape. Prepare to laugh a lot." Val isn't laughing right now. She's probably waiting to see how Ezra reacts so she can craft a similar response.

"Horror isn't really my forte, so this should be interesting. I usually go to the theater by the college. They play some good indie films there, and some classics, too." His deep voice reverberates through the car.

"I've always wanted to see a movie there," I say.

"Really? Val said you guys go all the time."

"We do?"

I check Val's face in the rearview mirror. Her eyes plead with me to just go with it.

"We do," I say emphatically, searching for words. "I just always fall asleep ten minutes in. So technically, I've never seen a complete movie there." I hope some part of that made sense.

"I admit some of them can be slow, but there are a lot of gems."

He pulls into the shopping center, which has gone to sleep for the night. The bright, sparkly lights of the movie theater light up the area like a casino. "Wow, I haven't been to a multiplex in ages. I'm going to stick out like Alvy did in L.A.," Ezra says, nudging Val's arm.

"Who?" she asks.

"Alvy Singer," he says. The name doesn't ring a bell to me or Val. "From *Annie Hall.*"

"Oh, right!" Val says.

"You okay?"

"Sorry, long week."

That makes Ezra chuckle. Their hands meet again on the middle console. Val exhales. Color flushes back into her face. He finds a space not too far from the theater, throws the car in Park and smirks at Val.

"What?" she asks, blushing.

"Nothing," he says. "I guess I was just looking at you."

And the cycle continues.

The unexpected rain made the movies the place to be for half my high school tonight. The concession-stand line stretches almost to the ticket booth. I give Ezra money to buy my ticket and dread the next step. The social obstacle course. I walk past groups of kids I see every day in the hall, alone. I don't know if it's true, but all eyes seem to be on me, sizing up my social profile. *I'm here with friends,* I want to tell them. *Just act cool, Becca.* In my brief glances at the onlookers, I notice lots of couples. I suppose that's standard for Friday night at the movies. Val and Ezra wait in the ticket line, hand in hand.

I feel better once the movie starts. I can leave my current world behind and focus on astronauts getting killed in intricate and gruesome ways.

Well, I thought I could.

But Val and Ezra insist on putting on their own movie. They can't just hold hands and be done with it. It's a process, with the necessary buildup. Their slightest moves distract me. Ezra strokes her arm while Val pretends to watch the movie. Then he puts his arm around her. But he won't stop there. Next, they hold hands. But I guess that isn't taking advantage of their bodies being so close to each other. So she leans against him, stroking his arm. But then he chooses to rub her thigh, which means she can't lean against him. She resumes her regular position. But a hand on her leg isn't enough, so he throws his arm back around her shoulders. Their bodies are like puzzle pieces not fitting. On-screen, a buff guy gets a tentacle through the eye socket, and I have no idea why.

I tap Val's shoulder. "Bathroom," I whisper. I do the crouch-stand and shuffle out to the aisle, where I can see that my theater is all couples, all mimicking some version of Val's and Ezra's moves.

I step into the lobby, and my night instantly gets worse. A line of moviegoers wait for the eight-thirty showing. Mostly from my school. Huxley and Steve stand in the middle with their entire social circle. Shouldn't they be someplace cooler than the movies?

I avoid eye contact and beeline to the bathroom, ignoring my peripheral vision. All I see is the bathroom, my salvation, my lean-to in this storm of awkwardness.

I bump into someone, a lady with her son. Their popcorn spills onto the red plush carpet. A preshow for the line.

"I'm so sorry."

"Watch where you're going!"

"Sorry!"

I glance over at the line. Of course. I am right in front of Huxley and Steve.

"Rebecca."

"Hi, Huxley."

"Are you here alone?" Her hair is dry. Steve's hair is dripping water onto his soggy shoulders. His umbrella lies at his feet.

"No, I came with Val and Ezra. They're in the movie. In the movie theater."

"Oh. That's nice they let you tag along with them," she says.

Addison and her boyfriend, who's at the local junior college but creepily still comes to all the Ashland events, snicker to each other, and I feel heat creep up my cheeks.

The mom I bumped reappears. "Hey, they charged me a refill fee for the popcorn. Three bucks. You're paying for it."

I'm not hallucinating: everyone in line is staring at me.

My mouth turns into a cotton swab. Sweat beads behind my ears. When I go to my ten-year high-school reunion, they'll introduce me as that tagalong girl who spilled a child's popcorn.

"Nice one, Rebecca," Huxley says.

"We used to be friends!"

She nestles herself against Steve's broad chest, and he closes his arms around her. That's her response, and I get it loud and clear. Other girls in line hug their boyfriends, so grateful they're not me.

I hand over the money and get this old woman out of my life. Forget the bathroom. I race back into the theater.

I stumble down to my row and find Ezra and Val making out. I guess they couldn't wait to get rid of me. I tap Val's shoulder, but she's too entwined with Ezra to notice. I'm standing in the aisle. Yet another batch of my classmates gawk at me. "Sit down!" one of them hisses.

These two aren't budging. I sit in the empty row behind them. I try to concentrate on the movie, but all I can see are my best friend and her boyfriend slobbering all over each other.

We used to be friends.

Tears well up in my eyes. Thank goodness I'm in the dark. Val and Ezra's quest to gobble each other's faces off overtakes my peripheral vision, but finally, the action onscreen wins out. The two remaining astronauts fight the evil queen, whose tentacles swirl around voraciously. She chases them through the spaceship, and because of all the brains she's sucked out, she knows how they'll think. She's smarter, faster and completely ruthless. But because of their small size, they can squeeze into a rescue pod, blast off, nuke their spaceship and kill the queen. This stupid movie totally transfixes me, opens up a new worldview in my mind. I feel like I'm right there with the astronauts, and I want to cheer at the top of my lungs when the spaceship blows up. It's like divine intervention that I came to see this movie on this night.

I have to vanquish the evil queen.

# 11

I don't have to do any thinking for Huxley and Steve's gossip dossier. As soon as I get home from the movies, I race up to my room and dig out my notebook. Everyone at school, including teachers, knows their history. It's an essential part of the social curriculum. I create from memory, the words spilling out faster than I can write them down. My pen whips back and forth on the page.

I combine their dating histories, because they've only ever been with each other. How adorable...and boring.

Huxley Mapother & Steve Overland

Dating History:

- Fall 7th grade (Huxley)/Fall 8th grade (Steve)–present
    - Steve—new student, played football. Huxley—nice and normal, then met Steve and became popular and demonic.
    - Eating lunch together by end of second week.

- Were seen at parties together by mid-September.
- Publicly confirmed relationship with article in school paper = the decline of modern journalism.
- PDA Level = ELEVATED
    - Held hands in school, kissed in the hall, nothing obscene.

Confirmed rumors:

- Winter sophomore/freshman: Steve—Got so drunk off tequila that he threw up on Huxley.[1]
- Fall junior/sophomore: Huxley—went on acai-berry diet and dropped 6 lbs before homecoming coronation.
- Fall senior/junior: Huxley and Steve window-shopped for wedding rings.

I stop writing. My hand is shaking. After over four years together as the top couple in school, do they really have no other rumors? No fights, no scandals? Huxley is a master of controlling her PR; you would never guess that Steve's family is scheming to rip them apart. In a school of fifteen hundred kids, why is there so little gossip about the biggest couple? Their relationship cannot be as perfect as it seems.

Diane and I form a battle plan over leftover pizza the next night.

---

1 That one is my favorite.

"I hate that the middle of the pizza never gets warm in the microwave. The edges are burning, but then the middle is still ice-cold," she says. But she eats it anyway.

My gossip dossier and yearbook are laid out on the dining table. My parents are at a bar mitzvah tonight, so we don't have to plot in private. "We have a better chance of getting Steve to dump Huxley. There's no way she would ever dump him."

"I'm not so sure. He's not going to be a big football star next year. His sex appeal is going to drop."

"He's going to Vermilion for her," I say. "And she'll probably join him when we graduate."

"That's bleak."

"Never underestimate the power of a whipped guy. He has a breaking point. She doesn't."

"Dammit!" Diane wipes a clump of sauce off her sweatshirt. A red splotch covers the *g* in *Rutgers*. Just one of many. "And since his family hates her guts, he's probably looking for any excuse to get rid of her. Now you need to work this angle, try to talk to his parents maybe."

"I don't think so," I say. I leave families out of my breakup schemes. I do have *some* ethics, despite my line of work. I pace around the room, careful not to knock into any of my mom's antique vases.

"What if he thinks she's cheating on him?"

"I doubt she would cheat on him, and he knows it." Huxley's face circles in my mind. Why would anyone break up with her? I think about all those picturesque moments she and Steve share during school. Her life is like a movie, every detail staged so that girls can aspire to be her. If you are her friend or boyfriend, you have to know your lines. And as I learned, if you don't fit the part, you're cut.

"What if she thinks Steve is cheating on her?" I ask.

Diane chugs the last of the Coke. "He wouldn't."

"Yeah, but if we make her think he's cheating?"

Diane puts down all food and drink and gives me her undivided attention. "Go on."

"If Huxley suspects he's cheating, she'll freak out and try to assert more control over him, which I think could drive him over the edge. But it has to be long term, a slow build. If we try anything easy, like a dirty text, she'll see right through it." My mind is in overdrive, imagining the possibilities.

"That could work, but who would be the other girl?"

My mind grinds to a halt. No girl in school would dare go after Steve. They know he has Property of Huxley Mapother stamped on his forehead. And I don't hate any girl enough to make them the unsuspecting other woman. My memory wanders to seeing Steve on his first day of school. So cute, so charming, so tall. He had no awkward prepopular phase like Huxley. There's no way she was his first girlfriend. It's not humanly possible. Guys like him don't sit on the market. There had to be someone before her, someone he left behind in Leland, his old town.

"His ex-girlfriend," I say.

"He has one?"

"They always do."

We go upstairs to Diane's computer to look at the photos in Steve's Facebook profile, but I don't have access. I'm not cool enough to be his friend in any context. All I can see on his page is his main picture: he and Huxley cuddling by a lake at sunset. It may seem like one of those candid pictures, but Huxley probably waited all day to get that shot.

"Great," I say.

"I have an idea," Diane says. "It's a bit old-school, though."

"They keep this stuff?" I ask in a hushed voice.

"Yeah. It's public record. All towns have them," Diane says at her regular volume level. The librarian at the reference desk shushes her.

The smell of old books stirs in the air, and I feel smarter just inhaling it. A giant clock hangs on the back wall, as if the Leland library is a timepiece for an old giant. Diane's finger scans shelf after shelf of town records until she finds bins labeled "Yearbooks: James Whitmore Junior High School" on the bottom.

"Of course they're on the bottom," I say. It takes both of us to pull the bin onto the floor. We scramble through Leland history until we find the relevant year.

I immediately flip to Steve's yearbook photo, for proof that I chose the correct book and to check out how young he looks. When I see his buzz cut and chubby cheeks, I laugh, even though he looks adorable.

Diane and I turn through pages of sports teams and clubs and faculty, all things I would care about if I actually went to this school. I'm amazed at how dated the pictures and people look after only five years. Then again, it has been five years. That's almost one-third of my life.

We reach the "Out and About" section. Real candid pictures of students around school. I can instantly tell who's popular by how many shots they're in. Steve pretty much has his own section. Multiple photos feature him and a lithe blonde with big eyes and a warm smile that makes me believe she's as friendly as she seems.

Angela Bentley.

A picture of the two of them eating at lunch sews it up for me. He's picking pepperonis off his pizza and putting them on hers. She's ripping off her crusts and placing them on his plate. It seems so routine for them. They give each other fake suspicious looks, hamming it up for the camera. "Angela and Steve: cutest couple ever!!" reads the caption. I have to agree.

"You were right, B," Diane says. She leans against the shelf, strumming her finger against an encyclopedia. "Do you think he still talks to her?"

"They're probably friends on Facebook. They seem too nice to have had a nasty break-up." I bring myself back to the present, away from reminiscing about someone else's junior high. "Maybe I can get into his phone and send her a message."

"He would delete it before Huxley saw it, and if she did see it, he would deny sending it. And anyway, how would we know any of this went on? They aren't like the normal couples you deal with. They're stronger and more secretive. I'll bet none of his friends know about Angela."

Diane looks at me for an answer, but I don't have one. She's right.

"You need to dig deeper," she says.

"What do you mean?"

"Undercover."

"Pretend to be friends with Huxley and Steve?" I wave off the suggestion. "No way."

"Really just Huxley. You need to get past their facade and join their inner circle. The more time you spend around her, the greater chance you have of seeing or hearing something you weren't supposed to."

"It would never work." There's no way Huxley would ever be my friend. Not again. The thought of spending time around her turns my stomach.

"Why not?"

"Huxley's mean, but she's not stupid."

"You said she's having auditions for the Student Dance Association. If you get on her squad, you'll have access to her for hours. Then we can get a better sense if the plan is working."

"Do you really think she'll tell me anything?"

"Didn't you two used to be friends?"

I slam the yearbook closed. "I'm not doing it, Diane. This isn't your business. It's mine, and I'm not doing it." My voice wobbles, but I remain stern.

Diane doesn't say a word. She was off at college when Huxley started cutting me out, and I only told her about it after the fact, like it was a petty high-school anecdote. We weren't as close back then; her world was revolving around Sankresh.

"You can do this." Diane breaks the silence. This time, she remembers to whisper. "Not just for Mr. Towne, but for all the people at your school who are treated like second-class citizens. You're going to expose this relationship for the pile of crap that it is."

# 12

"Rebecca, I didn't expect to find you here."

"Well, here I am." I stretch my arms out wide, then snap them back to my sides. I take deep breaths through my nose. I can do this.

The cafeteria looks different emptied out. Peaceful. No battle lines. Just a room with tables and chairs. Huxley sits behind a table with a sign-up sheet. Even after a full day of classes and acting superior to fifteen hundred of her peers, she is still fresh faced.

"You want to join SDA?" Mockery and judgment, her specialties, coat every word. SDA is a dance color war at Ashland created to provide a less gymnastics-centric alternative to cheerleading. We are split into two teams—green and white, with squads performing dance numbers set to a mash-up of new and old songs.

"Yes, I love to dance."

"You do?"

"You know that."

Huxley crosses her arms and leans back in her chair. Yep, she remembers, although she wishes otherwise. How dare I bring up a time when she was merely mortal.

We used to take lessons at the Frances Glory Dance School for Girls. Frances was a petite, old woman with a shock of white hair that looked like lightning in the night sky. She spoke in an indecipherable accent that Huxley and I were obsessed with and would impersonate during school. Frances always placed us in the back of routines because we were so tall. She used to call us her Telephone Poles. Or rather *Teelehfohna Pooles*.

"That was years ago," Huxley says. "And if I remember, you stopped going."

*Because of you,* I want to tell her. Dance class lost its luster when she got in with Addison and the other popular girls. The memory comes back, so vivid. I shove it to the back of my mind.

"You never forget those skills. It's like riding a bike."

"SDA is slightly more complicated."

"You're right," I say right back, hoping I didn't just stick my foot in my mouth.

Huxley gracefully swishes her hair behind her shoulders with a flick of her head. I wish my hair did that. "Rebecca, the Student Dance Association isn't some fun little club. It's a serious commitment for serious dancers. I'm not sure it would be the best fit for you."

"Everyone's allowed to audition. Let me show you what I got." I try to remain cheerful. I take more deep breaths.

"Fair enough."

She turns on the music. A dance remix of the Olympics theme plays, a bass-heavy rhythm pulsing beneath the brass fanfare. I tap my foot to get the beat.

"Ready when you are."

I perform a choreographed number I crafted from my Frances Glory memories (the happy ones) and watching old Britney Spears music videos. Huxley and I used to do this all the time, in her basement. We even posted a few of our performances online—and then quickly took them down. I practiced the moves all weekend, pulling certain muscles out of early retirement. I spent hours twirling, quick ball-changing, 5-6-7-8ing in my room until this routine was burned into my brain. I doubt other auditioners created such intricate routines, but I had to be immaculate to get Huxley to remotely consider me.

I turn and gyrate and try to make Britney proud, every move precise. I find myself enjoying this, remembering that once upon a time, I did have some type of athletic talent. I guess I still do. I dip forward then strike a pose for my finale.

"Thanks," Huxley says stoically, as if I'd handed her a coupon on the street. She doesn't make any notes on her pad. Her mauve pen lies there, matching her shoes. I doubt that is a coincidence.

*Thanks.* That's it? I catch my breath and feel soreness in my calves while Huxley remoisturizes her hands. A whole weekend wasted for nothing. Why did I think there'd be any fairness here?

"Thanks!" I nod and put on a beaming grin. I can't question her. That's a one-way ticket to instant rejection. "I'm going to keep my fingers crossed all week. I'm really excited!" I say. Maybe I can score some last-minute brownie points. I hate giving Huxley this power over me, but I keep saying *Alien Queen* over and over in my head to stay focused.

"We'll post team rosters on Thursday."

"Great!"

After an awkward moment of silence, I realize she's done talking. I collect my bag and jacket.

"You're really excited? About joining SDA?"

"Yeah. I've always wanted to do it." That lie didn't feel as forced for me. I did enjoy doing that routine, and perhaps under different social circumstances, I would have danced my heart out for SDA.

"It just seems so unlike you." Huxley sizes me up, her eyes scanning from my comfortable, fashionable flats to my recently combed hair. Okay, I freshened up during last period. You don't audition for SDA looking like you just went through six hours of classes. "You're not one for school spirit. You haven't done any dancing since the seventh grade. Yet you waltz in here and deliver a flawless routine. Just out of the blue. It seems... It's interesting."

Panic rises in my throat, wringing my mouth of all moisture. I knew I sounded too chipper to pass for normal. My mind scrambles for an answer.

"I don't know. People can change," I say. Huxley doesn't buy my excuse. Neither do I.

I get an idea. It seems so obvious, like it was sitting patiently, reading a magazine, waiting for me to find it. I grab a chair and sit across from Huxley. I can smell the sweet, honeysuckle scent of her hand cream. Time to level with her.

"It does seem interesting, right?" I ask.

"Yes."

"Between you and me, I'm not doing this to cross it off my high-school bucket list. I have an ulterior motive." I lean in and lower my voice. "I strongly believe that joining SDA will help me meet guys."

Huxley's spine goes upright. She raises an eyebrow at me. "You...want to meet guys?"

"Yeah. All the girls in the group have the best boyfriends, you especially."

"They do."

"It's either this or cheerleading."

"Don't do cheerleading. Those girls are sluts." She grins and nods, liking this change in me.

"Honestly, if anyone can teach me how to land a decent boyfriend, it's the girlfriend of Steve Overland." I cringe and wait for her response. I might be laying it on too thick. But a glance at her face tells me Huxley is lapping this up.

"Rebecca, what prompted this?"

"I've thought a lot about what you said in English class, about what you always say. And you're right! I was just too scared to love, and I only hated relationships because I wasn't in one. But I'm ready for that to change." I place a hand over my heart, mimicking every rom-com heroine. "Guys will like me if I'm in SDA."

"They will. Having the right type of well-roundedness will make you appealing to the right type of guys. And plus SDA is a lot of fun."

"It looks fun. I love the costumes. What's this year's theme?"

"The Olympics." She points at the stereo, and it makes

sense. "Each routine will represent a different sport. I want us to mix in those athletic movements with the choreography."

"I like it." And when I think about it, I actually do like it. Huxley glows with pride. She isn't president of SDA just for the power trip.

"This is all so unexpected."

"I know. When it comes to guys, I prefer to learn from the best."

That makes her blush. "I don't know."

"I must sound like such a weirdo, but I am ready to turn over a new leaf." I stand up and gather my things. She doesn't stop me. "Huxley, I know things are different between us now, but from one telephone pole to another, I could really use your help."

Another awkward moment of silence commences. This time, Huxley breaks it. "Okay," she says. Huxley smiles at me, a genuine smile. I can see all her shiny teeth.

"Thank you so much," I say, sounding like a peasant addressing a queen. But it's necessary to let her believe she's totally in control. "Where should we start?"

Huxley checks the clock on the wall. "Not now. I have to meet Steve."

"Hot date?"

She gives me an odd look. I guess we're not at the jokey friend stage yet. "Steve works at Mario's Pizza on Monday nights, so I hang out there and keep him company. It's usually dead there."

"How sweet."

“I love spending time with him, even if he is just folding pizza boxes. You’ll know the feeling soon.”

“You go there every Monday night?” I ask.

“Yes. It’s a good place to do homework.” She sticks her pad and mauve pen in her bag. She carries around fewer books than Val. “Rebecca, do you have heels at home?”

“Yeah.”

“Start wearing them.”

I barely wave back when she says goodbye. I’m too distracted by the break-up scheme that just popped into my head.

# 13

My dad will never throw away a coupon. One drawer in our kitchen is stuffed with discounts for every product and restaurant you can imagine: food, groceries, clothes, big-screen TVs, dog food even though we don't have a dog. I spend a good half hour rummaging through envelopes brimming with unredeemable offers until I find it. The background is a Sicilian-slice graphic: Half off any large pizza at Mario's. Valid Mondays only.

"Becca, what are you doing down there?" my mom calls from the staircase. "You're going to be late."

I shove the coupon in my wallet and grab my gym bag. My heels click loudly against the floor as I race out the door.

In the middle of eighth period, I receive a characteristically in-depth note from Val.

O. M. FREAKING. G.

I don't have to wait for her when class lets out. She jumps in front of me and cups my shoulders.

"Becca." Val breathes heavily. She zones in on my eyes, trying to communicate telepathically. I'm lost.

"Val."

"Becca." Kids file around us in all direction. "Becca."

"Use your words."

"Ezra. Told. Me. That..." Val stomps her feet, about to burst. "He can see himself falling in love with me. Falling in love! With me! Ezra! The cutest nonjock, nonsenior guy in the school."

My stomach knots itself like the rope I could never climb in gym class. She has yet to apologize for treating me like carry-on luggage at the movies, and I see now that she never will. Just because Val is in a relationship doesn't give her permission to be a crappy friend.

"Um, hello?" Val says. "Thoughts, comments, concerns?"

"What does that even mean?"

"Obviously it's too soon for us to be in love. But he can see himself falling in love with me."

"Why is he giving you the advance notice? If he's going to fall in love with you, then he should just let it happen. Is he saying that he could fall in love with you as like a test? 'You're on track to be fallen in love with by me. Keep up the good work'?" I throw in a thumbs-up.

"I think you're overthinking this. He's telling me that our relationship—P.S. I'm in a relationship. With a boy! How cool is that?—our relationship has the potential to go the distance. I think that's exactly what he means. Right?"

I check my watch. It's getting dangerously close to two-thirty. I pull Val down the hall as we continue our analysis.

"I don't know," I say. "But that's a really weird thing to tell someone. And really soon, too. Did he just blurt it out?"

"It's not something you just blurt out," Val says. She tells me about their Saturday excursion to Fort Lee, where movies in the 1910s used to shoot. "Hollywood before Hollywood," he told her. Before filmmakers wised up and migrated to sunny Los Angeles. Ezra gave her a personal tour of one of the soundstages. Val found it boring after the first hour, but she loved how into it he was. Ezra probably lit up like a department-store Christmas display describing everything.

Val looks me over. "You don't seem happy."

"For you? This is great," I say with all the excitement of a eulogy.

"Real convincing. You're my best friend. I thought you would seem more excited for me."

"I am. I just... Things are different now."

"They aren't. I just have an addition in my life."

"I know." And I know it's not true. I check the time on my phone: 2:27 p.m.

"I gotta run," I say. "Maybe we can hang out later?"

"Can't. Ezra and I are studying tonight. Where are you rushing off to?"

"Practice." My walk quickly morphs into a jog.

"For what?" Val asks, but I'm already gone.

My clicking heels reach a piercing pitch and echo down the hallway.

* * *

I enter the gym at 2:35 p.m. Forty sets of eyes stare at me, but nobody says a word. They are embarrassed for me. I keep my head down and scurry to the bleachers. Since when do clubs start on time here?

"You're late," Huxley says.

"I'm sorry. I didn't know you started right at two-thirty."

I take a seat in the front bleacher.

"Stand up," she says. "You can sit when practice is over."

"Are you serious?"

She glares at me with the fire of a thousand tanning booths. I'll take that as a yes.

I do as she says. All the girls have a perfect view of me. Now even the guys on the scenery crew stop what they're doing to gawk.

Huxley turns to the other dancers. "We only have the gym for two hours a day, and there are eight routines to master in six weeks' time. So when I send an email saying practice begins promptly at two-thirty, I mean it." She cocks an eyebrow at me.

Message received.

She turns on her smile, all traces of nastiness gone. I sit down.

"Rebecca, I didn't say you could sit yet."

It's only the thought of her relationship crumbling, of her sitting at a lunch table alone and forsaken, that propels me back to my feet.

"Our next order of business is to choose what sports each squad will be representing. Every captain came up with one sport. And this year, to make the process more democratic, I will be choosing sports at random from a hat," Huxley says, unaware that that isn't democracy.

She chooses first, exaggerated excitement on her face. "My squad, our sport is...curling? What's curling? Who put this in here?"

Meredith Arturro, captain of one of the lesser squads, steps forward. "It's like shuffleboard on ice."

"Shuffleboard isn't in the Olympics."

"But curling is. It's big in Canada."

While they go to someone's laptop to verify curling's existence, my squad mates talk among themselves. Ninety percent of their sentences begin with "My boyfriend."

"My boyfriend has the most adorable golden retriever."

"My boyfriend is taking his driving test next week, and he's been practicing like a maniac."

"My boyfriend and I went to a sushi restaurant, even though my boyfriend hates Japanese food. And I told my boyfriend that sushi is amazing, but my boyfriend was like 'I'm gonna puke if I have to put one of those things in my mouth.' So my boyfriend just got chicken. At a sushi place! Ugh, my boyfriend."

They wait for me to join in the conversation. I stand there with my mouth gaping open. "I didn't know they serve chicken at sushi restaurants."

The girls humor me with smiles, then continue their deep conversation.

Across the court, the scenery crew nails together the first of the sets. Each dance routine gets its own sets that wheel across the court to emphasize what the theme is. I guess the school had to find a way to open SDA up to guys. I spot a familiar face painting Olympic rings on a canvas.

"Hey."

"You're in SDA?" Ezra asks. Sweat forms around his temples. Flecks of paint dot his face and arms.

"I am. I live to dance."

"Me, too, but I find the costumes too binding," Ezra says, matching my penchant for sarcasm. "So I paint."

"You paint." I look at his masterpiece thus far. The rings are squares layered with jagged brushstrokes. Painting is not his medium. "Looks good."

"Yeah right." He dips the brush in more paint and steadies his hand on the canvas. That doesn't do the trick. "I'm directing the interstitial videos for the show, but since that's technically part of the scenery crew, I have to help out. At least I was able to sucker some of my theater compatriots into helping out, too."

"Yeah, you need someone to paint over all your strokes," his friend Jeff O'Sullivan says.

"I'm more Kubrick than Kandinsky, I guess."

"You're doing the videos? That's so cool," I say. The SDA captains, and their boyfriends, act in video skits to introduce the show and then each routine. They are usually the only ones who find them funny, but I have faith that Ezra can create something nongroanworthy. "Hopefully they'll be better than *Starship Alien II*."

"*Starship Alien II* had some redeeming qualities, surprisingly." Ezra's face brightens, as it does whenever movies come up.

"Yeah, it was under ninety minutes." I may have liked the

movie more if I didn't have to watch him and Val mash their faces together. I shudder at the memory.

"I'm with you," Jeff says, flicking back his thin, blond hair. He'll probably be bald by the time he's thirty, poor guy. Luckily, he's been dating Carrie Kirby since freshman year, and she doesn't seem to care. They're one of the few couples I can think of that seem to have lives outside of each other. Shocker. "My favorite part is when it ended. And when that scientist took her top off."

"There were some genuinely scary parts. And the movie had a good romantic subplot with Tony and Victoria," Ezra adds.

I throw my head back with laughter. "Oh, please! They have a one-night stand, and then he's madly in love with her and sacrifices his brains to the aliens? That's what I hate about romance in the movies. A guy looks at a girl once, and suddenly he's in love."

"It happens. There's that moment when you see someone and that feeling hits you. It's like you're noticing them for the first time."

"In the movies. Not in real life."

"You fall for someone in an instant, not gradually." Ezra taps his chest, getting more paint on his T-shirt. "The heart doesn't do gradual."

Everything Ezra says needs cheesy background music and sparkles. I wonder if his mom read him greeting cards as a baby. Jeff agrees with me and pretends to hold back throwing up. Ezra elbows him in the ribs.

"You could feel the attraction between Tony and Victoria," Ezra says.

"Ezra, do you even know what a one-night stand is? Victoria only felt one thing inside her that night, and it wasn't love."

He nods, taken aback by a girl not talking like a girl for a second. "Here, let's multitask," and he hands me the orange paintbrush.

"*Starship Alien II* wasn't a total abomination of cinema, but it definitely wasn't *Casablanca*," he says. Ezra talks like no other guy at school. It's refreshing.

"You got that right." My dad made me watch it on a snow day. He told me if I watched any more reality TV, my brain would rot, and it was time to watch something good. Usually I hate his movie recommendations, but I found myself captivated. Inspired by Humphrey Bogart, I went out the next weekend and bought myself a trench coat.

"You like *Casablanca*?"

"Yeah. It's a classic."

"Interesting," he says. He wipes up dripping paint with his T-shirt. "Now that had a great romance."

I take a break from adding curves to his square rings. "Just the opposite. It's one of the only movies where logic trumps love. Rick realizes that he and Ilsa had some fun times in Casablanca, but it's not serious enough to warrant leaving her husband."

"Not serious enough? When Rick tells Ilsa to get on that plane—that's love." Ezra makes the same pained face as my mom when she joined my dad and me for the final scene.

"Telling her to leave with her husband and never come back is love?"

"He cared about her so much. He wanted her to be safe and live a happy life above all else, even if it wasn't with him."

"Or he realized that their fling wasn't worth ruining their lives over. If he really loved her, capital-*L* loved her, he wouldn't have let her get on that plane." I point my brush at him.

"Let's agree to disagree." He turns back to the canvas. "What about *Titanic*? Easily the most romantic film of the past twenty-five years."

"I thought film geeks were supposed to have good taste in movies," Jeff interjects. "Man, we really need to get you to a Michael Bay film, stat."

"It's still a classic."

"Jack and Rose? That was just a vacation fling," I say. "He teaches her how to spit, she sees him in a tux, and suddenly they're soul mates? Nope."

Why do none of the movies girls at my school love have happy endings? One half of the couple either dies or moves away. But they can't get enough of those films. *Titanic, Shakespeare in Love, Atonement, The Notebook, A Walk to Remember,* every other Nicholas Sparks film known to man. My classmates want a relationship, yet they idolize movies where couples never wind up happy. I don't get it.

Ezra turns back to finishing his rings. "You must love *The Wizard of Oz,* then."

"What? There's no romance in that one."

"Exactly my point." He smiles and his eyes do the awkward shift up and to the left like a child asking for a cookie. Val's right. It's adorable, from an objective standpoint.

Huxley has begun speaking again. I have a minor panic attack. I drop the brush into the paint can.

"I have to go," I say.

Ezra gives me a salute. "Thanks for your help."

"Really, thank you," Jeff says. "It actually looks good."

I spin back around. "You guys do know that there's no orange ring in the Olympics logo, right?"

* * *

Angie,

It's been too long. I'm working this Monday night—I'll give you extra pepperoni as long as you save me your crust ☺

I tuck the coupon into the note and stick them in an envelope. I stroll down my driveway in slippers, relieved to be out of those heels. I place the envelope inside the mailbox and turn up the flag. The wind pierces at my skin and pushes me back.

Oh, no, Mother Nature. You're not stopping me tonight.

# 14

The first three days of SDA have been a parade of pulled muscles, twisted ankles and missed cues. I didn't know it was possible for every part of my body to be sore. My fingernails. My earlobes. My index finger. They all throb like they're under a pain microscope. My teammates barely break a sweat.

Since I'm on Huxley's team, not to mention in her final dance number, I have to be the cherry atop the perfection sundae. Our number has to bring people to their feet. When I think we're Broadway good, Huxley finds the cracks. She's blunt, morally opposed to sugarcoating. In fact, we're not supposed to eat sugar or any complex carbohydrate while under her tutelage. I can tell, though, that Huxley's favorite part of being captain is getting to point out the flaws of other dancers. Especially me.

"Rebecca, on that first count, you start with your right

foot, not your left. Do you know the difference between your right and your left?"

"Rebecca, your leg has to go higher. You're not kicking a soccer ball."

"Rebecca, smile when you dance. You're supposed to be having fun."

"Rebecca." She cringes at the pouches of sweat under my arms and between my legs. "Never mind."

Is this her plan to mold me into datable material? Belittle and berate me on a daily basis while causing me excruciating pain? Did I join SDA or a cult? She sneaks looks among her friends, sharing a telepathic moment at my expense. I suspect that helping me was never her plan. I'm the entertainment, the thing that gets the team to smile while they dance.

The only thing that pulls me through practice is knowing that Monday is just a few days away.

"Spider-Man is a much better superhero than Iron Man," Fred says to his friends before shoving a handful of ketchup-drenched fries into his mouth. "All Iron Man has is a metal suit."

"At least he can fly. Spider-Man just swings. Do you ever wonder why Spider-Man doesn't fight villains in the desert or tundra? No buildings to swing off of," Howard says back as he bites off a chunk of soft pretzel.

They've been at this argument for the entire lunch period, and neither has chewed with his mouth closed once. Since Val went to eat with Ezra, I've had to embrace my new lunch-table role of token girl. Fred, Howard and Quentin, and their stacks of plastic-enshrined comic books, have taken over. At least I'm not eating alone.

"What do you think?" Fred asks me. "Iron Man or Spider-Man. Who's cooler?"

I shrug my shoulders. I'd be better equipped to explain the quadratic equation. "Well, Robert Downey Jr. is pretty funny."

"Booyah!" Howard yells. The other two slump back in their seats. This isn't terrible. It's nice not listening to a conversation about boys, shoes or our classmates.

I doodle on a copy of Huxley and Steve's homecoming picture. I don't touch Steve's face, but Huxley gets devil horns, blacked-out teeth and a thought bubble over her with "I'm a bitch" scrawled inside of it. It's juvenile, I know. And it's just a piece of paper. But I do get some pleasure out of seeing Huxley look like a redneck devil.

"So Val and Ezra are now official, huh?" Quentin asks me. He's the last person I would guess cared about Ashland gossip, but I suppose every student likes to stay up on current events.

"He's 'not into labels,'" I say, making air quotes with my fingers. "But, yes, they are."

"That guy has got some serious game," Howard says after chugging his can of Hawaiian Punch. "I don't think I've ever seen him without a girlfriend. Like not even for a day."

"I think someone has a crush," Quentin says. He mimes to Howard to rub the red off his teeth.

"No, I'm just saying. The guy always has a girl by his side. I'm in awe. I wish I had half his mojo."

"You wish you had half his girlfriends."

"Yeah, that, too."

I wait for Fred to chime in, but he's preoccupied with another table across the cafeteria. A sextet of guys, who look identical to my tablemates, huddle around a table oohing and aahing over something. A Rubik's cube? A *Playboy*?

"Jeremy Fowler brought in another one of his vintage Batman comics from the 1940s," Fred says. I shrug my shoulders. "It's like if a girl brought in a pair of Jimmy Choos, I think."

I close my notebook, hiding the picture. "I didn't know you were such a fashionista."

"I have a sister." His eyes drift to the other table again. "We all used to sit together. We even had this tradition whenever a guy brought a rare comic to lunch. None of us ate when the comic was out. We gave ourselves a twenty-minute time limit to flip through it, then we put it away and had lunch." He rests his head on his hand.

"What happened?" I find myself slipping into Break-Up Artist mode.

"Jeremy's grandpa died," he says, his voice dropping. "Jeremy was never a real comic fan. He just liked to pretend he knew what he was talking about, and we always kind of ignored him. He once mixed up the Green Lantern and Green Goblin!"

"Well, they're both green."

"Trust me. You don't mess those two up," he says. He shakes his head, getting worked up. "But then his grandpa died and left him this stash of vintage DC Comics. Out of the blue! The guys were salivating over them. Suddenly, he thinks he's lord of the lunch table and demands that we only discuss DC Comics, or else he won't bring in any of the old books. My boys and I—" he points to Quentin and Howard "—are Marvel fans through and through. We've had lively debates at our table." Fred gets more animated, leaning closer to give me the full scoop.

"But Jeremy said the table should only be for DC fans. Real comic-book fans. He had the nerve to say that! I said that's stupid, of course. So he put it to a vote. Since the other guys wanted to check out his old comics, they sided with him. The table voted and excommunicated us when we came back from Christmas break. Heath Ledger is probably rolling over in his grave."

"Well, why don't you do something about it?" I ask. Who knew boys could be just as catty as girls? I can feel the wheels churning in my head, a plan forming.

"He won't listen to what I have to say."

"Get him to sell the comics."

"He wouldn't do that."

"He would if the price were right," I say.

"I make eight dollars an hour at my parents' restaurant. I'll make him an offer he can't refuse in about fifty years."

That makes me laugh. It's refreshing when you find people at this school with a real sense of humor. I regain focus and catch a quick look at Jeremy. "What if his friends found out he was selling the comics? They'd be mad, right?"

"Selling vintage comics? That's sacrilege." Fred shudders at the thought.

"Perfect. Set up a fake eBay account for him. Or better yet, just contact him anonymously and say you'd be willing to pay for his cache. Not the big bucks, just a so-so amount."

"But I can't."

"He doesn't know that. You just need to catch him being interested, then casually show his friends that he'd be willing to give up the goods for some lowball offer." I shrug nonchalantly. These genius ideas just come naturally. "Even if it's not true, all you need to do is plant that seed of doubt, and the rest will take care of itself."

But Fred isn't bowled over. He looks, well, kind of freaked out. "That's, um, pretty extreme."

"Well, so is turning your friends against you and excommunicating you from their table."

"It's different." Fred shakes the thought from his mind and piles his trash on his plate. "I'm not going to sink to that level. I mean, I still have these guys," he says, patting Howard and Quentin on the back.

"You're right," I say. I stick my notebook in my bag.

I use the bathroom pass during seventh period. Steve's gym period. I tiptoe into the boys' locker room. The smell suffocates me. I pull my shirt up over my nose and breathe in the fabric softener. Why do guys smell so much?

Like with most areas of our school, the locker rooms have not been updated in thirty years. The lockers are narrow and rusty, the green paint only visible on certain ones. Nobody's backpack can fit in them, so they're left on the floor.

Bad for students. Good for me.

I find Steve's sleek, waterproof backpack in the back of the middle row. A Christmas gift from Huxley last year. It was meant for cross-country expeditions, not the halls of high school.

I open the locker above Steve's backpack with the V56 key. I hope his underwear doesn't fall out onto my face. I shield myself before opening.

I take the homecoming picture out of my back pocket and tape it on the back of the locker door. A crumpled mountain of clothes hangs precariously on the left hook. Once some of his friends get a glimpse, the news should wind through school. Little-known fact: guys are bigger gossips than girls. Girls will keep secrets from each other, but their boyfriends spill the dirt as soon as they hit the dugouts, court or locker room. They just don't get caught.

I haven't sneaked into the locker room since I had to break up Nathan Crane and Sarah Covington. Her friends couldn't stand what a snob he was and that he was turning Sarah into one, as well. Once Sarah found texts on his phone calling her incompetent and stupid, she gave him the heave-ho. I can't believe that was only a year ago. Any guilt I had about what I was doing disappeared when it turned out Nathan did feel that way about his girlfriend. He just loved being with someone who made him feel so superior.

Coach Kapnek's raspy voice echoes off the lockers. I squat down and hide at the end of the row. I peer around the corner into his office, where Steve is in the hot seat.

Still in my squat position, I waddle over to the wall by his door and situate myself behind a bin filled with used towels. No one said Break-Up Artists live glamorous lives.

"Chandler University is still interested," Coach Kapnek says. "They're a great school."

"There's only one reason they want me. Did you talk to Vermilion?"

"I talked to my friend there. They're offering nothing. But did you expect them to hand out a merit scholarship to a guy with a B average?"

Coach Kapnek's desk squeaks. He must've sat on top of it. What's with teachers at this school not using chairs?

"Are you sure about this, Steve? You can be honest with me. Do you want to play college football?"

I lean my head closer to the door.

"No," he says, barely audible.

"Can I be honest with you? I think you do."

"That's not my life anymore. It's time to move on. It's not like I'm going to go pro or anything."

"You never know. It's still a great opportunity, and once this door closes, it's never going to open again."

"Thanks, Coach." Steve bolts out of his office and, luckily, in the opposite direction of the towel bin.

I waddle back to my locker hiding place just as Coach Kapnek leaves his office. He stands in the doorway a few moments. I crouch down farther, behind a fat backpack, and keep my breathing silent and controlled. He takes a few steps in my direction and stops. *If you get caught, Becca, just say you're sleepwalking.*

He strums his fingers on the lockers. I squeeze myself into an even tighter ball behind the backpacks. Peeling paint lingers in my hair. I close my eyes, knowing if I look at him, he'll sense it and look straight at me.

Coach Kapnek exhales a gust of air and walks past my row into the open bathroom area. What do guys have against privacy? While he's busy, I make a run for it.

"Hey! Who's there?" he yells at the wall.

Do guys realize how ridiculous they look at urinals?

Movies and television have lied to me. Stakeouts are not fun and exciting. They are boring.

So boring.

Diane and I have spent the past three hours sitting in her car spying on Steve and Huxley at Mario's Pizza. I fidget in my seat, alternating between stretching my legs and sitting cross-legged every five seconds. That's almost as often as Diane changes the radio. No music can hide the sound of our growling stomachs. Skipping dinner to stare into a pizzeria was not my smartest move. At least we don't have to smell it.

We take turns with my dad's heavy-duty binoculars. The bridge of my nose is red and indented and stings whenever I hold them to my face. He bought them one Saturday afternoon because our neighbor's house was broken into. He wants to live on a safe block, and the package said these are the same binoculars used by Navy SEALs. Those men must have stronger noses than me.

Worst of all, there's been no sign of Angela, or her boyfriend.

"If I have to watch Ken and Barbie kiss one more time, I'm going to projectile all over the dashboard," Diane says.

"She will come. She has to. You don't receive a letter like that in the mail and then not do anything about it."

"What if she emailed him instead?"

I'm not that high-tech. I can't access his email or bug his phone. Computers are so unromantic, though. What girl wouldn't be a sucker for a handwritten note? It's so old-fashioned. She wouldn't ruin that vibe with a text message. At least, I hope not. "We'll find out soon enough."

A woman enters the pizzeria. Diane perks up. She looks through the binoculars. "False alarm."

She sinks down in her seat and twirls her gum around her finger.

"So, baby sister, will Val and what's-his-face be your next victims?"

"I can't do that." That thought did cross my mind a few times. And every time, I shivered with disgust. How could I call myself her friend after doing that?

"You thought about it, though?"

"Doesn't mean I'll do it. Have you ever thought about doing that to your 'friends'?"

"What's with the air quotes for *friends*? They're still my friends," Diane says. She switches out her gum wad for a fresh piece.

"Are you sure about that?"

"I care about them enough to let their relationships self-destruct on their own."

"What about Owen's birthday?" I ask. Before I left tonight, I saw an invitation for Erin's son's first birthday. It was in the trash.

"He won't notice my absence."

It's hard to call someone your friend when you won't acknowledge her kid's birthday. Diane used to love organizing birthday events for her friends. She would buy a cookie cake and decorate it herself with inside jokes. For Sankresh's twenty-first birthday, she planned a bar-crawl extravaganza with their friends. I saw photos where she put floating sparklers in his drinks. She was always let down on her birthday because Sankresh was never as creative as she was.

Diane senses my disappointment. "The invite was just a formality. They all just want to see what a mess I've become. It's cheaper than hiring a clown." She laughs at her joke.

"I think they'd be happy to see you." They were all so close in college, the girls felt like my friends, too. I look forward to leaving the dull cliques of high school behind and finding my own group in college like Diane did.

"I can't go," Diane says. Suddenly, the car gets quiet, like all of her sarcasm fizzled away.

"Why? Did you guys get in a fight?"

"Technically, no." Diane's face softens. "They've all moved on. And I'm still here."

"You don't have to be."

"I wasn't given that choice. I'll always be here." Her voice wobbles, but she doesn't cry. I don't think she has any more tears left after last year.

I want to say something, but it's not as if I have some magic answer. I can feel the moment passing us by. Just like Diane wants it to.

She brings the binoculars back to her eyes.

"Anything good?" I ask.

"Actually, yeah." She hands me the binoculars.

"It's Angela." I'm always shocked when my plans go, well, according to plan. It's funny to think people are listening to me, even if they don't know it.

"Where's her boyfriend?"

"I guess she didn't bring him."

"And she waited until they were about to close. Interesting."

It was.

Steve's face lights up with shock, but quickly shifts to pleasantly surprised. I wasn't expecting that reaction, until I realize that of course Steve wasn't expecting a ghost from the past to stroll in for pizza. Angela is apprehensive, but when Steve comes from behind the counter, she hugs him.

I narrate for Diane. "She is so nervous."

Her light skin shows off the redness flushing her cheeks. They have some harmless chitchat. No crossed arms or standoffish posture. Angela reaches into her bag.

"She's going to show him the note!" I say and slap Diane on the arm a few times. "Oh, wait."

Huxley joins their conversation, hooking her arm around Steve's. Angela removes her hand from her bag. Steve makes introductions.

"Blah blah blah. Wow, I've never seen such forced smiles."

"From who?" Diane asks.

"Both of them. They're acting like they're long-lost best friends."

"Keep your friends close..."

Angela orders a pepperoni slice. Steve boxes it up for her while Huxley hangs out by the register. She wants to get out of there as soon as she can. I don't blame her. I feel bad that I threw Angela into this, but it's not like I'm ruining her life. So what if she reconnects with an old flame? You can never have too many friends.

Diane notices I've stopped narrating. "What's happening?"

"Nothing," I say with a sigh. "Huxley went back to her table. Angela got pizza. The end."

Angela shares an awkward goodbye wave with Steve and Huxley. I stop watching. I guess my plan sounded better in my head.

"Sorry, B." Diane turns the radio back on and flips through three stations in ten seconds. She's probably a master at *Name That Tune.*

I know my plan wasn't foolproof, but I thought it would be somewhat idiotproof. I'm dreading SDA practice tomorrow now that I have nothing to look forward to. I replay the scene in the pizzeria in my head. A detail sticks out to me, and I almost leap out of my seat. How did I miss it? "She ordered a slice of pepperoni," I tell Diane.

"Maybe she likes it."

"She does, but Steve would always give her his pepperoni slices."

"Interesting."

But it's not enough, I know she wanted to say. I rest back into my seat. Diane takes my binoculars for a second opinion. She gazes into Mario's. A huge smile overtakes her face.

"What?"

Diane hands me the binoculars. I need both hands to lift them. She's giggling and shaking her head.

"What?" I ask. I zoom into the pizzeria. Huxley is doing homework, and Steve's wiping tabletops. The night ends with a whimper.

"Look at Steve."

He turns to a corner, away from Huxley to clean a pair of tables, and that's when I see it.

Steve is eating Angela's pizza crust.

# 15

For the next two weeks, my life consists of school, sleeping and SDA. My postpractice aches usually dissipate by the next morning, except on Fridays, when I feel like I barely finished a marathon. I've been so busy I barely pay attention to schoolwork or how little I see Val.

Huxley has fewer notes for me, only minute details that I totally missed. Ezra and I have shared plenty of eye rolls over her comments. However, she isn't trying to be mean anymore. It seems like she just wants every dance to be a work of art and won't settle for anything less. I've been working extra hard not to have two left feet. I get up an hour early to practice in my room. I can feel myself getting better. I'm dancing with confidence, not just trying to keep up. When the music starts, my body shifts into autopilot. Those old lessons from Frances Glory are coming out of hibernation. Today, finally, Huxley acknowledges my improvement.

"Your brain and legs seem to be on the same page today."

I blush, just a crumb-sized bit. I can't help it.

Huxley ends practice early to hand out costumes. She stands next to an open box, dabbing her temples with a towel. Even after two hours of choreographed sweating, Huxley's hair flows down her back like she just left the salon. I look like I just left the rain forest.

The girls gather in their usual cliques on the bleachers.

"It had devil horns and 'I'm a bitch' written above her," Ally Zwick whispers to Kerry Anderson.

"Whoa. Tell us how you really feel, Steve," Kerry says back. I've overheard some variation of this conservation buzz its way through school. I love watching my work elicit such a reaction.

Huxley holds up the costume: a tracksuit made for a stripper pole with matching fuzzy earmuffs.

"Nice, right?" Huxley says to a sea of nodding heads. They'll have no problem fitting into those things. "I had them add the earmuffs because curling is done on the ice, where it's cold."

She distributes them among the girls. Some hold them against their chests. If I had their toned bodies with curves in all the right places, I would be excited, too.

"This year, costumes are ten dollars," she says. That garners whoops and light applause. "I know. My dad and I found a great deal online."

"Oh, please," Ally whispers to Kerry. "I doubt her dad went bargain hunting."

I have to agree with Ally. Huxley's dad works on Wall Street, where he is very well compensated. Doing what, I don't know, but she used to show me pictures from his corner office with a view of the Statue of Liberty. They don't do discounts. They probably paid top dollar for these costumes and lied to the school board. Only the best for Huxley's team.

Huxley shuts the now-empty box. "These costumes are very...compact, so I recommend you take the money we saved and wax any areas that may be seen."

"Will shaving be good enough?" a girl next to me asks.

"Stubble is for boys."

My teammates spend the rest of practice trying on the stripper tracksuits. I'm not ready for that yet, so I pretend to read my history notes while envying their genes. Girls join Ally and Kerry's huddle. They glance over at Huxley across the gym before talking. My teammates chat in the same animated, overzealous style people slip into whenever conversation turns to gossip. It's a biological compulsion. Talking about others is the earliest form of entertainment, after all.

"Do you think she realized Steve worked there?" Tamara Boyle asks, shoving hair behind her ears every point-two seconds.

"Please. You don't take the interstate to get pizza." Kerry turns her head in a "come on now" way. "My boyfriend heard Steve was flirting with her."

"What? No way." Ally cups her hand over her mouth. "You think he would do that right in front of her?"

Kerry shrugs. "Anything's possible."

"That sucks," Tamara says, then reconsiders. "Though it would be kind of cute if he got back together with his ex-girlfriend after five years. It's like a movie I would totally drag my boyfriend to."

"Yeah, Snow White saves Prince Charming from the Wicked Witch," Ally jokes.

"Hey, guys, let me know if you need a different size," Huxley says behind them. "With the costumes."

Their faces turn white as they frantically trade "Oh, crap!" expressions.

"Sure," Ally stumbles out.

I shut my book. "It's really sad that you guys have such boring lives and low self-esteem that you have to resort to gossip. Some girl bought a slice of pizza. Chill out."

The girls stay silent. What can you say to that? In normal social contexts, I would have stayed quiet. But I don't care about being their friend. And a part of me felt uncomfortable listening to them. They were talking mere feet from the subject of their gossip. That's just sloppy.

I pack my backpack, square my shoulders and walk to another corner of the bleachers.

Once settled in my new spot, I glance over at Huxley. She's engrossed with a group of her friends. She doesn't look my way for the rest of practice.

It's not enough having to practice around dozens of the best-looking girls in school. I also have to share a locker room with them—in case I forgot how pale and blah my body is.

Huxley and a girl from the white team change next to me. I don't know her name, but I think it's the last name of a president. Madison, Taylor, Carter. Something like that.

"So Bari adamantly denies making that crazy-ass wedding binder," Madison/Taylor/Carter says.

"Who would do that?" Huxley asks. She slips on her wavy peasant shirt. Leave it to her to make a hippie staple look utterly preppy.

"She thinks it was a setup."

"Not this again," Huxley says.

"She's claiming it's the Break-Up Artist."

My back goes yardstick straight. I keep my head down as I dress.

"Derek thinks it was, too," M/T/C says. She chuckles and smoothes out wrinkles in her blouse.

"Of course he does."

"I don't know, though. I think maybe she's onto something. Whoever wrote that note in the stall could be real. When you think about it, there have been some strangely convenient break-ups at our school."

I'm so focused on listening, I don't notice that I put on my shirt backward. The collar chokes my neck.

"The Break-Up Artist is an urban legend," Huxley says.

"Aren't all urban legends rooted in truth?"

"Reagan, you are not this susceptible."

Reagan!

Huxley continues: "If that book was planted, then why aren't they back together? Spare me your conspiracy theories.

"Though, if Bari knew what was good for her, she would move heaven and earth to get back with him," Huxley says. She pulls up impossibly tight jeans.

"If they're meant to get back together, then they will." Reagan wraps her curls into a messy bun.

Huxley rolls her eyes. "Some things should not be left up

to chance. Guys like Derek Kelley don't come around every day. Now Bari is just another single girl. She's thrown herself back into the unrecognizable masses." Huxley shakes her head. "Her loss."

"That's a little harsh, Huxley. He's just a guy."

She leans in close to Reagan. "Do you think we would be friends if you weren't dating Mark Olawski?"

All cheerfulness evaporates from Reagan's face. She finishes dressing in silence and gives Huxley a polite nod before leaving.

Huxley and I are the only ones left in this row. I get nervous for some reason. She's said far worse to me.

"Rebecca," she says. She shoves her feet into uncomfortable yet oh-so-beautiful heels. "You've gotten a lot better out there."

"Thanks." I tie my sneakers. Huxley notices them. I unzip my backpack and show her my heels. "If I wore these after practice, my feet would fall off."

"Remember those golden slippers we got in Frances's class?" she asks out of nowhere. "Do you still have yours?"

I picture them, hanging out on my bedroom floor next to my desk.

"Yeah. I think so." For the sixth-grade level, instead of handing out trophies, Frances Glory decided to dye a pair of ballet slippers platinum gold for each girl. It must've been a last-minute idea because the paint wasn't dry when she distributed them. My mom called her up, irate that my leotard was spattered with gold paint that wouldn't wash out. She wasn't the only parent. For our class picture, we all wore our stained leotards.

“I think the paint finally dried like a year ago,” I say, and Huxley cracks up. It’s a real, hearty laugh that I haven’t heard in years and kind of missed.

Huxley thinks about the slippers, or the class or something. She sits on the bench and stares at the locker for an extended moment. I’ve never seen her be so introspective.

“You think someone’s your friend,” she says. “It’s a sad day when you can’t tell your closest friends something in confidence.”

Is she talking to me? Is she talking about me? I can’t tell. I’m not used to dealing with a sensitive Huxley. I’m out of practice.

“They don’t sound like much of a friend,” I say.

“I told my friends that stuff about Angela in confidence.”

“Well, honestly, the higher you climb, the more those around you want to take you down. One of the drawbacks of being happy, I guess.” I can’t believe I’m giving Huxley any type of sane advice, but I’ve met her friends, and I wouldn’t trust them either. Addison and Reagan and the rest of them, all reveling in their popularity but wishing they could ascend higher, wishing they were dating the quarterback. I realize that being queen bee is probably exhausting, and I’m impressed that she’s been able to keep it up this long.

“You’re smarter than this,” I say.

“Thanks.”

I remain frozen on the bench. I still have to put on my right shoe, but I don’t want to break this moment.

“I’m really glad you joined SDA,” she says. Huxley places her hand over mine, and I squeeze.

“Me, too.”

# 16

As I lie on my bed attempting to do math homework, I receive an unexpected phone call from an unexpected caller.

"Hey! Want to go ice-skating tonight?" Val asks me.

"Now?" It's 7:16 p.m. on a Thursday. I'm not cool enough to have a social life on a weeknight. I can barely scrape one together on a weekend.

She explains to me that the regional college opens up their rink to the public Thursday nights.

"Ezra and I heard about it from Jeff," she says. "We'll pick you up in twenty."

"I don't know." My eyes dart from my clock to the homework sprawled out on my bed to my sore legs. Not to mention the fact that I only ice-skated once, and that ended in blood, tears and stitches.

"'I don't know' means 'convince me more.' Fine. It will be so much fun! Maybe some guy will ask you to skate with him and hold your hand. It's a scientific fact that everything is more romantic on ice."

"What's your source? *Us Weekly*?"

"Come on, Becca!"

I won't lie. It does feel nice that my friend is so excited to see me. Val and I haven't hung out in what seems like forever. And I don't mind that Ezra will be there, too. Now that I've gotten to know him, I'll be spending time with two friends. It shouldn't be awkward, as long as they aren't munching on each other's faces the whole night.

"So what's up?" Val asks me for the second time in the car. I hate those generic questions. People use them on someone they don't know, not their best friend.

"Not much." I shrug my shoulders. When you go from sharing every minute detail to barely speaking for a few weeks, it's hard to know where to start.

Val never knew me in my Frances Glory days. We knew of each other in middle school, but we didn't run in the same circles. I don't know why I never became friends with her friends. Huxley didn't like them, and that was that. It wasn't until our eighth-grade trip to Washington, D.C., that Val and I had this unexpected-yet-profound bonding session. We sat next to each other on the bus, and four hours and three states later, we were friends. It's amazing how that happens. With most people, my conversations never go beyond small talk. But then with a very special few, I just click. We bypass meaningless chitchat. After five minutes, I feel like I've known them forever. I can't explain it. It's completely outside my control. That's what happened with Val. So it breaks me that we're stuck in small-talk land tonight.

"Oh!" Val says, a thought coming to her. I'm all ears. "Ezra and I ate at the best restaurant Sunday night. Have you ever been to The Alamo Steakhouse?"

"Aren't you a vegetarian?" I ask her.

"I was, but I'm getting back into red meat." She rubs Ezra's thigh. He grabs her fingers and squeezes.

"Ezra, you're *not* a vegetarian?"

"Don't let the hemp necklace fool you. I love me some cow."

"Interesting." Why did my alleged best friend not tell me she was getting back into red meat? I know it's just cow, but I feel a little betrayed. I look outside, and it's darker than usual. The college is on a hill away from neighboring towns. The students there call it Harvard on the Hill.

More awkward silence. Even though this is a two-door, she feels so far away.

"How's Tamara doing?" Ezra asks me. "That looked like a nasty fall she took in practice yesterday."

"Well, she's a sweet girl, but such a spastic dancer. She gets really dizzy really fast."

"You know what Jeff calls her, right?"

"Tropical Storm Tamara, and we thought of that name together." I cock an eyebrow at him through the rearview mirror.

"That's a good one. I'm curious what name you have picked out for Huxley."

"It wouldn't be ladylike of me to divulge."

He bursts into a high-pitched giggle. It's kind of awkward for him, but also kind of adorable.

Val spins around to face me. She smacks her lips together, an obvious tell when she's frustrated. "You joined SDA? Why didn't you tell me?" She eyes me then Ezra, as if she cracked a conspiracy.

"I thought I told you," I say, which I know is a lie. But why didn't Ezra say anything?

"She dances quite well. Huxley is putting her front and center in her routine," Ezra says. He and I laugh at the thought.

"I took dance lessons forever ago," I say.

"Cool." Val slumps down in her chair and strums her fingers against her thigh until we reach the rink.

Even with the crowds, the ice rink has specific rings for all groups. Families and kids stay on the outer rim. The more expert skaters go in the middle, where they can whoosh in wide ovals. The third ring belongs to couples, holding hands while they skate. The bright lights against the steaming white ice creates a dreamlike—and fine, romantic—setting.

Val and Ezra skate around and around the rink. Val has better balance than I thought, and she isn't playing the "oops, I keep falling" card, to her credit. They glide across the ice, their cheeks a rosy red.

I hug the wall and lurch my way forward. Two-year-olds pass me.

I'm so focused on not cracking my skull open that I don't see Ezra skate next to me. He taps me on the shoulder.

"Having fun?"

"Tons!" I say. "Can't you tell?"

He holds out his gloved hand. "Let's get you out on the ice."

"I am on the ice."

He shoots me a look and keeps his hand out. "You look like you're on a ledge debating whether to jump."

"I'm fine. I'm going at my own pace." I already feel like a third wheel. I don't need him and Val treating me like a Make-A-Wish kid.

"Let me take you on one loop, and if you hate it, I'll bring you back here."

Val cheers me on from outside. She sips on a Coke.

"Fine," I say. I slap my hand into his. He whisks us off. I tighten my grip until my hand whitens.

"Loosen up. You're so stiff."

I'm doing a skate-walk. My skates clomp against the ice. My body remains tense and rigid like the Tin Man.

"Don't pick your skates up," Ezra says. "Bring them up a little, then let them glide." He demonstrates and makes it look so easy. I have a minor heart attack as I stand surrounded by speed skaters.

He hustles back to me and takes my hand. "I got you. Let's try it. Keep your skates on the ice and push off."

I take my first glide. It's more of a walk-glide, like a checkmark. My next move has a touch more grace. Then I take more of a glide on my third try and fall on my butt. I want to punch the ice.

Ezra pulls me up. "That was good."

"I think I'll go back to the wall."

"We're not even halfway around yet. You still owe me a semicircle. Now, stop looking down at your feet. It's screwing up your balance." Ezra turns and is now directly in front of me. "This time when we skate, look up and right at me."

He takes my hands and some weird electric current shivers through me. His hands are clammy, but they give me a sense of comfort.

"What if you bump into someone?"

"You'll have to be my eyes. It's all on you, Becca."

I want to take off my jacket. I may be standing on ice, but I am sweating.

"Ready?" he asks.

I look down then pull my head up. I stare at Ezra. His hazel eyes and round face pull me in immediately. It feels weird making such direct eye contact with him. It's intimate even though it's not supposed to be, like he's viewing some secret part of me. But it becomes hypnotic, and I start to notice details. A faint scar on his jaw. The redness of his lips. Eyebrows that slope down and trail off to the ends of his eyes. Do all eyebrows do that?

"You're doing great," he says.

Apparently, I'm gliding across the ice. A wave of exhilaration courses through me, unlocking me from chains of tension. The cold air whips across my face. Ezra has a wild constellation of freckles above his cheek. His eyes keep penetrating into mine, and it's making me flustered and I want to look away but I can't. I wonder what he sees.

I forget that Val is on the sidelines, that dozens of people are skating all around us, that there's noise or light or anything else in a five-mile radius of us. I'm sucked into a trance, and I have to get out.

I push past him and skate to the far wall under the scoreboard. Ezra calls out to me, but I lean my body against the ledge and catch my breath.

Outside my area of the rink, I am snapped back into reality when I suddenly notice Steve. He leans against the wall next to the emergency exit. His wide-eyed smile is on full display.

Angela stands beside him, laughing at every word he says.

# 17

To: Robert Towne
From: Le Break-Up Artiste

Dear Mr. Towne,

Over the past month, I have made significant progress in the dissolution of Steve and Huxley's relationship. Huxley, and several of her close friends, are beginning to suspect that Steve is having an affair with an old flame. Doubt and worry are two of my strongest tools. Nothing ends a relationship quicker than making a person override their heart with their warped, paranoid mind. Or at least that's what I read on a Hallmark card once.
I will, of course, continue to keep you updated.

Sincerely,
The Break-Up Artist

The next day, SDA practice cannot come soon enough. In eighth period, I pull a fresh pen out of my backpack. When I sit up straight again, I find a paper football waiting for me on my desk.

LIFE = OVER

I crumple it up and toss it into my backpack. I don't look her way.

"Becca! Wait up!"

Val catches up to me in the hall after class. She heaves for air. Sweat mats her hair to her face. She would be so embarrassed if she knew that.

"What's up?" she asks in a fake, cheerful customer-service-rep voice.

I have places to be, so I give in and cut to what she wants. "Your life is over?" I don't act concerned. I'm 99.9 percent sure this is a nonissue revolving around Ezra.

"My life is spiraling into a supernova of chaos," she says. Worry clouds her face. "I don't know what to do."

Maybe this is serious. If we talk this out, I'll be late to practice, but I know my priorities. "What happened?" I pat her shoulder.

Val clutches her two books and one notebook against her chest. "Ezra and I were walking to first period, and when he dropped me off, I kissed him."

I wait for the rest of her story, but that was it. "So what's the problem here?"

"Haven't you been listening? I said *I* kissed *him*. He always makes the first move, but he didn't kiss me this time. I had to kiss him."

We speed down the side stairwell, our heels clacking against the steps as we get to the first floor. I check the time every few seconds.

"I'm not getting the problem," I say.

"I had to kiss him. Why did he not try to kiss me first this morning? I don't even want to think about how I looked, leaning over to lay one on my boyfriend, pulling him in for a kiss like I'm some kind of überfeminist freak."

"This is the twenty-first century. That's allowed now. FYI: we can vote, too."

"Funny," she deadpans.

"I'm sure it looked romantic." Or rather like a PDA nuclear spill.

"I didn't even tell you what happened four nights ago."

*You haven't been telling me a lot of things, Val,* I think to myself. "What happened?"

"We were making out, and Ezra wasn't kissing me back hard enough. I was being the more passionate one."

"How can you even judge something like that? He's a very passionate guy, I'm assuming," I say.

"I could feel it. He wasn't kissing like he used to."

"Used to? You guys have been dating barely a month—"

"Five and a half weeks," she says. "Almost two months."

I stop in the main corridor and do a massive eye roll for her rounding skills, and for my stupidity. "Are you serious?"

"I know! I'm kind of scared."

"Will you stop it, Val. Do you know how annoying you sound?"

Val flips from worry to pissed off in a split second. "Sorry for pestering you."

Usually I would be fine eye rolling, but I've reached a limit on frustration I didn't know existed. The words spring out of me. "You have. You just keep me around to listen to your fake problems. I'm not your friend. I'm your sounding board."

"I've always been here to talk. You just choose to bottle it up. I thought you were supportive of my relationship."

"If you keep thinking your relationship is ending, then maybe it is."

It's 2:29 p.m. I don't have time for this. Who knew that I would consider SDA practice a better place to be than talking to my friend? But she isn't my friend. She's turned into a relationship zombie, just like the rest of them. "I have to go."

I skulk off to the locker room. I can't wait to focus on dancing for two hours and forget this conversation happened.

I slap on a gigantic grin as I waltz through the gym doors. The girls are stretching. Now that we've all improved and become well versed with our routines, Huxley isn't such a stickler about starting on time. Stretching time has expanded into catch-up-with-your-teammates time.

I change quickly and join Huxley and a cluster of girls doing the V stretch on the floor.

"Sorry I'm late," I say. "I've felt pretty lethargic today."

"Late night?" Huxley asks.

"Kinda, yeah. I went out last night."

The stretchers lift their chests off the floor. I have an audience.

"Rebecca Williamson out on a school night?" Huxley asks. "I can't even fathom the idea."

"Oh, really? I went ice-skating. What did you and Steve do last night?"

The girls are more anxious to hear that answer than my nighttime plans. Huxley plays it cool and takes the added attention in stride. She's a pro at being popular.

"Steve had to work, so I just relaxed," she says.

"Where's there ice-skating?" Reagan asks.

I tell them about the college ice rink and my remedial skating. "But I did it," I say. "I even took pictures."

Before anyone can ask to see them, I grab my phone and pull them up. Pictures of me pretending to twirl, pictures of Val and me, of Val and Ezra, all enjoying an above-average Thursday night. I look like some magical fairy. You would never guess I could only skate in three-second spurts.

"Isn't it a nice rink?" I ask. "I am totally going back."

Reagan peers into the phone, squinting her eyes to see the real picture. Other girls follow suit. They trade suspicious looks with each other.

I hand them the phone and play dumb. "What?"

"Is that...by those doors...?" Reagan starts then cuts herself off. She looks at Kerry, who nods back at her. They hide their smiles.

"What is it?" Huxley asks.

"Yeah. What did you guys see?" I ask. Wow, I didn't think my acting was this good.

"Nothing," Reagan and Kerry say simultaneously.

Huxley and I trade confused expressions. Only hers is real.

"May I?" Huxley asks. I hand over my camera. She scans the photo and remains unfazed. "Looks like a fun time."

She hands the phone back to me. For all any of the girls know, she saw nothing.

Only I caught the slight narrowing of her eyes.

# 18

"Tom Hanks is such a creep in this," Diane says through a mouthful of cereal. *You've Got Mail* plays on the TV. Milk dribbles onto her pajama bottoms. "He finds out they're online pen pals but doesn't say anything the whole movie. He just uses that insider information to manipulate her into falling for him. And then he drives her store out of business. Oh, and he was dating someone else the entire time. But she couldn't care less. She's like 'La-di-da. I get to kiss Tom Hanks. Screw everything else.' It's kind of pathetic."

"The dog is cute." I mix the fruit in my yogurt and relax on the Throne.

"Yeah, the dog is kind of cute."

My mom charges into the living room fully dressed and shuts off the TV. She looks at Diane. "Get dressed."

"Why?"

"Erin's son's first birthday is today, and you're going."

"Benjamin Button? Isn't it technically his eighty-first birthday?"

I laugh. My mom remains dead serious, which makes me laugh more.

"Swing by Toys 'R' Us and pick up a toy for Owen."

"Actually, I was thinking of getting him a carton of cigs and a flask."

My mom stays planted in front of the TV, arms folded. She's not backing down this time. I cover my mouth harder to contain myself.

"Becca, do you really find this funny?" my mom asks. No, just awkward. She's looking for my support, but she won't get it here.

"Mom, why does Diane have to go? She'll send a card. How about that?"

"So you think it's fine that she cuts these girls out of her life?"

"Can you please stop talking like I'm not here?"

"Diane, you're going. No excuses."

Why is my mom being so adamant? Can't she see the fear in Diane's eyes?

"What else do you have going on today? Are you planning to waste your Sunday on this couch again? You could maybe look for a job and put your degree to work."

"Why do you care so much about someone else's baby?"

"Why *don't* you care? She's your friend! Do you remember them? Those girls who called you every day to see how you were doing. The ones who tried to surprise you on your birthday." My mom shocked even herself with her yelling. She sits down on the empty bit of cushion next to Diane and goes to pat her knee, but Diane pulls them up to her body. "I know they're in a different stage than you, but you're going to meet a great guy and it'll happen, one-two-three."

"Like Tom Hanks and Meg Ryan?"

"Exactly!"

Diane swirls her spoon around in the bowl, avoiding eye contact with Mom.

"You'll see your friends. You'll socialize. You'll have fun," my mom says.

"They can barely be considered my friends. I'm not going."

My mom swipes Diane's car keys off the coffee table and retreats back to her TV-blocking position. She's quick, sprightlier than usual. She prepared for a fight. "Fine, then," she says. "If you're not going there, then you're not going anywhere this month."

"You can't do that."

"We gave you that car. We can take it away."

Diane pulls herself off the couch, her skin making a Velcro sound against the leather. She scowls at my mom. "Fine."

"I think you'll have fun."

I leap off the couch. "I'm going with her."

"Good." My mom relinquishes the keys with ease, quickly returning to her nonconfrontational self.

Diane gives me a relieved smile, as if glad to know someone in this house is still on her side.

Diane zooms down the highway, one hand on the radio.

"This is going to blow," she says to me, to herself.

"Is it just going to be a bunch of people staring at a baby?"

"Pretty much. Marian may try to steal some of the attention. Heaven forbid it's not all on her."

"Didn't you tell me she got so drunk at Aimee's twenty-first birthday party that they took her to the hospital?"

"Yep. She was sobbing in the corner when we sang 'Happy Birthday.'"

I remember when I visited Diane at college and got to hang out with her friends. Aimee, Marian and Erin were like surrogate big sisters for that weekend. They had all lived on the same floor their freshman year with Diane, all joined the same sorority and all shared an apartment senior year. The "maxipad." Most of what they talked about were inside jokes that went over my head, but I found them hysterical. They were so cool and, in my head, still are. I would never tell Diane that, though.

We pull into a gated community filled with homes on Martha Stewart steroids. You can tell each new homeowner strove to outdo the last one. We drive down a road overlooking a pond. Diane parks on the street behind an SUV with a Baby on Board decal. Erin's house has a wraparound veranda, a nod to her Southern roots. Blue balloons tied to the mailbox wave in the breeze.

"Brace yourself," Diane says. She's trying to be funny, but I can see she's scared, and all I want to do is protect my older sister. "You may suffocate from all the smugness."

I think about the maxipad and how envious I was of a friendship like theirs. I carry a colorful abacus for baby Owen that we found on clearance. "They love you."

"They love the old Diane, the one scheduled to be married and living in one of these bland, ugly houses." She stares down the house. Sadness creases her face. She spits her gum out on their lawn. "Ready?"

Erin's house is full of Pottery Barn furniture, funky paintings and couples. Lots of couples. In fact, all couples. Everyone is in the same uniform. The men have on V-neck sweaters with a collared shirt underneath and jeans. The wives wear sweaters (not in the same color as their husbands; that's too obvious) and leg-hugging jeans tucked into their boots. Casually formal. We look too casual. Diane cleaned up well, but these women just sparkle. I can sense Diane's dread of having to walk through this minefield of relationship zombies. She lifts her head and forces a smile. It's like watching a car salesman, except she's selling her happiness to the doubters.

I follow behind my sister. Couples huddle together and exchange impassioned small talk. Diane receives a growing barrage of glances and outright gawking. It's worse than the looks I got at the movie theater. You'd think adults would be more mature. They peer over at us then back to their safe conversations, clutching on to their significant others, infinitely grateful that they were able to fill out society's checklist. This is my cafeteria in ten years, the next preordained step in their clichéd lives.

Diane and I charge through in our bulky winter coats. She leans into me. "I'll say hi to Erin, watch the kid crap its pants, then we'll go."

"Diane?" Aimee gets up from the couch. Her baby bump peeks out from a flowing blouse. Knowing Aimee, her water will probably break when she's leading a meeting.

Diane gives her an awkward smile. "Hey."

"I didn't know you were coming," Aimee says. She doesn't sound excited to see her friend. She seems nervous.

"I didn't know you were pregnant."

"Yeah. Seven months. We're waiting to find out the sex. We want to be surprised. Like I am right now. Wow! It's good to see you!" She pulls Diane in for a hug, which looks uncomfortable for all parties involved.

I catch a couple behind me staring at Diane and whispering between each other. *Look, there's that sad single girl,* I'll bet they're saying. But they don't have the malicious grins of gossipers. They seem nervous, too.

"Hey, Becca! I haven't seen you in forever," Aimee says. Her eyes scan the kitchen entrance.

"Diane?" Marian joins us from the basement. Her wedding ring could blind somebody on a sunny day.

"It's a minireunion," Diane says.

"We didn't know you were coming," Marian says.

"Well, I'm here."

Marian and Aimee trade glances. Their necks crane over me toward the kitchen entrance. It's like they have a competition over who can be ruder and more obvious.

"This is a surprise," Marian says. "You should've told us you were coming."

"Well, I didn't. Where's Owen?" Diane asks. A caustic tone overtakes her voice.

"I think she's feeding him. She's wearing white pants, too, the brave soul," Marian says. She twirls her ring on her finger, but has to move her middle finger to make it go around.

People crowd in the kitchen, giving away Owen's location.

I'm too scared to go inside. I fiddle with the abacus beads, sliding them back and forth.

"Have you seen the front porch? It's got this really comfortable rocking chair," Aimee says. She tries to lead Diane that way, but my sister refuses.

"What's going on?"

Marian's eyes bulge, and she looks down at her drink. Aimee, as usual, is the composed one. "The chair's nice. We want to catch up."

"Bullshit," I blurt out, without even realizing that my mouth had opened, startling all three women. I expected smugness today, but not nastiness. Yeah, Diane may be single, but why does that deserve rubbernecking?

"Diane."

I know that voice. Diane knows it better than anyone in this house.

My throat tightens as if my tongue fell backward. The abacus slips from my slick hands, and I grab it at the last second. Diane may appear totally fine to her former friends and acquaintances, but I notice her trembling hands. She shoves them into her pockets.

She turns around at a glacial pace, trying to delay the humiliation as long as possible. "Hi," she says.

Sankresh stands in the kitchen doorway. He strokes Priya's hand. The sunlight hits her ring just right. It's bigger than Diane's was.

The room is quiet. Owen's crying fills the empty space.

Memories and feelings from that day crash through the mental barrier I had erected. I want to go over there and strangle Sankresh. For taking four years of Diane's life. For being a coward. For using the "I've fallen out of love" excuse.

I make eye contact with Erin. She cradles Owen against her shoulder, and her husband cradles her. She looks down, nestling herself farther into her husband's arms.

Sankresh takes a step forward. "I didn't—"

"Know I was coming," Diane says.

Aimee rubs Diane's arm, but my sister shrugs her off.

Owen won't shut up. He's screaming no matter how much Erin bounces him.

"Let's go," Diane says to me, but I'm frozen. All the relationship zombies stare at her, except for her supposed friends. Maybe later I'll appreciate the irony.

"Becca! C'mon." She rips the abacus from my grasp and tosses it on the coffee table, where it clanks jarringly against the glass. The sound bellows in the silent room.

I keep my head down, focused on the heels of Diane's shoes. I don't shut the front door behind me. The street has a creepy vibe I didn't notice before. It's like the houses are watching us, waiting for us to leave.

"Diane! Wait!" Erin scurries onto the front lawn babyless.

"Let's go." Diane doesn't turn around.

Erin's heel gets caught on something—a piece of gum?—and she falls face-first onto the lawn. I want to help her. She's going to get grass stains on her white pants, and for some reason, that hits me in the gut. But I keep walking.

The car's raring to go. Diane peers over the steering wheel at Erin, her face softening with concern. I swear she's about to open her car door when Erin's husband races outside and scoops her up. Diane peels away from the curb.

I close my passenger door while we're halfway down the street. Diane seems ready and willing to crash through the front gate, but it opens automatically. After the first traffic light, Diane pulls off to the side of the road.

"Are you okay?" I ask. The answer's obvious.

Diane stares out the windshield. Then, out of nowhere, she punches the steering wheel. Over and over. Gasping for breath. Grunts and indecipherable phrases sputter out of her mouth like a blender without the lid. The punching gets faster, more frantic. I feel like I'm the one getting pummeled and now tears form in my eyes.

Finally, she stops.

Without saying a word, she turns the car back on, and we drive away.

# 19

I shouldn't be in school today. I'm in the cafeteria before homeroom trying to do some homework, but it's no use. There's no way I'll be able to concentrate. Owen's birthday debacle plays on a loop in my mind, and no lesson plan can steal away my interest.

Ezra and Jeff find me sitting here, but I'm not in the mood for human contact, especially from Mr. Romantic.

"Studying for homeroom?" Jeff says, adjusting his baggy sweater under his backpack. "Now that is dedication."

"So last night I found this article about the ending of *Casablanca,* and I hate to say it, but it actually gives your theory some credence." Ezra beams with excitement. He raises his eyebrows at me, awaiting my response.

I shrug my shoulders and go back to studying my history notes.

"I'll email you the article."

I nod, not taking my eyes off my notebook. I'm trying my

best to stay nice, but I just want the whole world to disappear right now.

"Are you okay?"

"Yeah."

Diane stayed in her room all night with the door locked watching old sitcoms. I stood outside her door listening for sounds of crying, but all I could hear was a laugh track. I wonder what Sankresh and Priya were up to last night. The guests at Owen's party were probably in stitches about the incident; Diane is probably their new favorite punch line.

"You sure?"

I nod. "I just have a test later."

"Isn't that always how it goes? I guess that explains why you're here so early."

"Yeah." The banging of her fists against the steering wheel still pierces my eardrums. Sankresh wouldn't know what that's like. Ezra wouldn't.

"I gotta jet," Jeff says. "I told Carrie I'd help decorate her friend's locker for her birthday."

"She needs to loosen that leash," Ezra says.

"Tell me about it!" Jeff waves and runs backward out into the hall. He would never do what Sankresh did to Diane. He's too scared of his girlfriend. Or maybe he would and just slink away. Maybe it's easier for guys to be weasels than actual human beings.

Ezra strums his fingers against the top of a chair. "Are you sure you're okay?" He readjusts his hemp necklace, waiting for me to say goodbye. His eyes do the up-and-to-the-left thing, like he's perpetually having a stroke. "Well, then. See you later."

I can't let him go like this. Guys like him have been let off the hook enough times. Monica had to nurse a broken heart while Ezra lived it up with Isabelle; now somewhere Isabelle is crying while he and Val bicker about who should stop staring. Why do people want to be in love when they know its side effects? Some really are that selfish.

"Ezra," I say. He stops at a neighboring table. "Did you even care when you dumped Isabelle and Monica? Or were you 'whatever' about it since you already had another girl lined up?"

All friendliness fades from his face. He goes into defense mode. "No."

"Are you sure? It seems like you follow a pattern and Val's next."

He digs his hands farther into his hoodie. A sign of guilt?

"Why don't you go back to studying?" he says.

"Just answer the question, Ezra. Val's my best friend. I want to prepare her if she's going to get blown off. Is there a time limit or do you just get bored?"

"What is up with you?"

"Do you even care about the people you hurt?" I shake my head in disgust. "You're all the same."

Sadness creases his face. I look at his drooping eyes and get a flash of the guy who helped me ice-skate. Ezra storms out of the cafeteria.

I chase after him, catching him halfway down the hall.

"What?" he asks, not wanting to know the answer.

I don't say anything at first, then, as if the words were waiting in the wings, I launch into the story about Diane and Sankresh and Owen's party.

"Whoa," he says. "That sucks."

"It's just... What happened with those other girls?"

He shrugs, his smooth, witty self in hiding. "Things just didn't work out."

"What does that even mean?"

He softens. His warm, hazel eyes laser into me like I'm learning to skate, although this time, he wants to show me something else. "We weren't in love."

"Not the love excuse."

"It's not an excuse."

"It totally is. Whenever somebody wants to get out of a relationship, but they don't want to say the real reason, they use the love excuse. How can such a strong feeling just go away? It's not a cold."

"You're not in love with someone when you start dating them," Ezra says. His face lights up. "You feel something for them, something different and special. It might be love. It might not. You hope that what you have develops into love, but sometimes it doesn't. It's all about taking a chance. Love isn't a mathematical formula."

"You're just giving people an excuse to do whatever they want. I love you...now I don't. I'm so tired of people using that to be completely shitty to each other."

"So you think I was shitty to Isabelle? We were both miserable by the end. We would hang out after school and not say a word to each other. I tried talking to her about how things weren't working, but she wouldn't listen. She wanted to stay in a relationship." Ezra licks his lips, making them stand out even more against his light skin. "Break-ups are never clean, never easy. Just because I wasn't crying in the bathroom doesn't mean I didn't care. No offense to your sister, but you only know her side of the story."

That last line stings, even though it may be true. Maybe Sankresh went through his own silent hell. I'll never know. It's an interesting thought. I only hear about one side of relationships from my sister and my clients.

The warning bell for homeroom rings.

Ezra pats me on the shoulder. His hand lingers a second too long. "I hope your sister feels better."

I hobble out of the locker room post-SDA. I have a sharp pain in my right foot like I pulled a mysterious muscle in my big toe. Huxley leans by the water fountain, checking her phone, waiting for other members of her crew. Girls give her goodbye waves and smiles, then immediately turn to each other and discuss all things Huxley and Steve.

"Oh, look, Huxley all by her lonesome. I wonder where Steve is," one of them whispers behind me.

"Delivering a pizza," her friend whispers back. They snicker.

From what I heard in the halls, Steve claimed he was delivering a pizza to a birthday party at the rink. Angela just happened to be there. I suppose that's possible, and that excuse may hold up in a court of law or other places where reason reigns supreme. But not here. I always thought girls at Ashland adored Huxley, but I guess she's like any celebrity. They're eager to see her fall.

I nod good-night to her, but then I stop. I see a great opportunity.

"How are you?" I ask.

Her olive skin gleams under the fluorescent lights, as if there's any light where she would look bad. "I'm fine." She seems surprised at the question. I'm probably the only girl in SDA to ask her.

"Listen, if you ever need to talk..."

Huxley perks up just a touch, and for a second, I see my old friend somewhere in there. "I appreciate it, Rebecca. But I'm fine."

"You know, the more you say that, the less I believe you."

Huxley puts her phone away. She walks with me, leaving behind Reagan and Addison in the locker room.

We exit through the set of Ashland's green front doors that haven't been locked yet. It's a mild night, a sign that spring will be here any day. Only a few cars dot the parking lot.

"I like you, Rebecca. You tell it like it is. It's refreshing."

"You know, you can call me Becca. Everyone does."

"I know."

I walk with her to her car, a white Range Rover. Her movable throne. I wonder how many people saw us walk out together. While I'm talking to her solely for research purposes, a bump in my social profile would be a nice halo effect.

Huxley scans my body, and suddenly I feel as if I'm in airport security. "I think you've worn the same makeup and clothes since junior high."

"I haven't."

She raises her eyebrows at me. Not the same *exact* makeup and clothes. I found a style that works for me and keeps me from sticking out. Or so I thought.

"I think a darker shade would suit you well." She holds her

arm next to my cheek to better imagine me a shade darker. I swat her away.

"Thanks for the tip."

"I think you'd look hot. Well, lukewarm. What are you doing right now?"

My mind scrambles for a cool answer. I can't let her know that my life is as boring as she thinks. But I'm already stammering, and Huxley and I both know the truth. "Nothing," I say.

"Do you want to go to Willowhaven Mall? We can get you some new base, and maybe a new outfit or two."

I'm sensing a trap. I back away slowly. "I'm having dinner with my family. They're expecting me."

"They can keep your food in the oven. It'll be worth it when they see your new wardrobe."

"I like my clothes. Makeup may be one thing, but you can't fault my fashion sense."

"Your clothes are too safe. When you joined SDA, I said I would help you find a boyfriend. This is much-needed step number one."

"It's late and Willowhaven is a half hour away."

"You don't expect me to go to Sunnyside Park, do you? That place depresses me." She steps up into her car, and I feel like she's six feet above me, stretching her arm out to help a poor peasant girl. "C'mon, Rebecca. Don't be such a wet blanket."

I'm tired of being one. Val wanted to give me this makeover so many times, but Val isn't around anymore. I get into Huxley's car and sink back into the deep leather seat.

We speed out of the parking lot. My excitement builds

for the mall with each street we cross. Huxley turns on the radio and cranks up an old Britney Spears song.

"Do you remember?" Huxley asks.

"The music video we made? Yeah. We took that off YouTube, right?"

"I hope so!"

Her hand is tapping against the steering wheel. My head is bobbing back and forth. I feel it building up. I just finished dancing for two hours, but I still have energy.

As it nears the chorus, I turn up the volume. "Five, six, seven, eight!"

Then we launch into our old choreographed routine, modified for sitting in a car. Every move comes flooding back, something I wouldn't have been able to do by myself. Some things you can only remember with other people.

Huxley does a dramatic hair flip at the chorus while keeping her eyes on the road. It's not until we get onto the highway that I realize how perfectly everything is going to plan.

# 20

Girls drag their boyfriends into Hit or Miss, but Huxley doesn't pay them any attention. She rummages through the racks on a mission.

"Oh! Try this on!" She pulls from the chaff a fitted, red-and-black-striped dress.

"That's so not me."

"Exactly the point." She holds it against my body. "You could actually have a decent figure if you stopped hiding it behind sweaters and cardigans."

"It's freezing outside, if you haven't noticed. Warm clothes are kind of a necessity." I hang the dress back on the rack. Just because I read fashion magazines doesn't mean I can dress like the models in them.

"That's why we wear coats." She pulls the dress back out. "Trust me. These are miracle dresses. They'll give your body some character, accentuate the parts of you that are lacking, like your hips, your butt and *especially* your—"

"Okay. I'll try it on." I cross my arms over my chest, though I hate giving her the satisfaction of being right—er, making an accurate observation.

Boyfriends sit in a row outside the fitting rooms, chained there. They probably carve tally marks in the chair arms, counting the hours until they are free. Tortured looks are etched across their faces. A short, stubby girl charges out of her fitting room in a leather skirt that does no favors to her thighs.

"What do you think?" she asks her boyfriend. Fear and exhaustion consume his face.

"You look nice."

"Did I sense hesitation in your voice?"

His lower lip quivers. "N-no. Did you want to get something to eat now?"

"No. Not until you tell me how this makes my calf muscles look," she says with an icy tone. I guess there's just no sense in buying something your boyfriend won't find you attractive in.

The salesgirl leads us to the handicapped room at the end. I hang up the beautiful but so-not-me dress on the hook. At least I have anonymity at Willowhaven Mall. Nobody from Ashland will ever see me in this. As I slip on the dress, I keep wondering why Steve isn't in that row of guys. Why is Huxley spending time with me and not him? If she were worried about him cheating, wouldn't she want to keep him under her thumb at all times? Maybe they're having a good laugh over these rumors, and the joke's on us.

I do a double take in the mirror. Is this really my body? I have boobs! My figure could be referred to as *womanly* in some circles. I flick my hair away from my face, treating the mirror like a *Vogue* photographer. Damn you, Huxley. You're good.

All the boyfriends swivel their heads to me, and they can't help but smile. Neither can I. And for a second, I picture any one of them getting up and throwing his arms around me. Short and Stubby snaps her fingers in her boyfriend's face, waking both of us up.

"I think we have a winner," Huxley says. She's already found two more dresses for me to try on.

"I can't afford all this."

"My treat! I love helping out those less fortunate." She hangs them in my room. Even though she doesn't care about the money, I still feel weird about this.

"Why are you being so nice to me?" I wish there was a better way to phrase that, but suspicion and curiosity seem to have disabled that part of my brain.

"Because where you see an ugly duckling, I see a swan."

She says it so sweetly, so innocently. It's a total punch in the gut. I go back to my changing room without saying a word.

We traverse the mall en route to Spritz, a new makeup store Huxley claims she discovered, which means in a week, every girl at Ashland will clean it out.

"So where's Steve tonight?" I ask as we stroll past the food court. Couples share fries and Cinnabons just as they would in the cafeteria—because food does not taste good unless it's being fed to you.

"He went to a Devils game with his family."

"You weren't invited?"

"I was, but with SDA, I didn't want it to be a late night. I'm having brunch with them on Sunday."

"You hang out with his family a lot?"

"Yes." Huxley fingers a scarf on a kiosk. "They're the best. His parents got me this bracelet." She holds her hand out and a simple gold link rings her wrist. It's a lovely gift from people who want her out of their son's life.

"Where's Val tonight?" she asks.

"With Ezra, probably." I try to sound as nonchalant as possible.

She pats my back. "Don't worry. We'll get you one soon enough," she says with a comforting tone. Like she thinks I'm jealous? Why does it always have to come to that?

Pulsating music and red-and-cyan track lighting permeate Spritz. Their selection is better equipped for a girl going to the club than to school. Huxley clearly isn't thrilled by the ambience either, and I'm not sure why she championed it. She soldiers on, waving me forward. She picks out a few lipsticks and dabs them on her palm. They range from a natural pink to streetwalker red. She holds them up to my face.

"A more natural shade would be best. Nothing drastic," Huxley says.

"Agreed."

"Let me see that lip gloss you've been using for the last million years."

I hand her my tube of ballet slipper–colored gloss. It's mild, but girls like me aren't out for attention. Huxley tosses it in the trash behind the counter. I don't say anything. We both knew that was coming.

"Let's try some cranberry shades!"

"That's way too dark. People in outer space don't need to see my lips."

"We can go lighter."

Huxley glances around the store. She locks in on the sales associate, a girl with her back turned to us. A waterfall of blond hair cascades down her back. She and Huxley could have a hair-flowing competition.

"Excuse me," Huxley calls out. "Do you have a tissue?"

The girl turns around. My eyes bulge, and my heart stops momentarily, a stark contrast to Huxley's steely glare.

"Hi," Angela says.

Neither girl seems nervous, or else they're hiding it really well. I want to crouch under the table.

"Can you get me a tissue?" Huxley asks. She holds up her lipstick-smeared hand.

"Okay."

Angela hands one over. Huxley rips it out of her palm. My heart thumps louder than the bass.

"Thank you. I didn't know you worked here," Huxley says. "It definitely suits you."

"After-school job. Just like Steve's."

I flinch at his name.

Huxley wipes her hand and flicks the dirty tissue on the counter. "I'm looking for a lighter shade for my friend. Somewhere between burgundy and light pink. Any suggestions?"

Angela gives my face a good once-over. Am I supposed to jump in? How do you referee a fight composed of backhanded comments?

"I would go with Ladybug—that's what I wear." Angela

smacks her lips together for effect. "Or Plumful, if you want something more neutral." She pulls out two tubes from her display case. She coats my trembling lips with Ladybug first.

"Too trashy," Huxley says after a two-second glimpse. She smiles at Angela. "No offense."

"Let's try Plumful," Angela says. She caps Ladybug.

"How was ice-skating?" Huxley asks her.

"Fun. I bumped into Steve."

"I know. He told me. He tells me everything."

"I'm sure he does," Angela says. A wicked grin slashes across her face.

Adrenaline pumps into my system. Screaming and hair pulling could commence at any time.

"Angela, contrary to what you've heard, history doesn't repeat itself. So stop trying," Huxley says.

Angela layers Plumful on me. It's a step up from lip gloss. But I defer to Huxley. Right now, only her opinion matters.

She nods approval. "We'll take it."

"Really? I think Ladybug looked better." Angela peers down at me. "Which one did you like?"

"P-P-P-Plumful."

Angela rings me up.

"Thanks for shopping at Spritz! Tell Steve I say hi."

Huxley waltzes out of the store, sidestepping customers quickly and efficiently. She doesn't wait for me. But I'm not far behind. I want to get away from that girl as much as she does.

Her pace slows as she nears the Gap, allowing me to catch up. She is all smiles; Spritz is now a distant memory.

"I'm sorry you had to witness that," Huxley says. "I couldn't face her alone. Let's keep this between us."

I nod. Now I get why she was so eager to take me shopping.

# 21

My family is about twenty years behind the times. We don't have caller ID, among other once-cool-now-commonplace inventions, so when I'm forced to answer the phone, I have to take my chances that it won't be some chatty relative like Aunt Lisa. Love her, but not the half hour's worth of questions she shoots at me—at least one of which is always if I'm "dating any boys."

I hear the phone ringing as soon as I come inside the house. I drop my shopping bags and pick up the kitchen line. Diane eats Wheat Thins at the table while flipping through a magazine. She never answers the phone. She has no interest in talking to whoever is calling, except telemarketers. Because when they ask "How are you doing?" it's not out of pity.

"Hello?"

"Hello? Becca?"

As if on cue, my throat becomes a dried-up lake, and I have to almost cough to get my words out. "Hi."

"It's Erin."

"And Marian, too!"

I yearn for Aunt Lisa's nasal voice, asking me where I'm planning to apply to college.

"How are you?" Erin asks. She tries to sound cheerful, but she's just as uncomfortable as me. "It was really good seeing you, despite the circumstances."

"Thanks."

"Is Diane there? We really want to talk to her. Did she change her cell phone number?"

I keep wondering why they are calling together. Two against one again. Always. "Let me see if she's home."

I hold the phone against my chest and mouth who's calling. Diane shakes her head no and turns back to her magazine. "She's not home. Can I take a message?"

"How is she doing?" Marian asks. "She won't answer any of our calls or emails."

"Sankresh and James are still friends, and we didn't think she was coming. Becca, I feel horrible about what happened." Erin's voice catches, and it shakes something deep within me. "We hope she's okay."

"Yeah, how is she doing?"

"I'll give her the message. I gotta go." I hang up on them and cradle the phone in my hands for a few seconds. Diane watches me as I put the phone back. "Maybe you should talk to them. They seemed sincere."

"They just want a laugh. If they really care, then why haven't they come to see me?"

Why doesn't Diane try to see them? I think to myself. She has a car. She's able-bodied. But then I remember how they all just stood there at the birthday. Watching the car wreck instead of preventing it. They let Diane and me get stared at like circus freaks. They don't know what Diane has been through.

"They don't care," Diane says. "Trust me."

And I do because she's my sister.

I wouldn't say that Huxley gave me a makeover. I wasn't some unfortunate-looking girl with acne who wore baggy T-shirts and ankle-length jean skirts to school. Rather, she merely tweaked and highlighted some of my preexisting features. So my first day at school with this new look isn't some game-changer in my social profile. Time doesn't stop, and some soft-rock song doesn't blare in the background. I get a smattering of double takes and overlong stares, but overall, the effect is negligible. I'm still that girl in your class, just in a sleeker dress. Only those who know me make any mention.

"Becca?" Val spots me from down the hall after first period. She pulls Ezra down the corridor with her.

"Becca, wow," she says. There's little enthusiasm in her voice. She sounds deflated, almost hurt. "You look good." She musters up some excitement. "I can't believe it!"

"Yeah. I made some minor adjustments." I try to catch Ezra's reaction, but there is none.

"You went shopping and didn't text me?" Val asks. I doubt she would've come, not if she was with Ezra.

"Huxley took me."

"Oh. I didn't know you guys were friends again." Val's voice has a twinge of jealousy in it. Now she knows what it's like.

"Yeah. We've really bonded during SDA."

"Great." Val leans her head on Ezra's shoulder. "Doesn't she look great?"

He runs his fingers through his puff of hair and shakes his head. "Meh."

I know he's joking, but it still hurts. It would've been nice if he responded like the guys at the store.

Val elbows him in the ribs. He throws his arm around her waist and pulls her in close.

"You don't think she looks beautiful?"

"She always has. A new dress doesn't change anything."

"I gotta go." I walk to second period, blushing the whole way.

My lunch mates openly gawk at me, which I take as a compliment.

"Wow," Quentin says. "You look great." I can tell his eyes are struggling to stay north of my cleavage.

Fred blushes as he attempts to rip open a ketchup packet. I must really look nice, or they must really never talk to pretty girls.

My phone buzzes with a text message from Huxley. Rebecca, come sit at my table. And throw out that cookie.

She needs to join the CIA right now. Her observation skills are too perfect. I take my food and walk across the cafeteria. I pass the row of garbage cans and toss away my cookie. Val shoots me a quizzical look from her and Ezra's love nest. She's surprised about where I'm going as much as I am.

I pass Bari's table, and instead of Derek next to her, it's

Calista. They have what looks to be a heart-to-heart while sipping on Diet Cokes. Bari rubs Calista's hand soothingly. It's just two people talking, but I can only imagine what—or who—they're talking about.

Sunlight fills Huxley's corner table. Her friends and their food gleam. Some part of me cares about sitting with Huxley and her friends. It's the same part that's intrigued like a science experiment. It will be something different.

"How's the salad?" Huxley asks me. She bought the same one.

"It's what you'd expect."

"Is there a rule that says cafeteria food has to be inedible?" she asks.

I stand next to the full table, feeling more awkward by the second.

"Addison," Huxley says. "Get up."

Addison looks up from her magazine. She's prettier than most of the models in it. Her curly red hair bounces on her shoulders. "What?"

"You're in Becca's seat."

"What are you talking about, Hux?"

"You don't sit here anymore."

Addison laughs it off as a joke, but Huxley continues to glare. She waits patiently for Addison to stand.

"Are you kidding?"

"No. I'm not. You don't sit here anymore." Huxley is statue still, poised to attack if she needs to.

"I thought we were friends," Addison says.

"Me, too. But when things I tell you in confidence happen to spread throughout the school, it makes me question our friendship. I thought I could trust you, but apparently, I can't. How can I continue eating lunch with you when looking at your face makes me lose my appetite?"

Huxley doesn't flinch or misspeak. I feel like I'm the one in trouble.

"This is crazy. I have never said anything to anyone. I swear."

Steve squeezes his girlfriend's hand in support. The rest of the table is riveted.

"Raise your hand if Addison ever told you any personal stories about me and Steve, or Steve and Angela," Huxley says.

Slowly but surely, every person at the table raises a hand. Addison scrunches her face up, feigning outrage.

"This is a witch hunt! Don't worry, Hux. I have plenty more stories to share." Addison stacks up her books and flees out of the cafeteria. She leaves her tray on the table.

Huxley grins at me and motions at the empty chair. "Sit!"

The conversations at Huxley's table are mundane, yet because popular people are saying them, I somehow find it more interesting. These are the celebrities of my school, and I'm seeing them in their natural habitat. I know it sounds dumb, but I feel sort of cool for joining them. Who knew being popular could be so easy? All it took was some lying, manipulation and moderate dance skills.

The girls talk about fashion and celebrities; the guys talk about sports. They play their gender roles well. My seat is in the middle, so I toggle between both discussions.

"Steve-o, what do you think about armadillos this time of year?" Greg Baylor says through a mouthful of mac 'n' cheese. He's burly with shaggy blond hair. You might mistake him for a caveman.

"What are you talking about, dude?" Steve asks.

"This scout at Chandler University called me last night. He wants us to come down and check out the campus for a weekend." Greg shoves down another forkful of food. I wish I could eat mac 'n' cheese without thinking of the caloric consequences.

"Us?" Steve asks. Huxley's ears perk up. She checks out of the girls' conversation.

"Yeah, man. He's still interested. Are you going to eat that?" Greg points to my salad roll. I nudge it over. He takes it in one bite.

"Really?"

"You gotta come. Chandler University made it to the Sugar Bowl last year. And I heard that campus is wild." He raises his eyebrows quickly, as if we didn't already know what he meant.

"He's still interested?" Steve asks.

"I just said that."

Steve gazes at the rapidly diminishing mac 'n' cheese while he thinks it over. I'm sure he's picturing multiple scenarios of the weekend, all of them like a Girls Gone Wild video. The corners of his mouth turn up in a smile.

"I bet he'll bring up that scholarship offer again," Greg says.

"He's too late. Steve's already going to Vermilion," Huxley says.

"Is that a done deal?" Greg asks.

I remember Steve's talk with the coach. If he can't pay for Vermilion, then nothing's a done deal.

"Pretty much," Steve says. Huxley rubs his shoulder.

"Pretty much? Come check out the school with me. One weekend won't kill you, Steve-o."

"I don't think it's a good idea," Huxley says. "It wouldn't be fair to waste the school's time and money when he has no intention of going."

She rests her head on his massaged shoulder. Steve thinks it over and taps his fork against his empty plate.

"It's up to you, man." Greg licks his disposable plate clean, then crumples it into a ball.

"I'll pass. I already know where I'm going to school." Steve turns his head to a beaming Huxley, and kisses her smack on the lips.

I make a quick dash for my locker before sixth period. Since we can leave lunch a few minutes before the bell rings, I usually can zip down to my locker then all the way to health class without being late. I round the corner of the science hallway. Formaldehyde fills my nostrils. I stop dead in my tracks when I come to my corridor.

Val leans against my locker. She's crying.

# 22

“Can we talk?” she asks. Her eyes plead with me not to brush her off.

“What’s up?”

She scoots back from my locker. I drop my book bag on the ground, and I swear the floor tiles crack.

“I really like your new look. Remember I told you to use a darker base?”

“Thanks.” I squat down and take out my morning textbooks. I can’t remember the last time we were hanging out together sans Ezra. It seems like a decade ago.

“So how’ve you been?” she asks.

I feel like I don’t know this girl anymore. How did we get this out of the loop? I throw my books back in my bag. I’ll run down here before seventh period. This is torture. “I have to get to class.”

“Wait.” Val grabs my book-bag strap. Her voice breaks. “I miss you.” She wipes her nose with her blazer sleeve.

"I've been here."

"We've drifted."

"That wasn't me!" I didn't ditch anyone for a guy.

And now I'm crying, too. I miss the Val who talks in only run-on sentences.

"I know," she says. "I'm sorry. I don't want our friendship to end over a guy."

I'm pleasantly surprised by her self-awareness. "Me neither."

"I want us to stop having awkward conversations whenever we see each other. That's not us!"

"It's not!"

I hug her. That's the first certified-Val thing she's said to me in a long time. We smear the tears off our faces.

"I promise to rein it in with all my Ezra talk," she says.

"So even you've noticed it?"

"I'm telling you, Becca. It's like a vortex. You don't even realize you're getting sucked in. Having a boyfriend is such a rush, and it makes even boring parts of my life exciting. And so I think that everything in my life is going well. I thought we were great this whole time. But then I saw you hanging out with Huxley, and you sat at her table. And I realized that something wasn't right."

I drop my backpack on the ground with a thump. She smiles, like she missed hearing that thump or something. "How are things with you and Ezra going?"

"Fine. I don't know. I get that he's a movie buff, but that's like 80 percent of what he talks about. Between you and me, it's getting old."

“Maybe your relationship has run its course,” I say, hoping for a breakthrough.

“No way,” she says. She doesn’t give it another thought. That doesn’t matter to her. I want to ask her if she truly loves Ezra, but I won’t. Our friendship is too fragile for probing questions right now. I find myself getting frustrated with her again, more than I have after past relationship discussions. Now that I’ve gotten to know Ezra, he deserves someone who appreciates his movie-buff personality rather than someone who tolerates it for the sake of avoiding singledom. He’s looking for something special; Val’s looking for a plus one.

I get into my locker and make the necessary book swaps.

“So be honest with me,” Val says. “Is Huxley a better friend?”

“No,” I say. An automatic response. I couldn’t hesitate for a second or else Val would never forget it. “Unless you find backhanded compliments endearing.”

Val laughs, happy that her top spot on my friend list is secure. “And what kind of a name is Huxley anyway? I’ll bet her real name is something like Heather, but it was too bland for her taste.”

The bell rings, and for some reason, that makes us laugh harder.

When I get home, I find an email from Mr. Towne waiting for me, burning a hole through my inbox.

I need a REAL progress report. Let’s chat.

I roll my eyes at the email. Is he my dad asking how my homework is coming along? None of my clients have required a progress report. They have faith in me that I'll get the job done. But then, they haven't had to wait this long for results.

"Things are taking a little bit longer," I tell him on video chat. "But I am making progress."

His gray eyes stare coldly into the screen. He leans back and rests his arms on his gut. "It's been almost six weeks since we last spoke. You can't give me radio silence like that. One snarky email won't cut it."

What kind of metrics can I give him? I don't exactly work in statistics. *Trust the process,* I want to tell him. *Couples aren't destroyed in a day.* Still, I nod in agreement. "I'm sorry. I'll keep you updated."

"So after six weeks, you're only just 'making progress'?"

"These things take time. Do you think Huxley is just going to give Steve up that easily?"

"At this rate, you'll have them broken up by their silver anniversary." He squirms in his office chair, like a kid in a waiting room. He's probably not used to working with a teenage girl, especially not one in a costume. "Listen, college acceptances become binding by May 15. If Steve gets locked into Vermilion, then that's it. His life is over. He'll be stuck with her forever."

I'm not the first person to think that, but hearing a grown man say it feels slimy. He's not a member of Ashland's social world. He doesn't have that right to care about gossip.

"You have one month," he tells me before disconnecting.

* * *

I relay our conversation to Diane. I want to quit this assignment. It used to stimulate me; now it makes me uneasy.

She lies on her bed, painting her toenails a funky neon shade of green. With her Rutgers sweater still on, she looks like a Christmas decoration.

"You have to keep going," she says.

But it doesn't seem that simple anymore. I keep picturing Huxley by the water fountain, that forced smile plastered on her face while her supposed friends gossip about her demise mere feet away. None of them care that she's busting her butt to make this SDA show spectacular. How will it be once she and Steve are kaput? That's all people will talk about until finals. It's not like other couples where the dumper and dumpee can mend in relative obscurity. That forced smile will become a required part of her wardrobe.

Diane senses my confusion. "Don't tell me you feel sorry for this girl?"

I throw myself onto the bed, making Diane smear a green streak across her foot. This is why I hate getting involved in my subjects' lives. I need distance to perform a break-up. You don't see hit men sharing family albums with their targets.

"I mean, we're kinda-sorta-maybe, on some level, approaching the near vicinity of being friends again," I say, though I know we're a bit closer than that.

"Of course you are. Who else does she have to turn to?"

"Exactly."

"This is all part of the plan, but it's not real. Not for either of you." Diane blows on her feet. "You're a spare-tire friend."

I fold my arms over my stomach.

"No, not that spare tire. You're a temporary replacement. If you stop your plan and Huxley and Steve patch everything up, do you think she'll still want to be friends with you? Her lemmings will come running back to her, and you're going to get ditched. She won't need you anymore." Diane shrugs her shoulders. I didn't come to her for a sugarcoated answer. "She's done it to you before. Don't let history repeat itself, B."

I was blinded by her popularity, by the choice lunch table. But Diane's right. She's so right. We're not real friends. Real friends don't treat you like a social pariah to hide the fact they were ever friends with you. I *am* her spare tire. That's what happened with Diane's friends, too. When Sankresh dumped her, they stopped calling the house after a few weeks. They put in a little effort to show they weren't completely heartless. Then it was back to their more-significant-than-Diane others.

And Val. I don't let myself think of what will happen if things pick up between her and Ezra.

"You okay?" she asks.

"Yeah," I say with firmness in my voice. I know what I have to do.

Ashland High is way too trusting. The faculty can't be dumb enough to actually believe that students will use the bathroom pass to go to the bathroom. But still, nobody stops me as I walk out of school and into the parking lot. Nobody's around to raise an eyebrow as I pull a wire hanger from under my zip-up fleece. And nobody approaches me when I squat down next to Steve's car. It's almost as if they think we're responsible adults here.

I unwind the hanger and slide the stick of metal down the passenger-side window of his used Jetta. I keep one eye on the school, and the other on the hanger. I jangle it around until it finds the car lock. I lift up slowly and...*click*. I can't believe that worked. Thank you, internet.

I crack open the door. My bathroom pass sticks out of my back pocket. The freezing wind of bipolar April isn't doing me any favors. No slow moves, I tell myself. Just do it and walk away.

I inhale a gust of the icy air and pull the condom wrapper and half-used tube of Ladybug lipstick from my front pocket. I place them under the seat, where they will wait patiently for Huxley's foot.

I can't help but smile. Maybe it's nerves or adrenaline or the sheer ridiculousness of my current situation, but I am loving my job right now. I find reserves of energy, a renewed purpose.

"Becca, you're freezing," Ms. Hardwick says when I come back to class.

"The heater in the girl's room isn't working. I'd bring a coat next time."

I shoot Huxley a Steve-sized smile on the way back to my seat.

# 23

"No, don't push it like a broom."

"But it is a broom."

Huxley demonstrates for Steve how to maneuver a curling broom. She shuffles down the court with it in front of her. Ezra films it all from the bleachers.

"Can we cut for a second?" Huxley asks him.

I sit behind Ezra watching through his viewer screen. I agreed to help him with the SDA shoots tonight, even if it meant staying later. Huxley wanted a team member to shadow him to ensure that SDA's vision (aka hers) comes through on-screen. Apparently, one year the video director reedited the footage to make it seem as if SDA was a lesbian cult. Ezra asked me to be the boom operator, which sounded cool, until I found out I have to stand the whole time and dangle a humongous microphone over Huxley's and Steve's heads. Ezra said he'd give me an associate-producer credit, whatever that means.

While Steve may be a novice with a curling broom, Ezra is a whiz with the camera. He's found creative ways to get different shots. He placed the camera on the basketball hoop to shoot overhead. He carefully stepped down the bleachers diagonally as he zoomed in on Huxley and Steve, creating this sweeping shot. He took Huxley's trite dialogue and made it halfway funny. What started as some mundane scene has morphed into a piece of art. It's inspiring and hypnotic watching someone totally in his element. Even now, he squats beneath Huxley and Steve, and frames the next shot through his thumb and index fingers, ignoring the sweat raining from his head. I wish I had a skill I could throw myself into so passionately. Unless you count break-upping, I don't.

"Then you say, 'Wow! The floor looks super clean now,' and give the camera a thumbs-up," Huxley says. "How does that sound, Ezra?"

Ezra stays mum, though I assume that he didn't write this brilliant script.

"I don't know—it sounds kind of lame," Steve says.

Huxley whips her head around. She grips the broom tight. "I think it sounds cute. Lighthearted."

"But not funny."

I steady myself behind my boom pole, in case Huxley begins breathing fire.

"What do you think?" she asks Ezra.

"Um..." Ezra searches for the right word. Well, the right word is *unfunny,* but he thinks harder. "We can tweak it if you want."

"So you hate it, too?" Huxley crosses her arms, ready to take her frustration out on him.

"No, I don't," Ezra stutters. Huxley doesn't back down.

"I think you two can sell it," I say. Heads swivel to face me. "I think if you say the lines like you're dead serious and take out the thumbs-up, then the audience will crack up."

"I like it," Huxley says.

Steve nods. "Let's do it." He motions for Ezra to get into position.

Ezra places his hand on my lower back. "You're a life-saver," he whispers. His lips brush my ear for a second, and I get more goose bumps than an R. L. Stine fan club.

I hoist the boom mic over my shoulder. Ezra calls, "Action."

Instead of saying his lines, though, Steve grabs Huxley from behind and spins her around a few times, a mischievous grin on his face. She screams from shock then, because she actually finds it exhilarating. He then spins her upside down. Her hair splays out in all directions and she's giggling and I don't recognize her. Huxley isn't Huxley for a second. She's just a girl having way too much fun with her boyfriend.

Filming goes for another hour before Huxley calls it a night. She and Steve head home while I help Ezra pack up his equipment.

I rub my shoulders. Holding a giant pole above my head for three hours is exhausting. But thanks to nonstop SDA practices, my body holds up better than expected.

"I think that went well," I say.

"Define *well*," Ezra says. "That's why they invented editing."

Steve and Huxley may put on a great show in the halls, but an Oscar is not in their future. He spoke in a monotone, visibly nervous around the camera. Huxley overacted every line like she was in charge of a pep rally. Ezra will have his work cut out for him. Still, they were sort of cute together, the way they sneaked smiles at each other. They knew how to play that up for the camera.

"But directors like Kevin Smith and Gus Van Sant used nonprofessional actors and it worked out well," he says.

"Right!"

"You have no idea who they are." He wraps a cord around his fist and secures it with a rubber band.

I shake my head no.

His mind is like a film encyclopedia; it's incredible. It's rare that you get to talk to an expert about something he loves. And Val finds this tiring why?

"How did you get so into film?"

"I don't know. I just did."

"That's not an answer. You know pretty much everything about film, and you're like a kid in a candy store behind the camera. You don't just fall into that."

"I just did," he says firmly. This is not up for discussion.

"I didn't mean to pry. I was just curious." I've never seen Ezra clam up like that. He's always so open. I disassemble the boom mic in silence and place the pieces in the case.

"I'm sorry," he says. He sits on the bleachers. His hazel eyes darken like the sky before a thunderstorm. He loads the camera into his bag. He gives me this look like he's ready to tell me something serious, but it's uncharted territory for two sorta friends like us.

"My parents had a really crappy divorce, like of *War of the Roses* magnitude," he says. I don't get the reference, as usual, but I stay quiet.

"I could hear the yelling from the driveway. I would be woken up at night by glass breaking. It was noise all the time." He fingers his hemp necklace. "So to drown it out, I would put on my headphones, pop a movie into my computer and escape. I was at the library every day checking out DVDs. The classics, and plenty of romantic ones so that I wouldn't turn into a total cynic. And I just became a movie buff by osmosis."

"I'm so sorry. I had no idea." All those times I've seen him in the hall and talked to him, he never gave a hint of coming from that kind of home. I wonder what other hardships my other classmates keep to themselves. I will never complain about my parents again.

"I survived."

He downplays it and shrugs off the attention, like people who've had real problems do.

"I can't even imagine." I sit down next to him.

"Yes, you can," he says.

"What?"

He runs his hand through his black hair, scratching at his neck. Up close, his hair isn't really a puff, but rather a dense, intricate network of shiny strands.

"What was it like, with your sister, after..."

My chest clenches. I forgot I told him about Diane. I brace myself for the onslaught of memories flying at me. "It wasn't pretty." I try to laugh it off, but my acting won't be winning any awards soon either.

"You can tell me." He puts his hand on my knee. His eyes widen with his plea. "Please."

I want to resist. Why dredge up the past? But then I look into his eyes. There's no hidden agenda, no curiosity for gossip behind them. He cares. The sound of Diane's screaming overtakes my ears.

"It was awful." My voice is barely above a whisper. "My mom and I were helping Diane into her dress when he called. She looked so beautiful. I was so excited, maybe even more than she was. Her friends did that 'oooh' thing as Diane was on the phone with him. The phone slipped out of her hand and made this clank sound on the floor. Her face just went blank, and she said, 'The wedding's off.'" My hands tremble and I shake them to make it stop. Ezra grips my knee tighter.

"She walked into my mom's alteration room and just stared at herself in the mirror for like ten minutes. She didn't say anything, just stared. Then she locked us out and started crying. But it was a screaming crying." I cover my ears, the sound throbbing inside my head. "My mom banged on the door, begging Diane to open up. Then she sank to the floor and started crying, too. It was like an epidemic. I'd never heard anyone scream like that." My voice gets wobbly, but I hold back tears. "And he has no idea what he caused. He probably doesn't even care."

Ezra wraps me in a hug. His wool sweater cushions my face. "I'm sorry."

It's such a generic statement, but what other wisdom could he provide? It works. His body is so warm and comfortable. I could stay here awhile, but I pull myself away.

"Wow. How did this happen?" I say of our Lifetime moment.

"You're just so easy to talk to," he says.

"You, too."

Ezra looks directly into my eyes, like he did while ice-skating. Again, I feel exposed. It's only eye contact, but it's like looking directly at the sun.

My phone rings, echoing through the gym. I am compelled to answer it.

"Rebecca, amazing news! I just received a text from Steve's friend Colin. He's gorgeous, and he actually wants to go on a date with you. I showed him your picture yesterday, and he said you looked beautiful. I told him you would go to dinner with him on Friday. I figured you didn't have any plans this weekend."

"That sounds great."

"You'll have to muster up more excitement than that on the date. Colin is a catch, and I think you two are going to hit it off."

"Thank you, Huxley."

Ezra puts on his jacket, turning his back to me. Huxley's talking loud enough for him to hear. I stare into my lap while Huxley gives me the details.

"Rebecca Williamson, enjoy your last days of singledom, if there's anything to enjoy about them." Huxley hangs up.

I contemplate what to say to Ezra, but when I look up, the gym door swings closed.

When I get home, I beeline to my bedroom. Diane asks how my day was, but I just nod and continue up the stairs.

Focus, Becca. Save your crummy-friend anxiety for later.

I go online, create a new email address and type away. I

glimpse my costume peeking out from under my bed. I'm not Huxley's BFF. I'm the Break-Up Artist. If I never tried out for SDA, Huxley would still be treating me like junk.

And Val. Ezra and I had a serious talk. That's what friends do. They talk. And put their hands on each other's lower back while talking. It's completely, Switzerland-style, 110 percent platonic.

I reread and tweak the email about fifty times until it's perfect.

To: AddisonG48
From: StevesDirtyLittleSecret
Subject: I know what Steve did last weekend.

Fun fact: Huxley found a condom wrapper and Angela Bentley's lipstick in Steve's car. (Ladybug's her color, if you were wondering.) I guess old flames die hard. I doubt Huxley has mentioned this to anyone, but as one of her closest, dearest friends, I'm sure you'll know how to handle this. I know you only want the best for her.

It warms my heart knowing she has a friend like you.

# 24

According to the website HuxleyandSteveCountdown [dot] com, Huxley and Steve have three-to-one odds to break up in the next month, seven-to-one odds to break up in the next week, and twelve-to-one odds that they've already broken up but are keeping it a secret. The site has become an obsession at Ashland, with anonymous posts speculating about their demise.

"Don't people have anything better to do with their time?" Huxley asks me on the phone.

I multitask between playing the friend role and getting ready. I pose in front of my mirror wearing a cerulean one-shoulder dress that falls just above my knees. Who knew I could put myself together so well? "Just ignore it. They're all jealous that their lives aren't as interesting as yours."

"Why are people cheering for the destruction of my relationship?"

"Because you're popular and they're ugly." I hook in dangly earrings. "Why are you letting it bother you?"

"I'm not," she says, but I sense hesitation in her voice. The gossip and rumors have infiltrated her mind. "Steve told me nothing's going on with Angela. He says that stuff in his car was planted."

"You should believe him. He wouldn't lie to you." I paint my lips with my Plumful lipstick.

"You're right." She tries to mask her worry and play it off like it's a stupid joke. I can't give her peace of mind, not if I want my plan to succeed. But when I think about it, I don't have peace of mind to give. I don't know if I buy the coincidence that Steve randomly bumped into Angela at the skating rink. Sure, lots of kids' birthday parties take place there, but it seems too convenient.

"Do you know why he and Angela broke up in the first place?" I ask. "Do you really think it was distance?"

"Steve says things just didn't work out. But that's guys. No specifics." I'm surprised he gave her that much explanation. "Do you think Steve's cheating?" Huxley asks me quietly, and I can only imagine how tough that was for her to say out loud.

"I don't think so." I don't sound convincing. I fan my hair out. It falls down my face in waves. Another great trick Huxley taught me. "Do you?"

"No. Are you excited?"

"Yeah, I guess." I looked up Colin Baker on Facebook, and he is good-looking. Tall, athletic, smart, full brown hair, wire-frame glasses and a killer smile. Guys like this shouldn't statistically exist. They shouldn't be single ever. And they shouldn't be interested in me.

My phone buzzes with a text from Val. You busy tonight?

And then my stomach squeezes into a tight ball.

I spent Friday dodging Val in school. When she came up to me after Latin, I bolted for SDA practice, where I avoided Ezra's stare. But halfway through my routine, I realized that nothing had actually happened. We had one semiserious conversation where we got a little emotional, and we were tired. It was a long day. No big deal. It passed. There's nothing more to read into it. He's dating my best friend, and they're happy.

Happyish.

Still, to be sure, I didn't talk to him after practice.

"So where is Colin taking you?" Huxley asks.

"Windows on the Water." The restaurant is perched on stilts on the Hudson River overlooking the New York skyline. I checked out their menu online and gulped when I saw the prices.

"That will be so romantic." Huxley sighs heavily. "The beginning of a relationship is always the most exciting. I remember when Steve and I got together. There was a party at Travis Weber's. Steve and I sat on one of those wicker porch benches outside, drinking Coke. He gave me his jacket to make sure I stayed warm. 'Bittersweet Symphony' was playing inside the house. We were talking about the differences between our school and his old school. You know, that mindless chatter that neither person cares about because you know you're going to kiss any second. And then a travel-sized bottle of mouthwash fell out of his pocket."

"Real suave, Steve."

"Then there was a century-long awkward moment, and it hit me. I am going to get kissed. My life is going to change. I picked it up and asked, 'So what's this for?' Then he kissed me, and I just knew."

"You knew that you were in love with him?" I ask. I roll my eyes.

"Yes. I didn't know it was love at the time, but I knew it was something."

That something was a gargantuan leap in her social standing at the expense of our friendship. I didn't know about the mouthwash story. I had heard about their hookup at Travis's party secondhand. Not from her, of course. Does she really not remember what her life was like when they began dating? Has she suppressed it so completely that she honestly doesn't remember what she did to me? I keep these thoughts to myself. I'm so close. Once I break up her and Steve, I can fill in the gaps of her revisionist history.

The doorbell rings, and my heart jumps for some strange reason. This is just research, with food involved.

"Did I just hear a doorbell?" Huxley asks.

"You did." I peek out my window and see a guy in a blazer and jeans. I check myself once again in the mirror and take a deep breath.

"Come with me to Chris Gomberg's party tomorrow night. Prepare to be grilled in the car ride over," she says. "Good luck!"

"You, too. I hope everything works out with Steve." I hang up and jog down the stairs, which can be deadly in heels.

"Have fun tonight," Diane says. She leans on the banister with a bowl of popcorn nestled in her arm. "Try not to get pregnant."

"Thanks."

The doorbell rings again. I'm about to answer it when Diane pulls me back and scans my face.

"Don't get too excited, B. It's just a first date, and I can tell you how they end."

I open the door. Colin Baker flashes his dimpled smile. I didn't know those people in catalogs existed in the wild until now.

"You must be Becca," Colin Baker says. Even his voice is cute. "Nice to meet you."

I bite into the best salmon I've ever eaten while gazing at a luminous New York skyline. Meanwhile, a guy bursting with charm and good looks engages me in conversation about my life and seems genuinely interested. Can a Friday night get any better? No.

Then why do I feel bored?

"Curling?" he asks in disbelief.

"It's like shuffleboard on ice." I take a sip of my Diet Coke. "It's big in Canada."

He lets out a hearty laugh.

"Have you ever been to Canada? I once went skiing at Whistler in British Columbia. It was probably the nicest place I've ever been to."

"Nicer than New Jersey?" I ask.

"Let's call New Jersey a close second." Hearty laugh again. It's yet another adorable part of Colin Baker.

I glance at the skyline again and try to count how many buildings I see. Colin Baker is the textbook definition of great-boyfriend material. He would meet any girl's criteria. I should be kissing Huxley's feet for fixing me up with him, not tallying skyscrapers. But the thing is, Colin Baker knows a little bit about a lot of things, but he can't go in-depth on a topic. It amounts to pleasant small talk.

Or maybe this is what dates are like—a test to see if two people are compatible enough to transition into a relationship.

My ears perk up when Colin brings up Steve. Their families are friends, and the two have spent many semi-important holidays together. He tells me about fond memories of one-on-one basketball and Steve's impeccable barbecue skills. Steve seems like a good friend to have, popularity reasons aside.

"That's great that your colleges are near each other," I say. Colin is attending Drexel University in Philadelphia in the fall. I'm sure the admissions office swooned over him. "Are you excited that Steve's going to Vermilion?"

Colin gets an uneasy look and takes a sip of water. "It'll be great to see him."

He cuts himself off, but I gather he'd be willing to elaborate if I played it right.

"Yeah. It's a shame he's not playing football there. He's such a great athlete. I know Chandler University is still interested."

"They are?" Colin asks. He puts down his fork. "His family would love that."

"Really? They're not happy about Vermilion?" I ask in my most naive voice. "But it's a good school, and close by."

"And expensive. His parents can't afford it, and my dad heard that they aren't offering him a scholarship."

"He can take out loans."

"He'll be drowning in debt until he's forty. Truth is, Huxley's family can pay for it no problem. They're loaded." He jams a piece of steak into his mouth.

"Have they offered?" I sit at the edge of my chair. The candle on the table gives Colin an earthy glow.

"Not that I know of. Steve would be furious if she did."

"She'd be trying to help."

"But he'd be like their property. He already feels self-conscious being around the Mapothers. That would strip away his pride."

The waiter arrives with a fresh Diet Coke for me. I let him take away my plate. That's the most passionate Colin Baker has been tonight. Maybe I'm not the only one who wants to break up Huxley and Steve.

"I'm sorry," he says. He readjusts his glasses. "I like Huxley. I do. I shouldn't have said anything. What can I say? You're easy to talk to." His lip curls up slightly when he smiles. Cute. Add it to the list.

"I get that a lot."

Colin swirls his water glass around and gazes at me. "You are beautiful."

"Thank you."

"Want to go for a walk after dinner?"

We stroll along the Hudson holding hands, and we're not the only pair here. It's a parade of couples. New York glows in the moonlight, so peaceful from our viewpoint. This must be what every girl dreams of for a first date, so why do I still feel bored?

I want to kick myself for not floating on air. Maybe people melt over these empty motions because it's one step closer to being in a relationship, and I just know better. Colin is doing everything right, but it just seems like the logical order of a first date. I should feel nervous-excited, but instead, I'm just nervous.

Colin stops at a bench next to a magnifying viewer where I can see the city up close. He leans on it while I look into a window on the Chrysler building. "Have you ever seen the Chrysler Building up close?"

"I haven't."

This all seems like a setup from some romantic comedy. I'm by no means a date expert, but I see how things are lining up. The dinner, the walk, the quiet area.

And next up is the kiss.

I'm on a roller coaster, and we're slowing cranking toward the top. I think I'm having a heart attack.

*C'mon, Becca. You should be enjoying this.* Where are the freaking butterflies? I stare at Colin's disarming smile. Maybe if I concentrate, I can feel what he's feeling. Is he really feeling this? With me?

"You all right?" he asks. He holds my hand for support.

"Yes."

*He's holding my hand!*

Next stop: kiss. If we kiss, then we'll have to see each other again, and if we go on another date, he'll ask me to be his girlfriend, and then I'll be locked into being his girlfriend for who knows how long. Isn't that how it works? I know we're outside but somehow there are still walls and they are closing in on me and I am locked inside a tiny box with Colin Baker.

I return to the viewer. I stare intently at the Chrysler

Building for a good minute. I can't make eye contact. If I do, the roller coaster is going to teeter over.

"The city is so beautiful, I could gaze at it for hours," he says. That better be an expression. "Wow, you really like the Chrysler Building."

"Yeah, it's pretty. I've only seen it get destroyed in action movies." I press my forehead harder against the viewer. I can feel the metal on my skull. I'll bet Ezra could name at least five movies where the Chrysler Building got destroyed. He'd crinkle his forehead as he thought up the list, the eyes would go up and to the left....

*Pull it together, Williamson.* I grip the handles with the intention of never letting go.

Things go back to quiet. Until I feel his hands. Massaging my shoulders. I steel myself and think of janitors working in the Chrysler offices and those mops with the rectangular heads.

"It's so high up," I say.

He doesn't respond. Instead, he kisses my neck.

*Make it stop! Make it stop!*

*No, Becca.* You *stop. This guy is great. This is what you want. Why are you resisting Colin Baker?*

He caresses my fingers. No, not caressing. He's trying to unhook them from the handles. He's trying to turn me around.

The roller coaster is cranking higher. I can see the top.

I keep my fingers strapped on the handles. It'll be over soon. He'll give up. I am such a terrible person.

He reverts to massaging my shoulders. I can't talk. My

throat is closed for business. I fear that anything I say will be a trigger to kissing.

"Relax," he whispers into my ear.

"I am." My voice shoots up three hundred octaves. We're talking castrato levels.

"What's wrong? Is there someone else?"

"What? No!" I jerk around to face him, and my elbow makes contact.

Colin Baker holds his adorable hands over his adorable face and gawks at me with those adorable eyes.

"I'm so sorry! Are you okay?"

He pulls back his hands. Even his bloody nose is adorable.

# 25

Did I really give my dream date a bloody nose? Only crazy people and women on reality shows do something like that. *Was* there somebody else? Does that count Ezra even though he is taken? He may have been on my mind because of our talk, but I wasn't some mindless fan girl fawning over him like Colin Baker suggested. Because that would be crazy.

Right?

I bury my head into the couch cushion for good measure, to knock out the crazy.

"Becca, don't do that. Your makeup will stain," my mom says. She rubs my feet while us Williamsons sit around watching TV like an all-American family.

I get a text buzzing in my pocket: I'm outside.

I feel for the paper in my other pocket, making sure it's still there. "I'm going," I tell my family.

"You never said how it went with your date," Diane says. I don't know how to answer that question without turning red. She rests the container of hummus on her stomach. I wish she had plans tonight that didn't involve using her body as a snack table.

"What are you guys up to tonight?" I ask. I spot the calendar hanging on the wall. "Isn't tonight your anniversary?"

"It is. Thanks for the card," my mom says.

"Sorry." We all know how forgetful I am when it comes to greeting cards; as far as character flaws go, it's pretty minor, and my parents just laugh it off nowadays. "Aren't you doing anything to celebrate?"

She peruses her *People* magazine. "There's something about Iraq on TV tonight your dad wants to watch."

"Iran–Contra." He gestures to the TV.

I grab a pretzel log on my way out the door. "Don't party too hard," I say, although it'd be nice if they would.

Huxley's Range Rover waits by the curb. She scowls at me when I step in.

"Did you have fun disfiguring Colin Baker?"

Huxley zooms down Radburn Avenue, going at least fifteen miles above the speed limit.

"I am beyond livid." She flicks streams of hair behind her shoulders. Her sleek legs peek out from her tight skirt. She is dressed to party.

"I sent him an email apologizing," I say halfheartedly. I can't give her an explanation because I don't have one. And Ezra is not an explanation. "How's he doing?"

"He's fine. Luckily, you have very little upper-arm strength." At a stoplight, she checks her makeup in the rearview mirror before shaking her head at me. The condescension is annoying, but not unwarranted. Hearing her chew me out makes it real. I ruined my date with Colin Baker.

"He has his senior yearbook photo next week, Rebecca. What were you thinking?"

What *was* I thinking?

"I am so sorry."

"He's Steve's family friend. They must think I'm unhinged for associating with you. He took you to the nicest restaurant in Bergen County." Huxley does some more head shaking. She's not done, though. She swerves into the right lane and makes a sharp turn. I clutch my seat belt.

"I tried. I just don't get it." She's half talking to me, half thinking out loud. "I said I would find you a boyfriend, and I did. Guys like Colin don't come around that often."

She makes it sound as if he was my only ticket to freedom, some once-in-a-lifetime chance, rather than my first first date. "Huxley, he's a nice guy. I just didn't feel a connection." Such a cliché, but so true. If Colin went to Ashland, he would be one of those people who you say hi to in halls and talk about that one class you have together. We just couldn't break past the small-talk barrier, even without my distraction.

"You don't throw that away, not someone in your position."

"What do you mean?"

"Let's be real. Colin would've done wonders for your status. He's flawless boyfriend material, and he was into you."

"But I wasn't into him. Is that not allowed?" I sound pleading. I'm on trial here, for being single in the first degree.

"No. Not when your social life doesn't have a pulse. It's

like you want to be alone and miserable forever, Rebecca. Like you're trying to prove a point or something."

The fact that she can spew venom without blinking is sickening. My blood boils. I was just a charity case to her, never a friend. I can't wait for this all to be over.

"Well, I am done helping," she says. "Enjoy spinsterhood."

"I forgot what an expert you are on relationships," I snap back. "Where's Steve tonight?"

I catch her off guard. "He went ahead with some friends."

"I hope nothing happens between you two. I'd hate to see you return to your old status."

Darkness covers the town. The streetlights provide a waning, yellow light. We turn onto Chris Gomberg's block—a peaceful, rambling street. Except for the thumping bass emanating from the third house on the left. Huxley parks down the street, to protect her car from scratches and random acts of vomiting.

We cram into Chris's house, along with what seems like the rest of Ashland High. Kids set up camp on the stairs, in the halls. Huxley gets her share of looks and double takes when we arrive. Kindling for the rumor fire.

Chris's parents are present, but not supervising. His dad pumps the keg while reminiscing about his high-school glory days. Huxley and I push through to the kitchen, where Chris's mom acts as bartender. She pours Steve what's probably his fourth shot of tequila. Guys crowd around Steve, egging him on.

"C'mon, Stevie Wonder! You can do one more shot," she says. Her tank-top strap falls off her shoulder. If it weren't for her leathery, tanned face, you would never know she's an adult.

"I don't know," he says loudly. He chugs the rest of his beer. "Beer before liquor makes you sicker."

"Beer before liquor. Get drunk quicker!" She high-fives nearby guys.

"Don't worry, Hux," Greg Baylor yells. "We're keeping an eye on him." Then all the guys burst out laughing.

Huxley purses her lips as her controlled expression slips away. She grabs my hand, and we squeeze up to the bar.

Mrs. Gomberg sprinkles salt on Steve's arm, sticks a lime in his right hand, and the shot glass in the other.

I weave through the crowd to get close to Steve. The mob of drunken classmates smothers us. He's so trashed, he doesn't feel me snatch his phone from his pocket. I use my coat to hide my hand.

"On the count of three. One...two..."

Huxley swipes the shot glass out of Steve's hand. He gives her a puppy-dog look like a child whose favorite toy was taken away.

"Steve, can we go somewhere and talk?" Huxley asks.

She pulls him to an oversize chair in the living room. Everyone at the bar groans. The fun police came. Steve swoops out of Huxley's grasp and runs back to the bar, downs his shot, then casually strides back to his girlfriend.

As the bar area erupts in cheers, I splinter off and go to the upstairs bathroom. I only have a few minutes before Steve realizes he is phoneless. The door is locked, and a girl slurs out "One second" from the other side. Great. Can't she just pee in the front bushes like a proper drunk partyer?

Two minutes later, she pulls open the door and I am face-to-face with Isabelle Amabile, Ezra's ex-girlfriend. What's the protocol between ex-girlfriends and friends of current girlfriends? I think the rules state we're supposed to hate each other. Girls have to hate each other whenever a guy is involved. That's a mandate or something.

"It's all yours." She steps aside and holds on to a picture frame for support.

I walk into the purple-tiled bathroom, but Isabelle shoves her hand in the doorway.

"Tell Val to watch out." She wags her finger in my face.

"Excuse me?"

"It's not going to last. He'll find some flaw, then another, then someone else, and abracadabra. He's gone before you know it."

My face contorts into a grimace, and now I have no need to hate her. I just pity her.

"Actually, he's a really great guy," I say.

"He's a creep."

Trying to convince her is pointless. Never argue with a drunk, Diane once told me. You will always lose.

"Move on, Isabelle." I slam the door in her face, lock it and sit on the edge of the Jacuzzi.

I find my Zen place before taking out Steve's phone. I remove the piece of paper from my pocket and begin to type in Angela's number. However, the number pops up before I can finish. It's in his contact list, hidden under "Aunt Mabel." There's a chain of text messages attached to it. I read them about twenty times and hold on to the edge of the Jacuzzi for support. My head spins, and I haven't even had a drink yet.

Angela: Hey, thanks for the coffee.

Steve: It was so good seeing you.

Angela: When are you going to tell Huxley about us?

Steve: Soon. I promise.

# 26

It's weird when you find out your suspicions are correct. I knew from a young age that the tooth fairy wasn't real. But I still felt a pang of disappointment when my dad woke me up cramming a dollar under my pillow. It's not always fun being right.

I step over couples making out on the stairs. These parties are the same as school dances, just switch out booze for dancing.

"Becca?"

Fred waves at me from the bottom of the staircase. What's he doing here? Did Ashland's social strata get rearranged while I was in the bathroom?

"Hey." That sounded awkward. "I didn't know you'd be here."

"Likewise. I helped Chris pass bio last semester, so I got an invite. It's like I'm infiltrating some secret underworld."

"I know how you feel."

Fred brushes his hand across his wild hair. Upon further review, he's one makeover montage away from being decent-looking.

"You know, the lunch table isn't the same without you."

"Too much testosterone?"

I spot Steve semiconscious on the couch. His phone presses against my leg, and it won't be long before he's eager to drunk dial.

"I have to go. I'll see you around."

Fred tries to say a farewell, but I'm already charging into the foyer.

I navigate my way through the crush toward Steve, picking up snippets of chitchat. These are the same conversations I could have in the halls at school. Why are we here? So that other kids can see that we got invited to this party? I guess it's not about what you talk about, just that other people see you talking.

Steve is loosely clutching a beer he's too drunk to drink. I lean on the couch arm and rub his shoulder for friendly support. I slip his phone in between the couch cushions.

"How's he doing?" I ask Huxley. She brings him a glass of water.

"He's fine. He just has to learn when to stop."

If only she could see his phone, then she'd realize just how true that was.

I settle on a spot, watching the beer-pong game. This way, I can seem social without having to talk to anyone. Zach Hershkovitz has to pull Ally Zwick in for a kiss every time before he shoots. It all screams *superficial.* Steve and Huxley in training. My phone buzzes with a text from Val.

You busy tonight? Let's hang out! I'm going through Becca withdrawal.

This is the second night in a row that she's texted me to hang out. Ezra is probably busy, and I ponder what he's up to. Maybe at the indie theater with Jeff and other guys, catching up on classic cinema, engaged in an hour-long debate about an old movie with the guy selling popcorn, his eyebrows bobbing around his forehead as he makes his case, eyes beaming.

*Stop it!*

Mason Carroll sinks a Ping-Pong ball in the back left cup. The crowd goes wild, and he chest bumps his partner. I put my phone away. I'll text her later. I'm taking a sabbatical from Val's histrionics tonight.

I lean against the fireplace mantel. My head rests next to a picture of Chris, his girlfriend and his parents at the beach sipping margaritas.

"You're in my history class?" Bari asks, though she knows the answer. It's less awkward than asking my name. She and Calista share the chair beside me. They're skinny enough to make that work.

"Yeah, and Latin."

"I heard it helps with SAT stuff. So not true," Bari says.

I look down at my cup as Calista gives me a once-over. My ridiculous Break-Up Artist costume seems to have been effective since she just goes back to drinking. The girls confer among themselves, then stare at me again. I pretend to care about the game.

Bari taps me on the shoulder, and a shock of nerves rushes through me. "Have you heard of the Break-Up Artist?"

I strain to remain nonchalant. "The what?"

"There's this person, the Break-Up Artist, going around breaking up couples. She created that stupid binder and planted it on Derek. I would never make that. Now people think I'm crazy! She needs to be stopped." I smell coconut rum on her breath. "She's probably some pathetic fat girl who got cut from the cheerleading squad or something."

Calista nods supportively. "Calm down. We'll find her."

I guess Bari only figured out half the story.

"I thought that was an urban legend or something," I say.

"Nope. She's real. We found out she also broke up Michael Mulroney and Kimber Diaz. Made Michael look like he was stealing from her!"

I act intrigued even though breathing has become a little more difficult now. My memory of digging through Kimber's purse while she was in the nurse's office rears its ugly head. I take a sip of beer to hide the red flushing through my face.

"Well, I haven't heard of her."

"You will. We're going to find her. We're pretty sure she goes to Ashland." Bari tosses back the last sips in her Solo cup. "I can't wait to expose that bitch."

The beer pong stops. People shush those around them as the commotion in the kitchen becomes clearer. Faces light up as they pass the news to others like a current of electricity. It can only mean one thing: fight. I join the crowd flocking to the living room for a better view.

"I love fights!" Bari says. They do make parties worthwhile.

We find a pocket of space behind a papasan chair. My jaw tumbles to the floor when I see who's in the ring.

Ashland's favorite couple. And Angela.

Greg Baylor holds back Angela's boyfriend from clobbering Steve.

"What the hell's the matter with you, dude? You think you can mack on my girlfriend?" the boyfriend asks. "I'm going to destroy you."

He tries to push through Greg, but there's a reason Greg's one of our best football players. Steve grabs a kitchen chair for support. The situation is sobering him up fast.

"What are you talking about?" Huxley asks. She turns to Steve. "What is he talking about?"

"I don't know!"

"Don't act dumb. I saw the text you sent her tonight."

"What is he talking about?" Huxley asks. She struggles to keep order. Having spectators is probably killing her inside.

Angela's boyfriend rips the phone out of her hand. She's letting him do all the talking. He reads from her phone. "'Angela, I need you. Come to Chris's party. I'm ready to tell Huxley about us. I love you.'" He tries to dodge Greg but no luck. Mr. Gomberg helps Greg out, the most mature thing he's done tonight.

My classmates go nuts, conferring with each other about the message. I was not expecting her boyfriend to quote me. Why would she show him the text?

Huxley can't keep it together, not after that, not with the audience commentary. Nobody cares to notice that a lone tear forms in her left eye. It bobbles on her lashes before falling down her cheek. That's all she lets out. One tear.

This is probably for the best. I sped up a conversation they were bound to have in the future. Right?

"Hux, I didn't write that," Steve says. He tries to hold her hand, but she pulls away. "I promise."

"But it's from your phone." Huxley sits down on a chair and takes deep breaths.

Steve pats his pants. "Where is it?"

"Found it," Addison says by the couch. She hands it to Steve. "Sounds like a drunk text to me." She waves hi to Angela. "I love your lipstick. What shade is that?"

"Why don't you shut up!" Steve yells. I didn't know he had such darkness inside him. He runs back to Huxley and kneels beside her. "I—I don't know. I was super drunk before—maybe I did...but I didn't mean it, Hux. I swear."

Angela steps out from her boyfriend's shadow. I can see her heart breaking all the way from here. "What about us? You don't write something like that and not mean it."

"There is no us, Angela!" Steve screams. "You broke my heart! You cheated on me with that asshole. Don't you remember?"

Angela glances away.

"I remember." Her boyfriend smirks. Mr. Gomberg pushes him against the fridge.

Steve turns to Huxley, frantic. "We talked. That's it. I hadn't seen her since I moved, and I had to get some things off my chest." He looks deep into Huxley's eyes like a puppy who piddled on the floor.

"So you reminisced while ice-skating?" Huxley asks. She's tossed aside the composed facade. When your life implodes in front of the whole school, what's the point in keeping it?

"I was delivering pizzas to a birthday party, and she happened to be there."

"Happened to be there?"

"Yes! All we've done is talk. I promise. Don't listen to what everyone else is saying. Listen to me." Steve is pleading with the intensity of a man on death row. I thought he would've given up already.

"You're disgusting," Huxley says. She stands up and heads for the front door, ignoring the stares and smartphones.

Angela's boyfriend knocks Mr. Gomberg down and lands a punch to Steve's jaw. He hits him again, and Steve spits out blood on the freshly mopped kitchen floor.

What have I done? A broken heart is fine, but not a broken bone. I never meant for there to be blood. I feel like part of me deserves to be on that floor.

Greg yanks Angela's boyfriend off of Steve and slams him into the bar. Bottles of top-shelf liquor shatter on the floor. He and Mr. Gomberg pin him down. Angela runs over to comfort Steve. He swats her hand away. Dark circles outline his eyes. He stumbles through the archway after his girlfriend, half-drunk and sweating, holding his cheek.

"HUXLEY!" he yells at the top of his lungs. I follow the crowd back to the beer-pong table for a better view. Huxley pays him no attention. Steve musters his strength and stumble-jogs to the front door, falling into a ficus plant. He hops back up and slams his hand against the front door, keeping it shut. Huxley turns her back to him.

"Don't do this, Steve. Just let me out."

"No." He spins her around and grabs her by both arms.

He has the most intense look on his face I've ever seen in person, like he's talking directly to her heart.

"You know what I realized after seeing her again? That she didn't break my heart."

"Glad to hear it."

"She didn't break my heart because I realized I was never in love with her. I thought I was, but then I met you."

"What...?" Huxley starts, then takes in the spectators. For once, she's not prepared for this type of attention. "Actually, it doesn't even matter anymore."

She tries to release herself, but Steve won't let go. He could have any girl, all of whom are less prissy than Huxley, but he doesn't let go.

"I'm not going to keep defending myself. Nothing happened. You can believe me or you can't. But it's the truth." She tries to free herself, but he won't loosen his grip. "I love you, Huxley. I always have. I look forward to every moment I get to see you. I think about that way you tilt your head and smile at me at least fifty times a day. You make me feel like I'm walking on the moon, and I don't want that to end. I love you so much. You can believe me or you can't. But it's the truth." Tears flood his face, but he doesn't care.

The entire house is silent. I'm sure girls are finding this ultra-swoonworthy. Honestly, so am I. His words turn the lights on in some corner of me. It's not some movie I can laugh at. It's real life, real emotion, happening right in my face. And all I can think is how much I want to see Ezra right now.

Steve steps away from the door. But Huxley doesn't leave. She kisses him.

The house erupts in cheers and *awws*. Girls smooch their boyfriends.

He hugs her so tight he may snap her in half.

"I miss Derek," Bari mutters under her breath.

My heart is beating full-on out of control, and something like electroshock therapy runs from my scalp to my big toe. I can't string together a thought. They keep getting scrambled in my brain, and Ezra keeps popping up, like I'm searching for a radio station in the middle of nowhere and getting the same one every time. I have to get out of here.

I sneak behind Huxley and Steve still kissing and out the door. The cold air brushes against my skin and provides a fleeting moment of composure, but then the confusion returns. I walk to the corner of the street and take out my phone. A groggy voice answers.

"Can you pick me up?" I ask. I don't know what I'm thinking. Am I thinking? I may feel an iota of what Steve feels, but I can't tell. I can't decipher this.

I talk myself through it. *Okay, Becca, you got a little emotional. That happens, but you're out of there.* I must appear like a crazy person talking to myself on a street corner at 2:00 a.m. I spend the next twenty minutes calming myself down. That was an emotional scene, and it left me a little frazzled. It happens. I'm not made of stone. But then Ezra pulls up in his car. Just seeing him through the windshield flips the electroshock/cardiac-arrest button inside me.

I get into the car, and my body goes numb with nerves.

"Looks like some party."

"Uh-huh."

"Are you okay?"

"Uh-huh."

It's the only word I can remember. I can't look at him directly, so I stare at my trembling hands.

"Becca, seriously, are you okay?"

"I think we should kiss," I say.

He doesn't say anything back. He smells nice for just rolling out of bed. I sniff the cologne on him. Another sign this is a bad idea.

"I don't know what I'm... You're really cute. And I'm sorry I called—"

He shuts me up with a kiss, and the confusion disappears.

# 27

Love is in the air at Ashland. The school has been nonstop buzzing about Chris Gomberg's party. They sigh over Steve's bloody declaration of devotion to Huxley, but all I hear is my plan blowing up in my face.

I'm in the minority. Instead of the dramatic kiss at the party, there's a different kiss I can't stop thinking about.

Ms. Hardwick blabbers on about some book. When I look up at the chalkboard, I see Ezra's lips coming at me.

In comes Steve, carrying Huxley over the threshold as the bell dings. "Here you go, Ms. H. Your top student!"

The girls and Ms. Hardwick *aww*. Am I missing the girl gene that forces me to *aww* whenever I see something corny? Or was there a mass lobotomy I wasn't invited to?

"Oh, Steve. Put me down!" He grants her wish. Huxley smoothes out her outfit. She's wearing one of Steve's blue dress shirts cinched at the waist with an oversize belt and black tights. Only Huxley makes the ensemble look chic and not trashy. Yet another reason why I need to go back to hating her.

"Steve, you're late to class!" Ms. Hardwick says.

He shrugs and runs his finger down Huxley's arm. "It was worth it."

Another round of *awws*. *Okay, you two rediscovered your mutual infatuation with each other. Moving on...*

"Go!" Ms. Hardwick crosses her arms, finally laying down the law.

He pecks Huxley on the lips. "I'll see you later." He rushes out the door.

"That is so embarrassing," Huxley says, not meaning it. "I'm sorry for disrupting class, Ms. Hardwick."

"It's all right. Please get to your seat, Huxley. We have a lot to cover today."

"Sure thing."

I've created a monster.

I make a mad dash to my locker before lunch. I will buy a Snickers at the vending machine and eat it in the library today. Between Huxley and Steve, Val and Ezra, and Bari and Calista, the cafeteria is the last place I want to be. And Snickers have unheralded nutritional value.

When I open my locker, a letter flutters to the floor. It stares at me, threatening me with its contents. Has someone guessed that I'm the Break-Up Artist? I pick it up. This is ridiculous. I can't be truly worried until I open it.

*I can't stop thinking about you. When can I see you again?—E*

I slide to the floor. He wrote it in cursive. There's something so old-fashioned about it, in a good way. My stomach churns with equal parts ecstasy and dread. Suddenly, I'm no longer craving a Snickers.

I receive the second note of the day in Latin class. This time, I know the author. I rip open the paper football. I'm nervous, but I can't wait. I have to know what she knows.

My body stops functioning, like cement was poured over it.

"Becca," Mr. Hoffman asks. "You okay?"

I nod my head yes, even though inside I'm screaming no.

WE NEED TO TALK
I KNOW WHAT YOU DID

I can't run out of class. She'll hunt me down.

When the bell rings, she takes my hand and leads me out of class.

"Val, I'm so sorry," I blurt out.

"Why didn't you tell me you had a date?"

"Colin Baker?"

"He sounds cute! Dish!"

A tsunami of relief washes over me. My date seems like forever ago. I refresh my memory before describing the guy and date to Val. I omit the broken-nose detail.

"He was a nice guy, but I don't think he was into me."

"I know all about that. Don't worry, Becca. On to the next," she says. We head through the cluttered corridor as kids race to catch their buses.

"I'm going to hold off for a little while on the dating front."

"Becca," she says, wiping a clump of mascara from my lashes. "You have to get back out there. So you had one bad date. Move on. You just have to keep searching, weeding out all the losers. Mr. Right is out there, but you can't just sit back and hope he finds you."

And then Val gives me the look, the look Diane warned me about. The look Huxley has perfected into a science. The "oh, you poor, pathetic single girl" look. Wide eyes, pouting lips. One of the biggest joys coupled girls have is giving their single friends dating advice. Just because they lucked out—and it's luck, nothing more—they believe that makes them dating experts. I'm sure it's one of the reasons Val worked so hard to land a boyfriend. She's always wanted to be on the other side of this conversation.

"Val, I just don't feel like dating right now."

"That's not a healthy attitude. There are so many great guys out there. Don't shut yourself off."

"I don't need your advice!"

Val leans back, surprised by my outburst. "Fine, you don't want my opinion. Let's get a guy's point of view. Ezra!"

With preternatural timing, Ezra walks down the hall at that exact moment. I wonder if he's been watching us, if he saw my outburst. My body clenches, bracing for impact. But I also can't wait to look at him again.

"Hey," he says to Val. I never noticed how cute his deep radio-deejay voice sounds.

"Ezra, tell Becca that she needs to get out there and keep dating."

Ezra and I look at each other, neither of us wanting to talk first. The thumping of my heart in my ears drowns out all ambient noise. It's just me, Val, Ezra and blurriness.

"I don't really think that's my place to say," he says.

"C'mon, even as a hypothetical," Val says. "She needs to keep dating. There are a lot of good guys at Ashland."

"I don't know," he says, his eyes drifting up.

"Can we not talk about my dating life?"

"Oh, stop. We're all friends here."

Ezra licks his lips. Awkward and adorable, for sure.

"What do you think, Ezra?" I ask. "Are there decent guys at this school?"

"There's a handful."

"Exactly, sweetie," Val says. "Well, more than a handful. Three and a half handfuls."

"But, you know," Ezra says. He waves his finger, a grin emerging on his face. "I don't think you should worry. I think if there is a gentleman interested in you, he will make it known. He wouldn't let you get away."

I grip my hanging backpack straps. "You think?"

"I have a feeling. He just has to wait for the right time, or until he can't wait any longer."

"It's all about timing," Val says.

"Good to know," I say. I take a calming breath.

"Thanks, honey," Val says to Ezra. "You're the best." She kisses him on the lips softly. Not like how I kissed him.

The only way to get my mind off the current drama surrounding my life is work. Not homework.

My other work.

Since it seems dangling another girl or guy in front of

their faces is useless, I have to take a new tack to split up Steve and Huxley. I have to look within. I browse pictures of them online. I can only imagine how much worse school will be now that they've patched things up. Everyone will want to be like them. Students will move heaven and earth to find a suitable soul mate. And us singletons will be ostracized even more. I can't let that happen. I click on a picture of Steve and Huxley in cowboy hats at some carnival, and the conversation I heard between Coach and Steve flashes in my mind. Then I remember Greg Baylor talking up Chandler University at lunch.

A half hour later, I waltz into Diane's room with my laptop. I'm thinking this will be my last case as the Break-Up Artist, so I better make it count. Bari and Calista are onto me. Who knows if they've recruited others.

Diane finishes folding laundry. My mom wants her to do more chores around the house, and watching talk shows doesn't count.

Without notice, the kiss with Ezra rears its ugly head again. Why do I keep thinking about him at the most random times? Is laundry some kind of subliminal trigger? I remind myself that I kissed my best friend's boyfriend. I could be stoned to death in parts of the world for that.

Diane snaps her fingers in my face. "What's gotten into you? Are you still hung up on that Colin guy?"

"No." Of course not. I have a new boy to fixate on. Is that true? This is how a girl becomes guy obsessed. Will I just keep finding guys to pine for, an addict perpetually in search of my next fix?

"Don't lie to me, Becca. I'm your sister. I used to change your diaper."

I have to tell somebody. I have to say what happened out loud, to somebody. And Diane's right. We are sisters. If I can't tell her, then who can I tell? Definitely not my best friend.

"I kissed Ezra, Val's boyfriend."

Diane snorts when she laughs.

"I'm a horrible person."

"You're only a horrible person if you enjoyed it."

She catches the extra current of shame rippling across my face. "Becca!"

This is bad. Even Diane is taking Val's side. Every rush of excitement I get from thinking back on it causes an equal and opposite reaction of disgust. What if Val finds out? What if anyone at Ashland finds out? Is there a scarlet letter for bad friendery?

"I don't know what to do," I say. "I can't stop thinking about it."

"That's easy. Don't do it again."

"What if I want to?" A week ago, I would've rolled my eyes and walked away from a person talking such nonsense.

Diane doesn't roll her eyes. Her expression turns solemn. I wonder if she knew this day would come eventually.

"So you like him?" she asks.

I nod my head. I don't know if there exists a tipping point for officially liking someone, but I believe I'm hitting the major criteria. Can't stop thinking about him. Uncontrollably smiling when I do think of him. Want to see him right now.

"He sounds like a creep," she says.

"No, he's a good guy."

"He's dating your best friend and openly pursuing you. I don't have a dictionary on hand, but I'd say that's a creep."

"It's not like that. You don't understand." I picture the way Ezra acted with me, so delicate and sweet. He didn't have a secret agenda. Diane only views people's actions in black-and-white—mostly black.

"Will Val understand? You do realize that if you want a relationship with lover boy, your relationship with Val is over." Diane scowls at me, taking this very seriously for someone not involved. "Are you going to be one of those girls who happily ditches her friends for a guy?"

That leaves a bruise.

"It's not like I meant for this to happen. It just did. I'm still trying to make sense of it, and I thought I could talk to you about it honestly. I thought for one day you could drop the whole 'everybody sucks' mentality."

I set my laptop next to her. "Can you just make the call? I wrote out what to say."

Diane gives me a disappointed look, as if I must always view her life as a cautionary tale. She peruses my script.

"And use a Southern accent."

Diane dials Steve's house. She rests her feet on the clean-clothes pile.

"Hello, Mr. Overland? How are you doing today? I work for Coach Robert Latham at Chandler University. I was calling to find out if Steve is coming down next weekend to check out our lovely campus....He hasn't told you about it? Teenagers today!"

I stifle a laugh at Diane's over-the-top accent. She's watched *Steel Magnolias* one too many times.

"Greg Baylor had mentioned Steve was visiting next weekend during our open house....News to you? Well, here's some news *for* you. It's a great opportunity! All-expenses paid, meet with the coach and players, bunk in the dorms. I think he would really enjoy it."

Diane gives me the thumbs-up. We can argue, but she's always there when I need her. The definition of a Grade-A sister.

"...Of course. I understand. Absolutely discuss it with Steve, and just send us an email. You can even talk to Coach Latham directly, if you want. Don't even have to bring up talking to lil' ole me....Uh-huh. Sounds good. And tell Steve it's seventy-five and sunny here. You have a wonderful night, sir."

Love is in the air at Ashland. But not for long.

# 28

I'm woken up, not by it finally being light at this hour of the morning (hello, daylight savings!), but by the buzzing of my phone at five forty-five in the morning. From an unknown number. Curiosity overtakes grogginess, and I answer.

"Two-point-oh. Did I wake you?"

"Aimee?" Diane's friends always called me Two-point-oh, a newer version of my sister. Leave it to her to call apart from Erin and Marian. She always did her own thing, even if that included calling at insanely early hours. "Shouldn't you be sleeping?"

"The baby loves to kick."

"Wow! It'll be born before you're twenty-five. You'll be more of an older sister," I say with a laugh. I don't get why people want to have kids so young. I've heard your twenties are the best years of your life. Why do you want to waste them changing diapers? But Aimee always had a competitive streak, and if Erin could pop one out, then so could she—without gaining as much weight.

Wait—why am I making chitchat with my sister's alleged friend at too-early o'clock?

"What do you want?" I ask. That sounds rude, but she can attribute that to lack of sleep.

"I want to talk to Diane. We all do. This has gone on long enough. I don't know why Diane is so mad at us, but it's time to clear the air."

She makes it sound like Diane's some little kid having a tantrum. "It's been a tough year for her."

"I wouldn't know. She hasn't spoken to me."

"You don't know what she went through." My heart speeds up. I wasn't expecting a fight this morning. I stay on the defensive. Even though what Aimee's saying is technically true, like with my mom, Diane doesn't have anyone else in her corner. It's forever us versus the couples. "She was devastated. She was in shock for weeks."

"I don't know why," Aimee says.

That puts *me* into shock. No need for coffee. I am awake.

"The writing was on the wall for months with them. I'm shocked they didn't call it off sooner."

"First of all, *they* didn't. He did. Six hours before! If he knew from the beginning that his family wouldn't let him marry a non-Indian girl, then why did he continue to string my sister along?"

"A non-Indian girl?"

"Yeah. His family said that if he didn't marry an Indian girl, he would lose his inheritance."

Aimee doesn't say anything. I've heard of pregnancy

brain, where you forget certain things, but did she honestly forget about that? "Is that what Diane told you?"

"Sankresh just wanted some fun before finding a traditional Indian wife."

"Becca." She lets out a long exhale, like people do when they have to say something they really don't want to. "Two of his older brothers married white girls, and his family didn't say a word."

"Maybe not in public."

"Being Indian had nothing to do with it. You think he would've waited until just before the wedding to call it off? Trust me, that was the least of their problems, and Diane knows it."

"Then why didn't she break it off?"

"Because she wanted to get married." Aimee stops herself. "I'm sorry."

"That's not true." I grip my phone until I feel the plastic buckling. "It's not like you care."

"But I do! We all care! Diane is one of my best friends. Even though she won't talk to any of us, I still consider her one of my closest friends."

"Seriously?" I wonder why they kept trying, when Diane wasn't giving them anything back. Was their friendship really that strong?

"She was there for me when I was in a dark place, almost as dark as where she is now. It's a weird-ass bond we all have, and now she won't even talk to me. Do you know what that's like?" I find myself nodding without realizing it. Diane can be stubborn, but she needs the maxipad girls.

I have some time before I need to hop in the shower. "I know how you can see Diane again."

With ten days to go until opening night, rehearsals have been stretched an extra hour, which feels like an extra decade. Each minute is another challenge to not look over at Ezra, and to stop wondering if he's looking at me. In those moments (and there have been plenty) when I succumb to temptation and turn my head to him, he's distracted with painting or talking to his crewmates.

"Huxley, can we take a break?" Ally says, wobbling around. "I'm feeling a little dizzy."

"If you must," Huxley says, looking unimpressed. "Let's take a quick water break."

I'm relieved. Most of my hydration has sweated onto my clothes. I stumble to the water fountain with my empty bottle. Who knows what kinds of germs rest on it, but I don't care. Must have water.

Kerry fills up hers and Ally's water bottles. "Did you hear that another girl came forward claiming that she hired the Break-Up Artist? Urban legend, my ass."

"I think between her, Sarah, Bari and Calista, they should find her in no time," Ally says. I suddenly feel fully hydrated, but I can't move. I must keep eavesdropping.

"Seriously, how sad and pathetic do you have to be to break up couples for money? She must be uuugly." Kerry caps the bottles. "It's all yours," she says to me.

I check myself out in the reflection of my bottle. Isn't it sad and pathetic that people in relationships act so horribly that they force people to contact me? I inhale a gulp before filling up my bottle. When I finish, I jump back, startled that it's not a girl waiting behind me. It's Ezra.

I look at him. I have to. He's right in front of me. It's the perfect excuse.

"Hey," he says.

"Hi."

"I was just getting some water." He points at the fountain.

"Yeah. I just got some. It's good." I squeeze my bottle until the cap almost pops off.

"Good."

"Yeah."

"Um, you looked... You guys were good out there."

"Yeah. Ten more days."

"Cool."

"Yeah."

"Good," he says.

"I'm really excited." We're just two people having a conversation. Totally normal. Just talking about...I'm not really sure what we're talking about, but it's of the G-rated, non-home-wrecking-slut variety.

"I'm gonna get back to the squad and drink my water."

"Cool."

"Yeah." I run-walk back to the bleachers. I remember that I'm still thirsty and take a sip. I would love for us to kiss again. (Wow, I did not know what I'd been missing out on!) Instead, I pucker up to my water bottle and chug.

"Rebecca," Huxley says. I stop in my tracks. She waves me over.

I do as I'm told. "What's up?"

"I have a question for you."

"What is it?"

"How long have you and Ezra been hooking up?"

# 29

I peel pieces of the label off my bottle. “What are you talking about?”

“Don’t lie, Rebecca. It’s rude and it gives you premature wrinkles.”

I crinkle my brow, seized by worry.

“So does that,” she says.

“I was just getting water.”

“I didn’t just fall off the boat. I’ve never seen such a charged interaction between two people. Well, aside from Steve and me.” She does a quick stretch while I stand here awkwardly. “Now I get why you weren’t into Colin Baker.”

I think fast for a cover story. “It’s really embarrassing.”

“I can’t wait to hear it, then.”

I sit down on the bleachers and act mortified—head in the hands, et cetera. “He picked me up from Chris’s party since you obviously weren’t driving me home. I was stupid drunk, and I kind of threw up in his car." I laugh it off. "Like chunks of dinner all over his leather interior."

She holds up her hand. "No need to elaborate. I recommend you stay away from alcohol, Rebecca, if only because of the empty calories. So nothing else happened?"

"No." My voice returns to calm. The key to lying is convincing yourself that what you're saying is true.

Huxley calls everyone back to practice. Even though she thinks nothing happened, I still feel uneasy about her knowing anything. I get back into position, and with all my mental power, I concentrate on dancing. Not on Ezra.

Diane sits in my mom's throne watching a cooking show with a chef so thin I doubt she ever eats anything she prepares.

"Hey," she says. "You can change it if you want."

"I have a question." My voice travels to helium levels. "Did Sankresh's brothers marry white women?"

"Wow. That was the non sequitur of non sequiturs." Diane is wearing her usual uniform of Rutgers sweatshirt and pajama pants, and I want to take her in the back and hose her down. I feel this disgust toward her creeping in, toward what she's done to her life.

"Did they?"

"Yeah, I think so."

"Then why was that okay?"

"Sankresh wasn't as strong as they were. He was kind of a pushover."

Maybe that explains why they were together as long as

they were. Diane mutes the TV and kneels on the Throne to look at me. "Becca, relationships are complicated."

"They can't be that complicated if I break them up so easily."

"Did you hear that?" I hear faint screams from upstairs, my mom's voice. Diane and I look at each other, verifying that we both heard it.

"Mom, are you okay?" Diane yells as we run into my parents' bedroom.

"If you don't stop that, we're going to call the police!" my dad yells.

Diane swings open the door. My mom and dad are screaming at someone out the window.

"Oh! My windows!" my mom says, feeling the glass. "If I find scratches, you're paying for them! Do you hear me?"

I race to the window and nearly die from simultaneous shock and embarrassment. Ezra stands in our backyard, next to our rusty swing set. Pebbles lie at his feet.

"What the hell were you doing? You vandalized my property!" my dad yells.

"I'm sorry," Ezra says. "I thought this was Becca's window."

"No, she's one window over. Couldn't you have sent her a text message?"

Diane pats me on the back. "It's lover boy."

"Who's lover boy?" my mom asks. She comes closer and whispers to me: "Is that the boy you went on the date with? He's not what I pictured."

"No!"

"You vandalized my property!" my dad says again. He repeats himself when he's angry.

"He's a friend of mine from school. I'll take care of this." I draw the blinds and sprint to my bathroom for an outfit check and a quick blush and lipstick touch-up.

I haven't spent time in my backyard in years. I'm too old to play here. It's a shame I can't donate the space to little kids in need. Ezra sits on a swing, probably getting tetanus as I speak. He digs his hands inside his hoodie. Our outdoor lights paint him in silhouette, and he's never looked cuter.

"I'm sorry for the fracas," he says. His voice sounds sexier than ever. I'm the only one that gets to hear it.

"Hey," I say. For some reason, it's the only word that comes to mind.

Ezra pulls me in for a kiss, and it sends a blast of electricity through me. "I can't stop thinking about you," he says.

"Me, too." But I'm also thinking of Val. I squeeze his hand, wanting him to squeeze back.

"You're incredible, Becca. I've never felt this way about anyone." He runs his hand down my cheek. It makes me shiver.

Ezra's phone chimes with a call, but he silences it before the second ring.

What if that was Val? I can't let myself get sucked into the vortex like the couples at school. Not when Val is sitting in her bedroom alone trying to talk to her boyfriend.

"What is it?" Ezra asks, noticing my giddiness deflate.

"I can't do this," I say.

"Val?"

I nod. "How is this so easy for you?"

"I feel awful, but I know I'd feel worse if I let you go. It drives me crazy being in the same halls as you, and not being able to do anything about it."

Does he prewrite these lines? Still, I can't help but swoon. They only sound stupid until a guy says them to you.

"What are we doing?" I ask. "I can't go behind my friend's back."

"We don't have to. If she saw how right we were together, she would understand. She wants us to be happy," Ezra says, completely clueless about his girlfriend. "I think she would be more upset if we kept sneaking around."

"She would be miserable, no matter what."

Ezra swings next to me. He laces his fingers into mine. I can feel his warmth prickling the hairs on my arm. "I don't want to hurt Val. But why should we both be miserable to make her happy?"

I pull back. Suddenly she's making him miserable? That's a bit harsh. Val isn't some third-world dictator.

"Bad choice of words," Ezra says. He reaches for my hand again. "Not miserable. Val and I just aren't right, not like us. There's chemistry between us. You have to see that."

I gaze up at the sky, reaching for some kind of answer. All I can see is the North Star and a few others fighting through the pollution and lights. I don't know how a field of science with beakers and boron came to be a relationship necessity. There is something between us. A natural comfort level and physical attraction. It's all brand-new, and maybe I should keep experiencing it. I want to.

I take a deep breath. "So what happens now?"

"I—I don't really know. I guess I'll start by meeting you

first thing in the morning at your locker, and we'll take it from there," he says. Ezra tries for another kiss, but I shuffle to the side.

"What about Val? You need to break up with her."

"I'll do it before homeroom."

"Ezra!" Even though we're outside, I feel walls close in on me. I need time to process what's happening. Does this mean I have a boyfriend? Isn't there more of a gestational period? I wish there was an instruction manual.

"The longer we wait, the more upset she'll be. We have to tell her."

"Eventually," I say. I leap off the swing set. I need to move around. "We have to wait. First, you need to break up with Val immediately. We'll play it cool for a few weeks so she can heal and I can get used to all of this, and then we can go from there." Ezra won't have a problem because people always blame the other woman. I may not be popular, but Ashland High won't be able to resist sinking its teeth into this gossip and piling on the dirty looks.

"What do you mean, 'go from there'?" he asks. He grounds his feet into the dirt. "You mean become official?"

"Sort of."

"I don't want to wait! I want you to be my girlfriend now."

"I thought you weren't into labels."

I prefer labels on my clothes, not my life. Why does it always come down to being in a relationship? I'm not sure I'm ready for that. I don't want to join the packs of relationship zombies at Ashland. I don't want to be known solely as someone's girlfriend, or begin all my sentences with "my boyfriend."

Ezra pats the swing next to him, and I sit down. His hands are clammy with sweat, and it's nice to know I have the power to make a guy nervous. "Becca, I know this is fast. But have you ever seen *When Harry Met Sally...?*"

I nod yes. It's one of the only Meg Ryan romantic comedies that doesn't make me groan.

He gazes into my eyes, and it's as if we're back on the skating rink. "Remember the part at the end, when Harry says to Sally, 'When you find the person you want to spend the rest of your life with, you want the rest of your life to start now'? That's how I feel about you. Not the 'rest of my life' part. But you are the girl I've been searching for. You're so different and interesting. This may sound crazy, but I can see myself falling in love with you."

I lunge forward and kiss him, one of those deep kisses where our faces mash together like peanut butter and jelly. With tongue, but not gross lizard tongue.

"I don't know if I'll be able to hold back touching you or kissing you every time I see you pass in the hall, but I'll try," he says.

I blush at the thought of Ezra being so ravenous around me. "Parting is such sweet sorrow," I say.

"Likewise." Ezra kisses me again. We need to block out a Saturday afternoon to do that more. He pulls back, but our faces are so close.

I get a weird feeling and look up at my house. Diane glares back at me, then quickly draws her blinds.

# 30

Even Ezra chewing food is sort of cute. I dart my eyes at him for a split second while I stand in line to pay for my food. School has an added layer of excitement now. It's a game we're playing—sneaking glances in public, finding ways to brush against each other in the hall—and I want to win.

"Hey."

I almost drop my salad. Behind me, Fred grips a tray with a Philly cheesesteak, potato chips and a regular Coke. I wish I could eat like that.

"Can we talk?" he asks. "In private."

"Sure." I sneak in a 1-2-3-look at Ezra while following Fred. We walk to the one pay phone left standing in school, possibly in the state. "What's up?"

"Are you the Break-Up Artist?"

My stomach squeezes into a tight fist. I knew people would be suspicious eventually, but never thought I'd be accused point-blank. I don't have time to prepare a story. Fred is drop-dead serious. He's just looking for confirmation.

"What? No."

"I saw you slip Steve's phone into the couch cushions at Chris's party. And then all that drama happened over the text messages. I started to think there was a connection."

"I didn't take his phone."

"And then I remembered your revenge plot for Jeremy's comics. The way you talked about it, it was strange, like you'd done it before."

My hands are slick with sweat. I place my tray atop the pay phone. I thought I was so clever, so cautious, but apparently, I'm not invisible to everyone.

"Becca, I won't tell anyone, but you have to stop." He pushes his glasses up his nose, and he seems more nervous than me.

"Stop what?" I can't even convince myself. "I'm not doing anything."

Deny, deny, deny. Fred's face sinks into a hangdog frown. He wants me to trust him, but I can't. I can't trust anyone with this secret. It's too valuable not to use. He would be a hero to the school, to every school, to Huxley and Steve. His social standing would skyrocket. He's too smart to not take advantage of that, and I won't let him.

"I'm going to eat my lunch. The period's almost over."

"Bari keeps snooping around. She's recruiting other girls who've used the Break-Up Artist. She's getting closer. Whatever you're planning, it's not worth it. Give it up."

I remain a locked fortress, and won't even give him a nod.

"Listen." He touches my arm then instantly pulls back

as if I'll bite. "I'm not sure why you're doing this, but maybe it's time to stop. You can't manipulate people like this. Relationships are tough enough."

"And how would you know? It's not like you've ever had a girlfriend." I pause, taken aback by my harshness. "Is the witch hunt over? Because I'd like to get back to my lunch table."

He shakes his head, more like a teacher and less like a friend. "Don't let me stop you."

I leave Fred with the pay phone, and I fight back all feelings of guilt. His wounded expression burns into my memory, but I push it down. I have to look out for myself.

This will all be over soon, I repeat to myself. My time with Huxley is supposed to be temporary.

"You look flushed," Huxley says. I take my usual seat across from her and her tiny green salad.

Greg horses around with Steve, punching his back and rubbing his shoulders. Huxley is not amused.

"Steve-o, we are going to tear up Chandler U! Like rip it from the ground. Start sleeping now, because this weekend is going to be nuts!"

Steve isn't as hyper as Greg, but he can't hide his dopey smile. He's restraining himself for the table. Well, for one person in particular.

"Aren't you already committed to going to Vermilion?" Huxley asks. "Isn't it unethical to go on this visitors' weekend?"

"I haven't formally accepted either school yet," Steve says. "My dad thinks I should check out Chandler before making up my mind."

“You weren’t planning on playing football, though. Have you told them that?”

“I don’t know. I shouldn’t completely shut that door, you know?”

“I thought your mind was made up.” Huxley keeps up her pleasant, sing-songy tone.

“I guess it’s not.”

The table gets quiet. Before any of their friends can second-guess the stability of their back-on relationship, Huxley scoops up Steve’s hands.

“You’re right. You shouldn’t close any door just yet. The weekend sounds amazing! I know you two will have a blast.” Huxley pecks his knuckles. He caresses her cheek.

“Thanks, Hux.”

Huxley pushes lettuce back and forth on her plate, and presses on one of her fake smiles.

Diane hates needles. In high school, she attempted to get her ears pierced, but flaked the second she sat in the chair. It wasn’t until her bachelorette party when Erin, Marian and Aimee got some Long Island Iced Teas in her and dragged her to a piercing place that she finally got them done. Sometimes, Diane needs to be pushed. Sometimes, she needs to be ambushed. I repeat this to myself as I sit in the living room waiting. I’m doing this for a good reason. Because I love her.

Diane walks into the living room, and the same look of hurt and betrayal that flashed across her face at Owen’s birthday party comes roaring back. Her shopping bags slip out of her fingers.

Erin, Aimee and Marian sit on the couch in various stages

of drinking coffee. I stand up from the ottoman, my hands clasped. "Hey, Diane. Look who came to see you."

Diane sits fully upright on the Throne across from them. If she were in etiquette class, she would get an A plus. I feel our track lighting beaming straight on me.

Erin and Marian seem as uncomfortable as me. Aimee, for once, is the quiet, passive one. Maybe it's the pregnancy wearing her out.

"I'm so sorry about Owen's birthday," Erin says to Diane. The words puncture the silence like a fire alarm. "I had no idea you were coming, Diane. We've tried a million different ways to get in touch with you."

"Finally, we decided to come over to make sure you were still breathing," Marian says, flicking red hair out of her eyes.

"I am." Diane rolls her bracelet around her wrist.

Erin looks at me for some help, but I can't step in. I have to stay back. This isn't my battle.

"Diane," Erin says, sounding more desperate. "Please talk to us. We've been worried about you all year."

"If you were so worried, then why are you only coming around now?"

"Why have you been ignoring us for the past year?" Marian asks. "We've called, texted, emailed. I think Erin wrote an actual letter and mailed it to you."

"But you never came by the house. That would be too inconvenient for you, wouldn't it?"

"No! Of course not," Erin says, always the people pleaser. Baby Owen is going to be one spoiled child. "It's just..."

"You've been too busy." Diane shakes her head in disgust

and points at Erin, Aimee and Marian. "A baby, an almost baby and a wedding. Who has time for the sad, pathetic friend?"

"You're right, Diane," Aimee says. "We were busy. Why would we visit you if you wouldn't even pick up the phone? We love you, but we can't put our lives on hold, and neither should you."

Aimee glares back at Diane. She's the muscle of the couch group. She possesses a bluntness and take-no-crap attitude that a woman needs if she's going to work as a publicist while eight months pregnant. I would never tell Diane, but I always admired her.

"What Aimee means is that we are here to support you, but you can't keep pushing us away," Marian says.

"No, that's not what I mean. What the hell is going on, Diane?"

"Why would you invite Sankresh and *her* to Owen's birthday?" Diane says to Erin. Her entire body is still, poised to attack if need be.

"Because he returns phone calls," Aimee says. "I'm not getting dragged down into your immature drama. It's time to grow up and move on."

Diane faces a wall of classic "I'm sorry you're single" looks. In the mirror behind the couch, I catch my mom's feet on the stairs. I want to join her so badly.

"It's so easy for you to judge. Need I remind you that if it wasn't for me befriending Bill senior year, you would still be single." Diane looks up to the skylight. Tears form in her eyes, and she's probably hoping gravity will push them back in. "The guy I loved broke up with me on the day of my wedding. You will never know what that feels like."

"It's not like you didn't see it coming," Aimee says. I want to throw her coffee in her face.

"What does that mean?" Diane says.

"Take off your rose-tinted glasses. There were plenty of warning signs, and you ignored all of them. Do you remember what happened at your bachelorette party? About two Long Islands in, you started crying about how you didn't know if you loved Sankresh or not."

I do a double take at Diane. I'm surprised she didn't add *dun dun dun.*

"I was drunk!"

"But you still said it."

"So I had a little bit of cold feet. I still loved him."

"Dammit, Diane! Sankresh tried to break things off months before, but you wouldn't have it. You knew he was such a pushover that you could talk him out of it. You were so hell-bent on getting married—"

"Get out!"

Before I have time to process this bombshell, Diane launches herself off the Throne.

"The only reason you guys came here was for a laugh. Oh, look how heartbroken Diane is. One year later, and it's still hilarious. Well, you know what else is hilarious? Erin's butt-ugly baby, Marian's flaming husband and that eating disorder you had in college."

Erin and Marian hop off the couch. Their shocked expressions quickly congeal into looks of pity. They lift Aimee off the couch. I bury my face in my hands, embarrassed enough for the two of us.

"You are pathetic, Diane," Aimee says. Her words sting my ears. "But not for the reason you think."

Once the women slam our front door shut, Diane whips her head around to me. I've never seen such darkness in her eyes.

"You ambushed me."

A hydrogen bomb has exploded over my smart idea. I didn't think this would happen, but I guess I don't know my sister as well as I thought. "I wanted to help," I say through tears. "Diane, you can't keep living this way."

"Do you think I want to? But how can I face anybody, when all they see is the jilted bride?"

"That's what *you* see."

What is she fighting against? It's like she doesn't want her life to improve. She just wants to keep hating Sankresh, and she can't hate Sankresh if any part of her life doesn't suck.

"Some sister you are. You steal your best friend's boyfriend, and you think that makes you some relationship expert? Thanks a lot."

I cry by myself in the living room a little longer before going to sleep. While lying in bed, I think about how beautiful Diane looked with pierced ears. She took them out right after the wedding, and the holes closed up a few weeks later. They didn't leave any scars. It was like they never happened.

# 31

While I eat dinner at the alcove with my mom—another dynamite Friday night—the strangest thing happens.

Val calls me. Actually calls.

I know right away something is wrong. Val is a texter, which is odd for a girl who loves to talk, now that I think about it. Did Ezra spill the beans about our kiss?

No—kisses.

Multiple kisses.

"Hey," I say, my voice tense with curiosity.

"What are you up to tonight?" Val sounds chipper, just like typical Val. Except typical Val wouldn't call to ask me this.

"Nothing."

"Becca! It's Friday night!"

I tap my fork against the counter. "What's up?"

"Do you want to meet up for coffee? I really need to talk to someone. The craziest thing just happened."

"What?" I ask, a little too impatiently.

"Ezra just tried to break up with me."

* * *

We rendezvous at Azucar, one of those hip coffeehouses that only exist near college campuses. A guy who would be cute were it not for the overdose of facial piercings slides a chai latte across the counter. I need to be here for Val, but I also want to be there with Ezra. A mishmash of emotions bounce around inside me like straitjacket-wearing psychopaths in a rubber room. It's annoying how much real estate thinking about Ezra takes up in my head. I want to stop, but it's like some sort of addiction that I keep lunging for.

"Roll it," I say the second my latte hits my hand. I sink into the plush purple couch next to Val. She stirs her coffee.

"Last night, Ezra sent me this email saying that he didn't think things were working, and that maybe we should see other people. And, sure, things haven't been as great as they used to be, but that's just the excitement of getting together wearing off. It happens to all couples."

No, I say to myself, only to couples who are together for the wrong reasons.

"I'm so sorry! What a slimeball. Through email?" I say. And on second thought, did Ezra really have to break up via email? Val deserved better. "You should've called last night."

"The thing is, I wasn't upset last night. I was in shock, but I didn't cry. I didn't believe him. It seemed so abrupt. I was not going to sit back and watch my relationship dissolve. So I devised a plan."

I lose my appetite for coffee. I should be the only one scheming on this couch. "What did you do?"

"I looked up quotes from movies that he loves and hid them around school, like a scavenger hunt for him. Under the piano in the band room, I hid a note that said 'Play it again, Sam' from *Casablanca*. He loves that movie, even though I fell asleep when we watched it. So he followed the clues around school until he ended up at my car. When I saw him walk up to me, I almost passed out or something. It was so romantic."

It was. And clever. Who knew Val could construct something like this? She would've made a great co-Break-Up Artist in another life.

"What happened?" I sip my latte.

"I said we've been building something together, and I cared about him so much, too much to just accept his breakup. He once told me that relationships were about two people taking a leap of faith, having that initial attraction and seeing if there was more to it. Well, for me, I knew there was more to it. And if that meant waiting for him to come around, then I would, because I know we have something special. And he'll realize it soon enough."

I clutch my latte until it dents inward. Since Val isn't in tears, I already know the answer, but I ask anyway: "So what did he say?"

"He pulled me in for a kiss. And it was...interstellar. Ezra's an amazing kisser."

*I know!*

I grit my teeth. My fingernail pokes a hole in my cup.

"So, crisis averted," Val says, back to her beaming self. Seeing her happy irritates me in a whole new kind of way. "Want to split an M&M's cookie?"

"No."

"What's wrong?"

"Val, can I ask you an honest question? Are you really into Ezra? Genuinely?"

"Of course!"

"No, you're not!" My yell attracts the attention of every college hipster and Mac enthusiast in the room.

"Can we please end the charade? You just wanted a relationship. You were desperate for one! It's so obvious."

Val places her coffee on the table. She's either way too calm, or I'm way too pissed. "It's not like that. Yes, I know I was a little boy crazy—"

"Understatement of the millennium. All you've done is lie and deceive and manipulate just so you don't have to walk down the hall alone. You needed a boy, and you got one. But that boy is a genuinely good guy who deserves someone who actually cares about him." The words stream out of me before I have time to process them. I'm so hot that my drink feels cool in my hand. My feelings about their relationship cannot be bottled up any longer.

"I can't believe my best friend is saying this. I never lied to Ezra," she has the audacity to say.

"Oh, yeah? Tell that to Annie Hall. Or why don't we reread the email you had me write?"

"You sound like a jealous lunatic. Do you have a crush on Ezra?"

"No!" I blush at the question, but my already red cheeks hide it.

"I don't have to justify my relationship to you," she says. She feverishly runs her fingers down her blond mane, as she always does when she's frustrated. "If you really think this is all fake, then why is Ezra still in the picture?"

I marinate on that but can't come up with an answer right away. Ezra wants *real* love. Why can't he see through this sham?

"Do you like him, or do you like being in a relationship more?"

Fresh tears bulge at Val's eyes, and a pang of misery stabs at me. Nothing is worse than making your best friend cry.

"Maybe I wasn't totally honest with him at first. I didn't want my lack of movie knowledge to ruin everything. But my feelings for him were always real." Val wipes her eyes with a napkin. The tears keep coming. "I always found that expression 'my heart skips a beat' so ridiculous. As if some guy could really cause that. But he can. Whenever I see Ezra walk toward me in the hall with that adorable smile, or see his number pop up on my phone, or hear his voice, I feel my heart stop for a second. Like it's sighing or something. And then my heart beats really fast. It's freaky mind-over-matter stuff, but really cool. That happens every time I see him."

Val stares at me with an intensity that I didn't know such a perky person could summon, one that tells me without any doubt that she is dead serious.

"I love him. I love him so much," she says.

Heat strangles my neck. I didn't know it was possible to be so furious at someone you care about so much. "No, you don't! How deluded are you? Your relationship is bullshit, Val!"

Before she can respond, I'm out the door, hitting the night air at full blast. A double dose of pain shoots through my chest. Not only have I made my best friend cry, but she's in love with a guy who doesn't love her back.

* * *

On the drive home, I crank up a news station on the radio. Maybe world unrest can distract me from the chaos that has become my life. I need to ignore the disgust I feel for myself.

I am in serious like with Ezra Drummond.

Even though he's still with Val for some unknown reason, I can't help it. My heart and mind are conspiring against me.

"I like Ezra Drummond!" I scream over the weather report. It feels great to say it out loud. And then the dread sinks in. I roll down my window. The breeze blows against my face.

How can I be with him and hurt Val? How can I let him stay with Val? Why do none of these options end with happily ever after?

My phone rings. The second caller of the night. I am never this popular.

"Hey."

"Hi, Rebecca. What are you up to this weekend?"

"Nothing."

"Rebecca! You honestly have no plans this weekend?"

I roll my eyes at the comment. I'm glad one aspect of my life remains constant.

"What is it, Huxley?"

"Do you want to go down to Chandler tomorrow?"

I don't think about the logistics, the lies I'll have to tell my parents or the sheer lunacy of Huxley's question. I've never needed an escape so badly in my life.

"What time are we leaving?"

# 32

On Saturday afternoons, most kids from Ashland are watching crappy movies on cable, running errands or working. (Maybe a scant few are doing homework, too. Maybe.) None of them are 35,000 feet up in the air lounging in first class, eating Salisbury steak and sipping on free champagne.

Except Huxley and me.

I told my parents I was hanging out with Huxley this weekend. I never specified *where* we'd be hanging out.

Huxley downs her second glass of champagne and peers out the window, something she hasn't stopped doing since we crossed the Appalachian Mountains. It's rare to watch her be so pensive.

"Are you okay?" I smack myself on the forehead. Dumbest question of the day. Let's try again. "Do you want to talk?"

Worry clouds her face. "I know there's not much we can do when we get there. I just need to see with my own eyes what he's doing tonight, if..."

"If he's having too much fun."

"If he's happy," she says. She glances out the window again. "If he plays football for them, I don't know if we'll make it."

"Don't say that!" The flight attendant gives me the stink eye while she refills Huxley's glass. She probably can tell I'm only in first class because of Huxley, not the other way around.

"He loves you. Remember Chris Gomberg's party?"

She nods yes, but without conviction. "Things will be different if he goes off to school."

"That's why you want him to go to Vermilion."

"I can't lose him."

She needs him close, needs the control. But I don't get why she's so intent on staying with him after he graduates. She'll graduate a year later and go off to college and find another boyfriend. Is her senior-year status at Ashland that important?

"Maybe you two should just call it quits now. Let each other start fresh. We have brand-new lives waiting for us once we get out of Ashland." I take a sip of my champagne. The bubbles tickle my nose, and I let out a Chihuahua yelp. The flight attendant shakes her head at me.

"I don't want a brand-new life. I like my life with Steve. My parents were high-school sweethearts. They both went to Rutgers, got married right after and settled down back in Ashland. As old-fashioned as that sounds, it's also incredibly romantic. They knew from the start what mattered the most. I want that with Steve."

Diane also tried going that route with Sankresh, but it backfired. The only time when the whole high-school-sweetheart story works out is when the two people involved don't think about it.

"Maybe you're meant for something different. Maybe that's not your life. You're smart, Huxley, and you're a born leader. Look what you've done with SDA. I think there's this whole interesting future waiting for you. Do you really want to chuck it for the sake of some relationship?"

"It's not just 'some relationship.'" She swirls around her glass of champagne, watching the bubbles, so contemplative, as if she's reviewing the past four years and making her own judgment.

"I began dating Steve for all the wrong reasons," she says. "I liked him because he was Steve Overland. Now it turns out I actually love the guy."

And I actually believe her when she says it. She sounds so natural about it, so genuine, like she's stating a fact rather than proving a point. Unfortunately for her, it's a fact that she can no longer control.

The warm breeze and amber setting sun of Dallas welcomes us. It makes me question living in a place that has snow.

When I turn my phone back on, I find a pair of text messages waiting for me.

Both from Ezra.

Can you meet up today? We need to talk.

I know how to fix what happened with Val. You're the one I lurve.

Does *lurve* count as the L word?

"Why are you so smiley?" Huxley asks me.

I shove my phone in my purse. Heat rushes through me, but let's just attribute that to the desert weather.

Our cab whizzes down the highway. We pass a steakhouse shaped like a cowboy hat. It's unabashedly corny, yet endearing. Steve would like it here.

"Who was that?" she asks.

"Nobody."

"I'm sure it wasn't."

"I wasn't smiley." I can't enjoy this. Not when every organ in Val's body beats for Ezra.

We drop our luggage at the hotel. Huxley sprang for a penthouse suite with a living room, kitchen and balcony overlooking the pool.

"My dad had points," she says.

I unfurl on the king-size bed and unwrap the mint on my pillow. It pays to be Huxley's sidekick. I sit up, a thought coming to me.

"Why did you ask me to come with you?"

Huxley stops hanging up clothes. How much did she bring for one night?

"I don't know. For some reason, when this idea popped into my head, you were the only friend I pictured joining me."

"Really? More than Ally or Reagan?"

"Yes. They would never go along with this. You probably think I'm insane for coming here, but you also get it."

It's true, in some odd way. I guess I'm used to scheming, but she doesn't know that.

"I know I can trust you," she says.

I gulp down a lump in my throat. "Thanks."

We change outfits, aiming for fun yet not very noticeable, and wash the smell of airplane off our skin. I crank country music on the alarm-clock radio, but Huxley's not in the mood to laugh. She focuses on getting ready. She's on a mission.

I release the dead bolt and open the door to the hall, but Huxley shuts it just as fast. She's nervous as hell.

"Don't worry," I say. She's so fragile and human. Any trace of the ice queen has melted, and I can see the girl I once knew underneath. "We'll probably find Steve sitting on a bench, bored out of his mind."

"Thank you for coming with me." She takes a deep breath, and I can tell she wants to say more.

"What is it?"

"I'm sorry."

I take my hand off the doorknob. "For what?"

"For ditching you. You were a good friend."

I don't have some huge emotional reaction where I grab her for a hug and cry hysterically into her shoulder while music swells. I thought I would if I ever received an apology, as if those words would magically fix the past four years. The damage can't be undone, but I'm ready to move on.

I open up the door again and give her a reassuring smile. "Let's go do some spying."

After walking around campus for a good forty-five minutes, a student in the middle of a Vegan Rights protest sneers and directs us to Sigma Tau Iota, the fraternity of choice for football players.

"Say au revoir to your brain cells," he said before returning to chanting. ("What do we want? Seitan! When do we want it? For dinner!")

The frat house could use a paint job, but its majestic front columns and wide balconies give it a powerful aura. This is *the* place to be tonight, probably every night. Packs of students glom on to every inch of the property, each of them with a red Solo cup in hand. It's two girls to every guy at this soiree.

The door's wide-open (well, actually there's no door), and we join the dense crowd. Sweat beads form on my forehead. This is Chris Gomberg's party times fifty, except nobody has a history here. People scope out Huxley and me, but not because they know us. There's no decade-long backstory branded on our foreheads. It's freeing having a clean slate for once.

We push into a narrow hall and enter the stream of people going somewhere. Huxley looks like she wants to bathe in Purell. I'll bet more than the heat and claustrophobia, Huxley hates not being recognized.

She peeks into a common room where girls and guys dance on plaid wingback chairs and an antique wood coffee table. My phone buzzes, and I remember that Ezra texted me earlier.

Where've you been? We need to talk. Can I see you this weekend?

"No sign of him," Huxley says.

I can't ignore him forever. I don't want to. I don't want to hurt Val, but this is my life, too. If she's such a proponent of love and relationships, then she will have to understand. Nobody's perfect, even best friends. I imagine Ezra and I talking about what happens next, and some more kissing.

I text back: Let's meet up tomorrow night at 8. I can't wait to see you!

"Who can't you wait to see?"

I try to hide my phone, but Huxley's too fast. I guess since we had a heart-to-heart, she believes she can know every detail of my life now. My face turns redder than a Solo cup as she scrolls through my messages.

"Wow, Rebecca. I had no idea."

"I'm not a home wrecker," I blurt out, which makes me sound super guilty. Looking for a distraction, I zero in on the keg and wait in line behind two guys with an aversion to grooming. We use their mushroom-cloud hair as cover in case Steve should come through.

"Do you love him?" Huxley asks, cutting to the heart of the matter.

I search for a definite answer. "I don't know."

"I thought you and Val were close friends."

"We are!"

"Would you throw away that relationship for one with Ezra?"

How is Huxley so good with questions? She doesn't mince words. Stalling, I glance to my left. A girl sips her beer and makes a stink face, then proceeds to pour out the rest of it on the carpet. I don't even want to see Huxley's reaction.

"'Throwing away' sounds so harsh. It's more complicated than that," I say.

“Not really. You are freely hooking up with her boyfriend. Why should she stay friends with you?”

“Because we’re best friends.” My head spins with guilt. I can’t live in a world where Val and I aren’t speaking. But does that mean I have to stay away from Ezra? I don’t want to live in that world either.

“I don’t know what to do. I can’t be with him, but I want to so badly.”

Huxley sizes me up. A satisfied smile is planted on her face, like she knows something I don’t.

“You don’t love him,” she says matter-of-factly.

Her confident tone ticks me off.

“You two sound like star-crossed lovers, and as you pointed out in English class, that makes you quote-unquote ‘full-on crazy.’ Knowing you shouldn’t be with Ezra makes you want him more.”

I’m shocked that Huxley was listening to me that day, and that she could quote me.

“Maybe Romeo and Juliet were in love,” I say.

“No. They weren’t full-on crazy, but definitely up there.” Huxley laughs at me, the first time she’s relaxed today. “What drew them together was the excitement of getting caught. That’s not love.”

“Or maybe they just fell for each other under really cruddy circumstances.”

“But what would’ve happened when things calmed down, when Romeo didn’t have to recite sonnets and get in sword fights? What would they be like on a random Tuesday? The couples that thrive on drama flame out the quickest. I’ve seen it a million times.”

I had a bunch of witty retorts, but they all fade away. I'm left gawking at my foamy beer, shocked that Huxley Mapother said something so...un-Huxley Mapother-ish. Do Ezra and I think we're star-crossed lovers? Maybe that's part of the excitement I feel when I think about him, knowing that I shouldn't be thinking about him.

"And also, I have a feeling Ezra is the first guy who was ever into you. Am I right?"

She may be right, but I still find it rude. She reads my clenched expression.

"I thought so."

He wasn't my first kiss, though. I made out with a guy at a Model UN convention last year. He was from Ghana—at the convention, not in real life.

Huxley clinks my cup, and we drink. Now I know what sewer water tastes like.

"This is all so new for you," she says. "I was in your shoes once, and I'm not condescending. I really was. I remember the mouthwash that fell out of Steve's pocket, and that moment when I knew he was going to kiss me and my life was going to change forever. It's so exhilarating. I think that's what you like about Ezra. You like that he likes you."

I scoff at the remark. "That sounds like Val."

"Well, that's why you two are best friends. You're so alike. Honestly, I'm kind of jealous of the relationship you guys have. I don't have that with any of my friends."

"I shouldn't throw it away." The epiphany knocks me to the ground. I don't care that I'm wearing a nice skirt. I sit cross-legged on the grimy floor, much to Huxley's dismay. She's right—I fell for the relationship crap, just like Val. Val just vocalizes what I refuse to say. I thought I was stronger than that. I thought I couldn't be duped.

I'm half relationship zombie.

"I know what you need." A guy in a baby-blue polo and cargo shorts grabs my free hand and pulls me up off the floor. He yells into my ear. I could get drunk off his breath. "You need. To do. A keg stand."

"A what?"

"It'll be good clean fun! I promise," he says in his Southern twang, which is impossible not to swoon over. It's the American version of a British accent.

"Um, sure."

He takes my hand. Huxley clutches my other hand and pulls me away. "No. You're not doing a keg stand. You're wearing a skirt, Rebecca!"

We hear a holler loud enough to overpower the noise, and Greg Baylor barges into the far end of the hall. Beer stains streak his Chandler University T-shirt, but he certainly isn't letting that get him down.

"It's the beer train!" he says to the three girls behind him. "Chugga-chugga, chugga-chugga."

Huxley and I turn away from him. We push through the tightly packed partygoers, who are magically parting for Greg's train. We keep our heads down as he gets closer.

He stops at the keg, while Huxley and I flee into the common room. We sidestep around grinding girls and pass a contemplative foursome of wallflowers who came to the wrong place for conversation. Rows of house photos line the room. In the photos, the boys look like respectable gentlemen. A guy in his underwear and a cowboy hat races past us, grazing Huxley's boobs.

Pictures can be so deceiving.

We squeeze into a circle three people deep that lines the dining room table. They're cheering something that I can't see.

"That was close!" I say.

"If Greg's here, then Steve has to be close."

Very close.

Like right in front of us.

In the center of the circle is Steve, taking body shots off two blondes in bikinis lying on the dining table.

He slurps down both shots without looking up and garners whoops and hollers. Some Southern guy even yells, "Yee-haw!"

Steve smiles so wide that his teeth may fall out of his mouth.

"I need some air," Huxley says.

Flying first class isn't as fun on the return trip. I can't enjoy my tortellini centimeters from an ailing Huxley.

I keep thinking about the couples I've broken up. I plot and scheme, but I'm never present for the personal anguish that comes with breaking up. I've never had to watch it firsthand.

"What are you going to do? Are you going to break up with him?"

Huxley locks eyes with me. Her misery has hardened into

determination. “No. I’m going to fight for the guy I love.” She sips on her water. “What are you going to do about Ezra?”

The pilot makes an announcement that we’re getting ready to land. It’s time to reenter reality, and I’m prepared.

# 33

Ezra meets me at a Dunkin' Donuts near my house. My heart has a mild gush when he sits down at the table. I can't help it. It's not fully on board with my head yet.

"Hey there! You've come out from hiding." He reaches for my hand. I yank it back into my lap. His eyebrows squiggle in confusion.

"We need to talk."

"This sounds ominous."

"It kind of is."

"Listen, I know you're upset about the whole Val thing. But it will get done."

I gaze into his hazel eyes one last time. They reflect the glint of waning sunlight pouring through the window. They're beautiful, and that's about it.

They're just eyes.

"I can't date you."

He slumps back in his chair and shakes his head a bunch. "I thought we had something."

"We did, but Val and I have something stronger."

"I really could see myself falling in—"

"But could you? Really?" I notice how easily he throws that word around. It seems like it loses its power the more it's said.

Ezra shrugs his shoulders, resigned to my decision, which he's figured out won't change. "I guess it's like the end of *Casablanca*. I have to let you get on that plane."

"What do you think would've happened if Ilsa didn't get on that plane? She and Rick would've gotten bored with each other once things died down." I rein myself in. I'm already breaking up with the guy. I don't have to ruin his favorite movie. "I'm sorry, Ezra. You're a good guy, honestly."

"Thanks."

That wasn't so bad. Maybe messy break-ups are only for immature people.

"I know I don't have any business asking you any favors, but this time, when you break up with Val, please do it in person. She's a good person, and she deserves that much."

"Who says I'm breaking up with Val?" Ezra takes a bite of his donut. He rubs the smear of chocolate frosting from the corner of his mouth and licks it off his fingers.

"What? But you aren't into her!"

"Val and I have had our ups and downs, but maybe there's something there."

"There isn't." Five minutes ago, he was all set to break up with her. *It will get done.* He was ready to cross it off his list like taking out the trash. Now he flipped a switch, and he's back on the "falling in love with Val" track?

"I have to give things a real chance."

"And then you're just going to dump her when something better comes along?"

"You make it sound so crass. I can't control the way I feel."

"You're disgusting." I was going to get something to drink, but now I just want to leave. This can't be the same Ezra I swooned over, but here he is, in all his selfish glory. "You think you're some expert on romance, but you don't know anything."

"You've never had a boyfriend. You wouldn't understand."

"You're right. I've never had a boyfriend. But you've gone through multiple girlfriends. Whenever things stop being all first kisses and warm gooey centers, you bail. You hit one tiny bump in the road, and you're on to the next." *He's gone before you know it,* Isabelle told me at the party. She was plastered, but still, she was right. He probably thinks one argument will lead him to the relationship his parents had. I shake my head, angrier at myself than him.

The high I had been on comes to a startling, crashing halt. "I'm such an idiot. I actually started to believe all that shit about love."

Diane has never been more right.

The real Ezra looks up and to the left. It's no longer cute. It just makes him look like a brat. He doesn't say anything back. He's not used to being criticized. He preys on girls so eager to be loved, so hungry for a boyfriend, they'd never say a mean thing about him. And my best friend is his current victim. He'll keep stringing Val along until he finds someone else. I won't let him give her any more firsts.

"I'm telling Val," I say.

"Telling her what?"

"Everything." I head toward the door. Ezra runs in front of me and blocks the passageway.

"Are you sure you want to do that?" he asks. "You think I'm the one she's going to be mad at?"

"You think she'll be mad at me?"

"Her best friend hooks up with her boyfriend behind her back. She'll never forgive you. I had a temporary lapse in judgment. I was upset by our recent fights and ran into your open, waiting arms. You should've known better."

He's right, and we both know it. He grins like a sore winner. What was I thinking?

"Do you think Val will willingly go back to being single?"

My eyes widen with shock. I made out with the scum of the earth. Multiple times.

"You are pathetic," I say, though I don't know which one of us I'm talking to.

My mom has a dinner plate covered in plastic waiting for me. She and my dad watch *Love Actually*—she on the Throne, he on the couch. Never cuddled together, of course. Maybe they have the right idea. They gave each other a normal life in the burbs with all the trappings. They didn't let some fruitless search for love constantly upend their lives.

"Becca, where are you going?" my mom asks.

I stop at the foot of the stairs with my dinner in hand. "I'm going to eat in my room. I'm really tired."

"Are you okay?"

"I just had a long weekend."

The phone rings when I'm halfway to the second floor.

"Becca, can you get that?" my mom asks. It will take an act of nature to pull either of my parents from their seats—a downside to owning comfy furniture.

I pick up the kitchen phone hung next to the fridge. "Hello?"

"Hello, Rebecca Williamson."

And I just stepped on a land mine. I grab the fridge door to steady myself. I know that voice, and I shouldn't be hearing it on the house line.

"Mr. Towne?"

I run into my mom's alteration room with the phone and lock the door.

"How did you get this number?"

"I'm not the best with technology, but I got a buddy who was able to track something called an IP address to your computer. Found your computer and your name as the registered user. As for your actual number, I just looked you up in the phone book." Mr. Towne speaks in a genial, chatty manner, barely concealing a menacing undertone. For the first time, I'm scared.

"I'd prefer if we kept our correspondence limited to email," I say.

"I wanted to, as well, but this is just taking too long, and I haven't heard from you in a while."

"I'm sorry. I've been really busy. But I'm taking care of it." I look at my hand, and I'm still gripping the doorknob. I can't move from this spot.

"You've been saying that for over two months. I feel like I'm getting the runaround, and I don't appreciate it. May fifteenth is this Friday."

I want to hang up. I never want to hear his voice again, never answer another break-up email. "I—I don't think I want to do this anymore," I say, trying my hardest to control the shaking in my voice.

"You're so close. Steve went down to Texas to visit this weekend. He's loving football again. But the kid got drunk and blabbed to everyone who'd listen about his girlfriend and how he's so in love with her and couldn't leave her."

Hearing that provides me with a fleeting smile. I wish I could tell Huxley. "I'll give you a refund."

"I'm not interested."

I pace around the room, hop in place, but I can't get calm. There's no protocol for when your true identity gets discovered.

"I think he's in love with her."

"You and I both know that's a boatload of crap. It's not love, never is," Mr. Towne says. "You agreed to do this, Rebecca."

My voice becomes more erratic. "Why do you want to break them up? Why can't you just leave them alone?"

"Are you rooting for the lovebirds now?" He lets out a hearty chortle that pierces my eardrum. "Let me provide you with better incentive. If Steve chooses Vermilion on Friday, then I will make sure that every student and parent and Burger King employee in your town knows what you've been up to, Miss Break-Up Artist. I don't think high-school life will be so much fun after that."

Before I can say anything, he hangs up. When I *69 him, his number comes up as unlisted. I go upstairs, walk into my bedroom without turning on the lights and crawl into bed. I pull the covers up over my head.

I march through Monday perpetually on edge. Each second of the day is spent mentally preparing myself. Ms. Hardwick drops her dry-erase marker, and I nearly shoot into the ceiling. She asks me if I'm okay.

"I'm fine."

Except for my life teetering on the verge of utter ruin.

At lunch, Greg will not shut up about the weekend at Chandler. He leaves out any mention of the party Saturday night. Huxley and Steve focus on their plates, both embarrassed for different reasons. It's sweet how much they care about each other's feelings.

Finally, after what seems like a week, the day is over. I pull Huxley aside before we get changed for the final SDA rehearsal. I sit her down on a bench by the main office, a place where nobody will interrupt us. I don't have to beg for a moment of her time anymore.

"Have you spoken to Steve about the weekend at all?"

"No. He won't bring it up. Which means he had an amazing time, probably with one of those blondes." Huxley hides her face in her hands.

"I have to tell you something. But promise you won't say I told you."

She springs back to life. "I promise."

And because we're such good friends, I trust her. "I overheard Steve and the coach talking a while back. Steve is having trouble affording Vermilion. They didn't offer him any scholarships."

I think back to my reconnaissance in the boys' locker room. I was so excited. I was so stupid.

"He never told me," she says.

"Maybe that's what's stopping him from going. Chandler University is probably offering him a full ride."

I study Huxley, watching as the wheels turn in her head.

"Do you think that's really all it is? Chandler has football."

"He'd only be going because he could afford it. He doesn't want football. He wants you," I say. I'm only telling a partial lie, but that doesn't make me feel better. My chest tightens. "He loves you, Huxley."

"My family could pay for it no problem. Steve would never go for it, though."

"Only if you made him ask you for the money."

Huxley strums her fingers against her knee as she contemplates the idea.

"If Steve goes to Chandler University, then you know what will happen to your relationship. Do you want to let him go over dollars and cents?" I stop talking. I can't be too pushy.

We sit there in silence for a minute. We hear the echoes of our teammates warming up. Huxley glances at me, a smile emerging, one full of hope.

"Steve does like surprises," she says. "Thanks for looking out for me."

Bile rises in my throat, but not before I say, "What are friends for?"

# 34

There's no time left. All my hard work pays off tonight. As unsure as I may be, I have to go through with it.

Tonight, I dance.

"I am going to have a talk with the principal. They have some nerve making girls wear this getup." My mom stares at me in my stripper-pole tracksuit costume. I should agree with her that this outfit is a total affront to feminism, but I look so good in it, I can't complain.

"It has to be like this, so we can dance," I say. I load up on hair spray to get my hair into the tight bun required.

"You wear it well, I guess."

"Thanks, Mom."

We pass Diane's room on our way downstairs. Her door is shut. I can make out the laugh track blaring on her TV. I hear it more often now, since Diane has given up the Throne. She's treating our house like a hotel, and I'm just another random guest.

My mom knocks on her door. "Diane, we're leaving for Becca's show. Are you coming with us?"

We trade looks, neither of us hopeful. My dad joins us, tapping his watch, but quickly he gets the holdup.

My mom has to knock on the door again to get a response.

"Yeah. Give me one second!" Diane yells through the door.

"I'm worried," my dad says, always a bit behind current events.

"Maybe it's Sankresh's wedding coming up," my mom says.

"Did you ever detect any problems between Diane and Sankresh?"

My mom's cheerful demeanor fades, and she gets serious, diplomatic almost. "No couple is perfect." I can sense the slight pain in her voice. I wonder if my parents knew it before they reserved a church.

"Why didn't you try to stop them?" I ask, anger rising toward my parents. Did they know this was going to happen? Why didn't I?

"We couldn't," my mom says.

"Don't worry. She'll get back on that saddle," my dad says, totally unaware of how girls think.

"What if she doesn't?" my mom asks. "What if she stays like this?"

"Single?" I ask. "I'd rather her be single and happy than married and miserable."

"But she's not happy."

The door bursts open, and Diane whooshes out in a wrinkled outfit. "You can stop talking about me. I'm ready."

* * *

Students and parents crowd the gym floor, looking for friends and seats. I gave my parents strict instructions where to sit so they'd have a clear view of me. Fingers crossed they remember.

Nerves and adrenaline inject an extra skip in my step. Fifth row up, Val and Ezra take a seat. I stare at her, hoping she will sense my presence, but Val won't make eye contact. She and Ezra canoodle in plain sight, their goal of proving me wrong no doubt bringing them closer together.

Huxley dumps out a shopping bag of Pixy Stix onto the locker-room benches.

"Get a boost, guys. I want 1000 percent energy levels out there," Huxley says.

Girls lunge at the sugar salvation. They rip them open and pour sugar down their throats. Some dancers rub the sugar on their gums and teeth. I will hold off. I don't want to crash before I go on stage.

"Rebecca." Huxley taps me on the shoulder. Her outfit has a blue, glittered streak across the front, letting spectators know she's the captain. Of course, most of them probably know that already. "Whatever happens tonight, I want you to know that you have surpassed all of my expectations."

I blush at the backhanded compliment. For a moment, I forget why I joined in the first place. "Is Steve ready for his video debut?"

"I don't know. We broke up." She says it quickly, getting it out and over with as fast as she can.

The statement pummels me in the gut, which is odd since I orchestrated their demise. I'm now free of Mr. Towne, free of her and Steve's reign over Ashland, free of the Break-Up Artist. But I don't feel like celebrating.

I put on my most convincing concerned-best-friend game face. "I'm so sorry, Huxley."

"He did not take too well to my family's donation to his college fund. If he wanted to be with me, he wouldn't care about the money." She shrugs. "Guys and their pride."

She doesn't flinch, like she was reciting a math problem for me. How is she so composed?

"Did you tell anyone yet?" I ask.

"They'll find out soon enough."

"Find out what?" Reagan sidles up next to us. She bounces in place.

"That the curling squad is going to have the best routine in the show!" Huxley and Reagan "woo" together, and Huxley joins her in bouncing.

Huxley stands atop the bench and whistles to get everyone's attention. "This is it, girls. You ready?"

The girls scream. I convince myself to mouth "yes."

"I can't hear you! Now I said, are you ready for SDA?"

They scream louder, piercing my eardrums, and run onto the gym floor. The crowd joins them in screaming.

I pull Huxley back to the lockers. "Are you okay? If you need to talk—"

"It's time to dance!"

I spot tiny cracks in her bubbly facade, but she patches them up. She has to.

She's the captain.

The night goes by in a blur. Girls dance in front of me, and

I applaud at some routines, but my brain has no connection to the outside world.

She will get over this, I tell myself over and over. She and Steve are not meant to be. If they were, then they wouldn't have broken up. This will all pass, and I will never have to do anything like this again. That's what I keep repeating to myself, anyway.

Before our number, the curling video of Steve and Huxley plays for everyone. Ezra edited it masterfully, and I cringe when I remember that night. Steve and Huxley have impeccable comic timing and adorable rom-com-worthy chemistry. The audience has the right responses at the right parts.

I peer over at Huxley. Squad mates glance back at her for real-time reactions. She doesn't disappoint. Huxley smiles bashfully, a wide grin that only I can see is fighting to stay up. Tonight, the suspicions will start because Steve isn't here. By tomorrow, his friends will know about the break-up. They'll tell their friends and girlfriends, who will spread the word to every person they know. You don't sit on this type of gossip. By Monday morning, at least half of the school will be all caught up and spreading the word. If you didn't hear the news this weekend, then that means you aren't popular enough. Don't worry, though. The story will wind through school rapidly, trickling down to the faculty no later than sixth period. At lunch, every student will be making sideways glances at their lunch table. Who will have to switch tables? Girls will look over their shoulders during class to catch a glimpse of Huxley. If she walks by a group of kids, and they get quiet, she'll know why. And she'll have to face that at least twenty times a day. Most will blame her for the break-up; girls always receive the majority of the blame. She'll be called a slut and prude in equal amounts; she'll be called a bitch for no reason. Side rumors and completely false stories will wind through the halls. And through it all, Huxley will have to maintain that same stupid, hollow grin.

The film cuts to Steve whirling Huxley around, when he caught her by total surprise. They are exposed in this genuine, intimate moment, where this vibe, this current, makes them glow, and they radiate pure, unadulterated happiness.

And there, under the basketball hoop, in my stripper-pole tracksuit, curling broom at my side, I begin to cry.

# 35

Monday morning is exactly how I predicted. It's always a letdown when you realize your peers are as shallow and transparent as you assumed. Though who am I to talk? I have gossip dossiers on half of them.

I sulk down the science hall, ignoring the foul stench of frogs. A group of freshmen are engaged in a conversation next to the locker. Guess who it's about.

"I heard she couldn't stand to be with him because he's not rich. She offered to pay for his college."

"That's kind of sick. She was probably paying him to date her this whole time."

"Wouldn't surprise me. She pretty much turned him into her personal puppet."

"Her hand shoved firmly up his ass. What a deranged bitch."

"Will you shut the hell up?" I slam my locker and pull rank for the first time in my high-school career. "Do you honestly think you know the truth about what happened? You probably heard it fourth- or fifth-hand, since you're not popular enough to know somebody with the real scoop."

"So what really happened?"

"Like I would tell any of you."

I almost knock one of them out sliding my backpack over my shoulder.

It takes a few corridors for my body to go back into Monday-morning mode. But as soon as I get to first period, the normalcy gives way again. This time to panic.

On the classroom door hangs a picture.

Of me.

In full Break-Up Artist attire. Mask, red graduation gown, black background. There I am, for all of Ashland to see. In big, black letters under my picture is the caption "Who is the Break-Up Artist?"

Flyers hang on every door in the hall.

Every hallway is papered with the flyer. I can't take them down. That would be a dead giveaway. This can't be Mr. Towne's dirty work. I already told him about Huxley and Steve. Besides, this seems too catty for him.

I survive the first half of the day by keeping my head down, literally. My peers must believe I'm deeply saddened by Huxley and Steve, or obsessed with my shoes. I watch classmates dissect and analyze the flyer in fourth period. Ms. Hardwick studies it with some girls before the bell rings.

"I heard she was behind Huxley and Steve's break-up," she says. "She has to be. It's all too convenient."

"That's what we all thought in my last period, too," another student says.

The bell rings, and Huxley is a no-show. I thought she would come to school today, but not even she can overcome this gossip with grace and dignity. Her social stock is in free fall.

I open my copy of *Beowulf* wide so that it covers my face. Did Bari plan to put up these posters to coincide with Huxley and Steve's break-up, or is this just the mother of all coincidences? I bank on my classmates' collective obliviousness. They would never suspect me. The girl who's just *there* doesn't do stuff like this. Most Ashland news items are like food poisoning: a vicious first twenty-four hours, and then they're gone. I just need to make it through today and pray for a pregnant teen to waltz through the doors tomorrow.

Come lunchtime, I plan to grab food and race up to the library. Huxley tugs at my arm while I walk to the cafeteria.

"Hey, wait up." No tears stain her face, but it's lacking its usual glow. She seems exhausted.

"You're here."

"I came in late. I figured I had a good enough excuse."

"How are you doing?"

"I'm fine."

Neither of us believes it. I cock my eyebrows at her.

"I feel awful."

Students stare at us as they enter lunch, and I want to hiss at them.

"I feel like I lost a part of myself," she says quietly but firmly, knowing she can't let herself give the audience a show.

"It'll get better."

"I don't think it will," she says. She glances at her and Steve's homecoming picture in the trophy case. Blocking her view is another flyer taped to the glass. She skims the contents, soaking in the picture and caption.

She looks back at me.

I can see her brain working. My spine tightens, and I can't move.

She laughs, almost on the verge of a giggle.

"What's so funny?" I ask.

"Some people need to get a life." I'm unsure if she's referring to the Break-Up Artist or the ones searching for her. But Huxley's already moved on. "Do you want to eat lunch in my car today? We can listen to the radio."

"That sounds perfect."

But she doesn't listen to me. Her eyes wander back to the flyer. She rips it off the glass and holds it millimeters from her face.

"Golden slippers," she says, showing me. "See there? The black sheet is covering a mirror, but she didn't cover the bottom. You can make out the golden slippers in the reflection. Those are the exact same ones that we got from Frances Glory."

Huxley jerks her head up.

It just clicked.

She stares at me in confusion, in shock. "Rebecca?"

"I'm so sorry." It's all I can say. I've lied to her enough. I can't do it anymore.

"Is this...? But you..."

"Yes...to everything."

"You...break up couples?" Her eyes go wide. More clicking. "Were Steve and I...?" The flyer rustles in her shaking hands.

I nod yes. I should've known this day would come. I just assumed I'd be mad that I got caught, not mad at myself.

"It was before we became friends again. And then I couldn't get out of it...." I stop myself. It's just excuses.

"Why would you do this? Why do you want to break people up? That's sick. You're sick."

My reasons might seem flimsy now, in the face of an upset victim, but they were reasons. "You don't know what it's like being single in this school."

"This has always been your M.O. I remember how bent out of shape you got when I began dating Steve."

"Shut up, Huxley." I'm tired of getting talked down to by people who think they know better. "I didn't care that you had a boyfriend. You ditched me and then treated me like crap."

"And I apologized! I even gave you a makeover. This is how you repay me?" She holds up the flyer. Like vultures, a crowd gathers around us, but I can't contain myself. These words have been waiting to come out for years.

"It was business. I became the Break-Up Artist because of people like you. Girls who treat other girls like they have some inoperable brain tumor just because they're single."

"You made yourself feel that way," she says. And maybe she's right on some level, but I'm not giving her any credit here. Huxley crumples up the flyer and throws it at my feet. "I'm going to get Steve back. I love him."

"What's going on?" Bari steps forward from the crowd.

Huxley holds the flyer next to my face for all to see. "I found the Break-Up Artist."

Now that I'm in the center, I notice that crowds don't gasp or buzz among each other at each development. They don't say anything at all, like they're watching a really good movie. (Movies...Ezra...ick.) They are riveted and won't even blink.

"You're the Break-Up Artist?" Bari steps forward from the crowd. Her blond roots are coming in, pushing the brown hair to her shoulders.

"Guilty," Huxley says.

"I'm sorry." I'm barely audible.

"No, you're sorry you got caught," Bari says. "How many couples have you destroyed? And for what, to make you feel better about being some pale, flat-chested, single bitch?" She points at the balled-up paper in her hand. "You are so messed up." She pushes me against the trophy case. Her petite body is a firecracker dangerously close to being ignited.

Calista hangs back in the crowd, avoiding eye contact with me.

"How dare you come between Derek and me. What did we ever do to you?" Bari asks.

"Why don't you ask your friend?" I say, my eyes darting to her former best friend. "I'm *hired* to break up couples." Bari whips her head around at Calista, whose head turns the color of Craisins. It's bad business to rat out my clients, but she started it.

"What are you talking about?" Bari says inches from my face.

"Was being with Derek really worth it? Did you even like being a brunette?"

I can smell the sweat off her, how badly she wants to lunge at me, and I am terrified. I can do catty and underhanded fighting, just nothing involving my fists.

"It's better than what you are," she says.

My heart speeds up, about to leap out of my body. Fear swallows me whole.

"Leave her alone!"

Val pushes Bari off me. She shields me from her and the rest of school. Her swishing blond hair flicks me in the face, but I'll take that over Bari's fist any day.

"She's not the Break-Up Artist. So stop the witch hunt," Val says.

"She already confessed," Bari says. "Some friend you got there."

Val turns around, and I have to watch her get her spirit crushed yet again. "Becca?"

I don't say anything. What can I say except the truth, and that won't help.

"I think this is a big misunderstanding. She's my friend. She wouldn't do this." Val pleads my case to the school, but it's useless. What defense do I have? I wanted to help people; but really I wanted to help them get revenge, help make others as unhappy as they were.

"Are you sure about that?" Huxley asks her.

"Yes, I'm sure!" Val says with absolute conviction.

"Why don't you ask her what she's been doing with Ezra?"

Every kid in the hall gawks at me, mesmerized. I am an overturned car on the highway, and they are crossing their fingers for a gas leak and explosion.

Val turns to me. She hesitates a moment before asking. "What is she talking about?"

I shut my eyes.

"Becca, what is she talking about?"

"It seems Rebecca got awfully close to your boyfriend. A little too close."

Val's eyes go wide with hurt and horror, and I can't take how defenseless she looks.

"Wow, you're a backstabber *and* a home wrecker!" Bari says. "Have you killed any orphans lately?"

I squeeze my eyelids as tightly as I can.

"Rebecca, I am disgusted with you on so many levels. How many innocent relationships have you ruined just to make yourself feel better?"

"I hate you," Val says. Her voice cracks with a sob.

I open my eyes. Flecks of white fill my vision. I'm squeezed against the trophy case, my personal space a distant memory.

"What's going on here?" Ms. Hardwick pushes through students. Bari turns her way, and that's my cue.

I free myself from her manicured clutches and race down the hall, ignoring the teacher calling my name. Tears fly off my face. I charge through the front doors to the parking lot, get in my car and drive off.

# 36

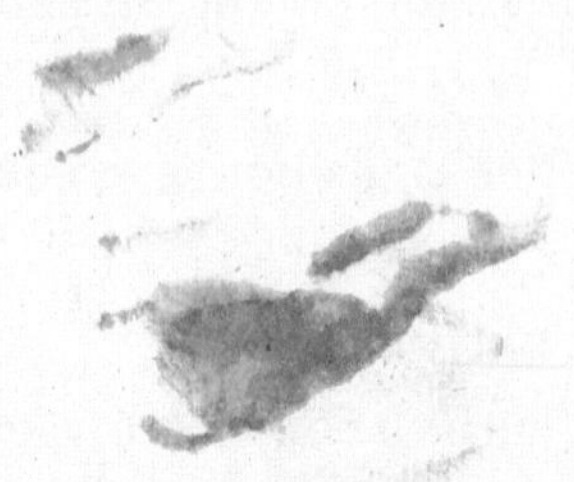

For the next two days, I stay home from school. On day one, I convince my mom that I have a bad cold. That night, I call Val's house and practically beg her mom to put Val on. To my surprise, Val doesn't hang up, and it takes me a few seconds to start talking.

"Hello?"

"Hi," I say back, completing the most awkward greeting in the known universe. Val stays quiet. I have to lead this. I started it.

"I'm sorry," I say.

"Sorry because you kissed Ezra?" I knew this wasn't going to be easy.

"Sorry because I lost my best friend." Knowing that it's come to this, that it's come to me saying that, straining to salvage this friendship or risk losing Val forever, causes me to tear up.

"We're still together. Not even you throwing yourself at him could break us apart."

"What? Throwing myself at him?" True, I kissed him first. But what about the notes, the freaking pebbles at my window? Apparently, Ezra has been teaching a class in revisionist history. "It's not like that, Val. I can explain."

"I'll pass," she says, so cold, like a cult member. "Some friend you are."

She's gone full-on zombie.

"Ezra's taking me on a Starlight Cruise Friday night to celebrate our relationship renaissance. We're stronger than ev—"

I hang up.

By day two, after I've received enough vicious emails and phone calls from my classmates, my mom doesn't put up a fight and tells the school that I have strep throat. In exchange for my truancy, I spill the details about being the Break-Up Artist. I know my mom must want to yell at me for doing something so mean and then demand I see a shrink for some heavy psychoanalysis, but to her credit, she doesn't interrupt me. She listens attentively, her hands cupped on her lap. She hides her disappointment and withholds her judgment. That makes me talk more, about Ezra and Val. No gasps from her. I wish I had known my mom would be such a good listener. I would have come to her with other issues instead of Diane.

On day three, I sit at the breakfast nook eating cereal at 2:00 p.m. Some milk dribbles off the spoon onto my sweatshirt, but I don't bother wiping it off. My mom comes out of her alteration studio and massages her hands. They are cramped from a long day of sewing, from day after day of dealing with demanding customers. All so she can provide me with a pleasant, comfortable life, one which I have just destroyed. I'm daughter of the year.

"I think you should go back to school on Monday," she says.

My stomach clenches when I think of school. Huxley's face. Bari's face. I keep picturing them glaring, ready to pounce. Val. I can't even imagine her face.

"I know you're scared, but you can't stay home forever."

"You could homeschool me."

My mom sweeps crumbs off the counter into her palm, then brushes them into the sink.

"I really appreciate your opening up to me about everything that happened, sweetheart. I think I've done a good job of listening impartially, but now I want to discuss why you found the need to be this Break-Up Artist person."

I sink my spoon into the cereal bowl, drowning it in milk. I knew this moment would come, but it's useless. She doesn't understand why. She can't understand because she's in the type of relationship that I would dissolve. She's Val in thirty years. "It's complicated," I tell her.

"I remember how stressful it was for me in high school. I was one of the last in my group of friends to start dating—"

"Mom, it's not about that!" Of course, it always has to come back to being single. That's the only logical explanation why girls do anything, right?

My mom slips her hand over mine and looks me in the eye. "I never had the best luck in the guy department."

"Mom, stop."

"But when I met your dad, I knew in an instant why it was never meant to be with any of those other losers."

"No! You didn't! You settled. Don't feed me this image of a fairy-tale courtship. You were single, Dad was single, you came from similar backgrounds, you wanted to have kids and live in suburbia. The end. It was never about love."

Mom stiffens up. She tries to take it in stride, but I can tell I just deeply offended the woman who gave me room and board inside her for nine months. "You don't think your father and I love each other?"

It sounds different, more serious, when she phrases it like that. "I know you guys don't hate each other."

"But you don't think your father and I love each other?" She's in disbelief, which confuses me. Have they seen how they act around each other?

"You never kiss. Dad will kiss you on the forehead once in a while, but that's it." I cringe, thinking about my parents kissing on the mouth, kissing like couples do at school. Yuck!

"When we were dating, our friends used to call us the romantics."

"Seriously? Now it's like you're siblings."

"Your father and I love each other very much. It's just that after twenty-six years of marriage, it becomes a different kind of love." My mom pulls a rag from the sink and wipes down the rest of the counter. She's always working to make things look nice, from bridal gowns to tabletops.

"You two didn't even go out for your anniversary."

"We've done the lavish anniversary events many times over. They become boring, and expensive. If your father wanted to, he could've taken me out to the nicest restaurant in Manhattan and then to a show. But we had both worked long hours that day. I know how much your father loves any show about war. And he knows that Brunello's is my favorite restaurant that does takeout. So we relaxed on the couch eating chicken cutlet and learning about Iran–Contra, and it was a great anniversary. I know it's hard to understand now. I'm sure couples at your school act much...differently. But that's what love is."

"It sounds boring."

"Welcome to real life. After the first dates and romantic gestures peter out, because they all will eventually, you have to be left with a person you still want to look at every day."

"And Dad?"

"I still do." She wipes the milk off my sweatshirt.

Maybe she was right. I think back to all those boring moments between my parents, and how they know every little detail about each other without even thinking. They weren't acting like anything. They don't need to prove to the world that they're in love with PDA and giant stuffed animals.

"Did you see the news?" She pulls the daily paper from the counter. "Steve Overland got a full scholarship to Chandler University. He even had a press conference with the coach there."

She shows me the article. I spit cereal all over the table. I recognize the coach. How could I not recognize the baby face and sparkly blue eyes? Chills crawl up my arm. Everything about him is utterly familiar, except for his name.

I clench the phone in my hand and shut my door.

“Hello, Chandler University Athletics,” the secretary says.

“Coach Latham please.”

“Latham here,” he says into the phone.

“Hello, Mr. Towne.” I try to sound ominous, but he laughs.

“Great job, Ms. Williamson,” he says.

“You’re not Steve’s uncle, are you?”

“You got me.”

“Steve’s family never had a problem with Huxley. You just wanted her out of the way so Steve would play football for your second-rate school.” I shake my head, shocked at my stupidity.

“Come this fall, we won’t be second-rate anymore.”

“You lied to me.”

“You’re giving me a morals lesson? You break up couples for money.”

“I thought I was helping his family.” I’m not some mercenary, splitting up couples no matter what. I always needed a compelling reason to take on a client. But is any reason really good enough?

“I’m sure you were. They didn’t want their son to languish at some nothing school because of some controlling girlfriend.”

“Better than some conniving coach!” My voice bounces off the walls. Nausea overwhelms me. I need to sit down.

“I told you what you needed to know to get the job done.

You should see Steve. I've never seen a kid so happy. You did the right thing."

I think of Huxley, who I doubt is as happy. And for what? So Coach Latham can get a nice Christmas bonus? "He was already happy with his girlfriend."

"Are you sure about that? When I spoke to him at the press conference, that was not the case. If they were really in love—" he laughs at the thought "—they would still be together."

I don't think any relationship could withstand the lies and manipulation I used to break them up. What would've happened if I hadn't interfered? What would have happened to all the other couples?

"I'm going to tell," I say.

"Who's going to believe you? You've been talking to Mr. Towne."

"I can track your IP address, too."

"I wouldn't tell anyone about our agreement if I were you." He lowers his voice, and a chill passes through the phone into my body. That wasn't some friendly advice. "I think it would mostly hurt you. Nobody will appreciate the sick after-school job you have going on."

"They already know."

"The damage has already been done, then," he says. "Trust me. You don't want this story leaving your school and becoming actual news. Maybe if you're lucky, you'll get me fired. But my coaching record, while not stellar, is still good. Another college will hire me once this blows over. The first win of the season will make this story ancient history. But you..."

I swallow hard and clutch the phone closer to my ear.

"This will follow you around forever. In college admissions, in job interviews, in relationships, in perpetuity. Everywhere. Do you want it to be the first thing people learn about you? Are you ready to be the Break-Up Artist for the rest of your life?"

I try to be strong and cold, but tears are running down my face. I want to scream at him that he is so wrong, that I can't wait to expose him for the scum he is. But sadly, he's right.

"Forget it, Becca. It's high school."

# 37

After three days of sleeping in, I am up for no reason by seven-thirty on a Saturday morning. I check Facebook and take a good gander at what people are saying about me. My classmates have a very limited vocabulary, but they know how to use it. I see an update from Aimee. She posted a picture of herself holding an infant boy, her new son. He's so peaceful, and smaller than a watermelon. I've never had the baby gene, but marveling at his big eyes and teeny fingers instantly makes me happier. I wonder if I'll ever have a friend who I'll know from singledom through motherhood. Maybe Val was supposed to be that friend.

That's not something you just throw away.

I barge into Diane's room. She's flopped on her bed like a corpse.

"Wake up." I slap her legs under the blankets.

"What? Becca, what's wrong?"

"We're going on a road trip."

"Where?"

"I can't tell you yet. Get dressed. And put on something nice."

"I'm going to pass." She falls back into bed.

I yank the blanket and top sheet off. She struggles to hold on to them, but I have better leverage.

"Be downstairs in half an hour."

"No!"

"Diane, trust me on this one." I drag her blankets out with me.

I drive past the endless strip malls and actual malls of Route 4. Only a handful of cars dot the road. Who in their right mind would be driving at eight-thirty in the morning besides us? Once we near the George Washington Bridge, she asks again where we're going.

I turn to her, a sly smile on my lips. "We're going to visit Henry Walter."

"Who?"

"Aimee's new son."

Diane perks up from her stupor. "She gave birth already?" She seems sad that I knew before her, but she reaps what she sows. "She's probably sleeping."

"That baby only sleeps in two-hour increments. I'm sure she's up."

"Becca, please turn around."

"Why?"

"Because I don't want to go."

Somehow, we hit traffic. At eight-thirty on a Saturday. Cars cram into E-ZPass lanes. We crawl past a shady motel that's probably been home to millions of extramarital affairs. Frustration builds within me, ready to shoot out at Diane. I keep the picture of Henry Walter in my head to stay centered.

"You're jealous. And angry."

"Excuse me?" Diane says.

"I'm your sister. If you can't admit that to me, then whom can you say it to? That's why you've cut off contact with your friends."

"I haven't cut off contact with them. That sounds so harsh."

"But it's the truth."

"It's not fair," Diane says, and I'm glad she won't fight me on this conversation. The words come easily for her. I wonder how long she's been wanting to say them. "If it wasn't for me, they wouldn't have met their husbands. I almost had that."

"But you don't." I have to be blunt. She has to take this needle. "You have to move on, or else you're never going to have a chance at it in the future."

Diane throws herself back in her seat and lets out a huge sigh. "Will this be my legacy? Diane Williamson, the girl who got dumped on her wedding day. Oh, and she also cured cancer. But more importantly, she got dumped on her wedding day."

"It will only be your legacy if you let it. You're frozen in time. What happened sucks, but you can't let it define you."

"When did you get so mature?"

"Getting ostracized from your entire school will do that to a person." I laugh it off. That stuff doesn't even seem important anymore. The cars unclog, and the steel archway of the GW Bridge towers in front of me.

"So why are you dragging me to see this baby?"

"Because you're lucky. Despite everything, you have three awesome people who still want to be your friend. Barely." I think of Val, and how my life feels empty now. I didn't realize it was full before. "You're going to have to do a shitload of apologizing, but they still love you deep down. You really don't want to give that up. Not over what happened with some stupid guy."

Diane gently touches my shoulder. "Thank you." Then she proceeds to wipe her nose on my sleeve.

When we get to Aimee and Bill's apartment, Diane does a shitload of apologizing. They call up Marian and Erin and that gives way to tears all around. They won't get back to full-strength maxipad friendship overnight, but some of the vibrancy that I remember from Diane returns. It's possible to see the girl who brought together three married couples lurking under the current Diane.

"You want to hold the baby, Two-point-oh?" Aimee asks me.

I get nervous, knowing I'm making myself responsible for a human being, but this isn't an offer a normal person would turn down. So I hold out my arms. "So is Henry technically Three-point-oh?"

"Three-point-oh. I like that," Diane says.

"Actually, wait a second," Bill says. He runs over and pulls out a bottle of mini hand sanitizer. "For the baby, Becca."

I squirt out some sanitizer and wipe it on my hands. I

stare at the bottle a few seconds more than anyone needs to look at one. The wheels have begun turning, and I know I must make things right. "Is something wrong?" Aimee asks.

"No." She hands over Henry, and he's even more precious in person. I don't know the kid, but I'm already in love.

"How are you doing?" Diane asks.

"So far, so good," I say. "Hey, can we stop at CVS on the way home? I have a plan."

"Sure. For what?"

"For getting Steve and Huxley back together."

# 38

I'm at school super early. Thankfully, only the janitor's here to judge me. I use my V56 key to get into Steve's locker, then Huxley's. Once I finish, I hold the key over a trash can, contemplating its fate. In the end, I keep it for now. For the memories.

And...you never know.

My next stop is our drama department's prop room, and I shiver in disgust knowing that this is Ezra's turf. I remember a couple I broke up last year, a pair of actors. All I had to do was go online and post bad reviews for one and glowing reviews for the other, and jealousy and histrionics took care of the rest. I yank a quaint wicker bench from a pile of random objects, perfect for an old lady's garden, and tug it back to our brand-new TV studio. The bindings for half of my textbooks are falling off, but at least Ashland has a TV camera that can zoom in.

I set up the bench in position, facing the shiny new camera. I pull up a side table, where I place a CD player and two cans of Coke that I'm hoping won't get warm and flat by this afternoon. I step back from my design and take in the odd contrast of the furniture against the green-screen wall. I've never been more proud of a scheme.

I wait in the control room during lunch, checking the clock obsessively, thinking that I may have the power to move the hands with my mind. But I don't. So I wait some more.

At noon on the dot, Steve peeks his head into the studio. No strolling in for him. I crouch down behind the control panel stuffed with buttons and levers. He checks out the bench, walking around it, really inspecting it. *It's just a bench,* I want to tell him. He realizes it's not electrified or rigged to explode, and sits down. He presses Play on the CD player, per the note. The slow strings of "Bittersweet Symphony" seep out from the speakers.

"Hey," Huxley calls from the entrance.

My breathing quickens, and I wonder if he feels the same. They are a beautiful couple to behold. Some people just fit right.

Steve stands up to greet her. "Hi."

"This is some setup," she says as she surveys the scene.

"I know."

"I forgot that you knew my locker combination."

"And you remember mine," he says.

She approaches the bench, but doesn't sit down. They both take a moment to look at the details. The Coke cans, the dark blue mood lighting.

"How long did it take you to do this?" he asks her.

"Me? Didn't you do this?"

"Nope."

"You didn't slip a bottle of mouthwash and a note to come here at noon into my locker?" she asks. She pulls both from her pocket.

He does the same thing. "You mean this wasn't you?"

They look around the TV studio. "Hello? If someone's here, you better come out," Steve yells to the room.

I clamp my hand over my mouth. I should've known there would be suspicion. I hear their footsteps getting closer to the control room. I find a cardboard box under the control panel and position it in front of me. Steve throws open the door.

"If someone's here, this is kind of weird."

*Just go with it,* I want to tell him. *You'll thank me later.*

He creeps into the room, right up to the control panel. I can smell the rubber on his shoes.

"Is this some kind of sick joke?" he says to no one, although technically, I guess he's talking to me.

"Steve," Huxley says. "Come over here."

He returns to the studio, and I go back to my spying position. "Why is there a bench here?"

"Steve." Huxley laughs softly. She pulls the bottle of mouthwash and note from her pocket. Steve does the same thing.

"The bench, the mouthwash. 'Bittersweet Symphony,'" she says.

His eyes widen in recognition. "It's like Travis Weber's party."

"Our first kiss."

"I was so nervous."

"I was more nervous. My teeth were chattering."

"I thought you were cold. So I gave you my jacket." Steve finds the jacket I carefully left across the bench and covers Huxley's shoulders.

"Who would go through all this trouble?" she asks. She sits on the bench. Their knees touch.

"Someone who wants to see us back together."

"Would you fall into that category?"

Steve shifts his knees away from her, breaking the moment. "Hux, why did you try to pay my tuition for Vermilion? Who does that?"

I see her tense, her guard back up. "Someone who cares about you. I was trying to help."

"Do you know how embarrassing that was? I know my family isn't as rich as yours, but—"

"You never complained before when you've come on family vacations and received Christmas gifts."

"This is different."

"Why?"

"Because I want to go to Chandler!" he blurts out. "I want to play football. I love playing football."

Huxley takes a deep breath and looks up at the mood lighting. "I know."

"But I also love you."

Their eyes are now locked on each other and having a separate conversation. Their bodies get closer, as if they're on conveyor belts, en route to the proper, inevitable destination. It's amazing how quickly they slip back into the groove. Maybe some couples can't be broken, no matter how hard anyone tries.

"I miss you," she says without her trademark Huxley poise. "You know, I think this is the first time we've ever really talked about this."

"I like it," he says. His strokes her hair behind her shoulder, and my heart does one of those gymnastics backflips. For the first time, I believe in Huxley and Steve.

"So what happens now?" Huxley asks. "What do we do?"

"We'll figure it out."

And then he leans in and kisses her.

I put my hand on the one switch I know how to use. It's a lever that can broadcast the image recording on the shiny new camera into the shiny new TVs around school. Proof that Huxley and Steve are indomitable. Proof that I'm not a completely horrible person.

But I take my hand away, and while they're making out, I sneak into the hall unnoticed. Even the number-one couple in school deserves some privacy.

# 39

The next day in Ms. Hardwick's class, a group of girls, including Ms. Hardwick, gather around Huxley's desk. They wouldn't be callous enough to be talking about me, right? Ms. Hardwick's still a teacher. I keep my nose in my textbook and eavesdrop.

"It was so sweet," Huxley says. "He left a note in my locker saying 'Let's work things out. Meet me in the TV studio at lunch.' And when I got there, he had re-created the scene of our first kiss. And I fell in love with him all over again."

The girls *aww*; some lean their heads on each other's shoulders. I remember wanting to bang my head into my desk after hearing and seeing all of Huxley's and Steve's sweeping fauxmantic gestures before. And now I created one. Life has a weird sense of humor.

"So is Steve still going to Chandler?" Ms. Hardwick asks.

"He is," Huxley says. The murmuring between girls doesn't faze Huxley one bit. "We're going to try the long-distance thing and see how it goes. Steve is an amazing athlete, and he needs to be on the field."

"Texas isn't that far," some girl says. "If any couple can make it, it's you two."

"We'll have to see. If we're meant to be together, then we will be together," Huxley says. Calmness coats her voice; she's just telling it like it is. "But I think we'll make it."

"Time to start class," Ms. Hardwick says. "Everyone back to your seats."

The crowd disperses, and I get a direct view of Huxley. I try to make eye contact with her. She doesn't look my way. She keeps her focus on Ms. Hardwick. I can't tell if it's a guise or her true feelings. Maybe she thinks our friendship was really a fake this whole time. I guess from her perspective, that's how it seems. I hope someday after graduation, when the chains of Ashland's social structure are lifted, when she and Steve are planning their immaculate wedding, we can meet up for coffee and laugh about this.

Until then, I turn around before I'm caught openly staring.

I face a cafeteria chock-full of sideways glances and cupped whispers. I've never been on the other side of it, the subject of the gossip, and I feel like a circus performer in front of a perpetually bored audience. They want more. They want the story to keep moving, to get worse. I hope for my sake that it doesn't.

I grip my tray, which is merely a prop. Past the scowls and stares and spotlight, I see one open chair.

"Is it okay if I sit here?"

Fred stares at me, and I feel myself shriveling up. But then he breaks into a smile, and I've never been so happy to see those straight white teeth. He removes his stack of comic books from the seat.

"Thanks," I say.

"We'll bill you at the end of the week," Fred says.

It's nice to be able to joke with somebody.

"I'm so sorry, about what I said to you. You were just trying to help."

"Hey, I'm obsessed with comics and I have little-to-no muscle mass. I'm used to insults. Besides, I figured you were in an in-too-deep situation, and I was right."

The first trace of my appetite returns. There are some decent people at this school.

"It'll get better," Fred says. "Some girl will get alcohol poisoning at the prom, and you'll be a distant memory."

"A girl can dream."

I officially hate this. Why can't people move on? I don't want to suffer through hate stares the rest of my high-school career. I hope they reach a breaking point before I do.

Fred's attention catches on something behind me. I turn to see Derek trudging through the double doors looking chewed up and spat out. He's scratching his five-o'clock shadow, and his clothes desperately need to be ironed. I have to look away. He's destroyed, and I operated the bulldozer.

"I did that," I say in disgust.

"No, you didn't."

"You're joking, right?"

"Nope," Fred says. "It turns out Derek didn't get into Princeton early decision in December. He got wait-listed, and his official rejection came while you were out." Fred finishes off his second slice of pepperoni pizza. "I guess they only let one kid in per high school. So, good for Bethann."

It really shouldn't, but watching Derek's misery gives me the warm and fuzzies.

"I'm still an awful person."

"Kinda," Fred says.

I guess I was asking for that.

"But not really," he finishes. He gulps down the rest of his Sprite.

"I am. I break up innocent couples."

"Why aren't Bari and Derek back together? They know you broke them up. They know it was all lies. But they're not dating."

"Because... I don't know." He has a good point. Derek shuffles past Bari's table without any acknowledgment of his ex-girlfriend. Bari doesn't even pretend to eat. She spins the straw inside her Diet Coke, matching Derek's gloominess sigh for sigh. Why aren't they sitting together? A girl like Bari savors moments like this, when she can be a support system for her former boyfriend.

"If they really were in love, then why didn't they patch things up? Huxley and Steve did."

Ashland's golden couple is back to finishing each other's sentences and meals. It's weird watching their table now knowing what actually goes on there, which is nothing spectacular. The same conversations and dull jokes.

And now that I think about it, my break-up methods weren't that genius. If these couples were meant to be together, then their relationships wouldn't have crumbled because of a flimsy text message or faked wedding binder.

I feel a weight lift off my shoulders. I don't consider myself the most awful person at Ashland anymore. I didn't destroy young love; I just sped up the inevitable.

But then I glance a few tables over at Calista, sitting with some girls but uninterested in what they're saying. She seems just as miserable as Bari.

"You're not all bad," Fred says.

I'm not all good either.

"Thanks." I smile for the first time today. My cheeks are sore from the constant stoicism.

"You're actually kind of cool." Fred scratches his eyebrow. "And I was thinking, maybe we could hang out, outside of school."

My reverie stops. I suddenly get nervous. This conversation just took a severe left turn, and it's flooding my mind with a million scenarios.

"Like a date?"

"That's one interpretation." Fred's cheeks bunch up when he grins. His eyes gleam in the fluorescent light.

"With me?"

He nods yes.

"Okay." I play it cool even though my arms and fingers tingle like I slept on them all night. I stand up. "I'm going to get some chips. I'm feeling hungry again."

Fred's grin follows me all the way to the cashier line. Melinda Jankowski taps me on the shoulder, engaging me in conversation for the first time since middle school.

"Thank you," she whispers to me.

"For what?"

"You broke up my friend Katie's relationship last year. I

wondered what made Charles dump her so abruptly. Now I know."

I cringe at the memory of impersonating Katie Derrickson on a blog about dealing with your boyfriend's impotency. Not one of my classiest moves, but it did the trick.

"You're welcome?" I say, unaware I had fans.

"He was such a jerk. He was telling Katie lies about us so she would stop being our friend. What a toxic pig. We were all beyond happy when they broke up," Melinda says. "So thank you, seriously."

I step up to the cashier and unfurl the two dollars in my fist.

"Actually, I got it." Melinda reaches across me and hands the cashier money.

"Thanks," I say, dumbstruck. The cashier has to remind me to take my food. "I wish everyone felt like this."

"Yeah, that's not going to happen," Melinda says. She pays for her meal. We walk back into the main room together. "But you do have a few supporters."

But there's one supporter I'm still missing, the one who's always supported me. I walk back into the expanse of the cafeteria. Val and Ezra are tucked in their corner table. They've probably forgotten I exist. She catches me gawking, and I scurry back to my nerds. Are we destined to be the next Bari and Calista? Is this how it ends?

I throw my chips on the table. Appetite lost.

No.

A feeling of determination and hope surges through me.

No.

Some relationships were made to be broken, but not all.

"What is it?" Fred asks.

I take out my Plumful lipstick and apply a fresh coat over my lips. "I have one last couple I need to destroy."

# 40

I'm surprised Starlight Cruises hasn't been sued for false advertising. This is the Hudson River, the border between New York City and New Jersey. There is no starlight. But I suppose Smog-Refracting-Light Cruises doesn't have the same ring.

Passengers board the dinner cruise. It's mostly sweet old couples who still wear suits and dresses for a night out. I park on the street and avoid the line of cars waiting for valet. I don't have time, and I can park my own car for free, thank you very much. Also, I need some walking time to psych myself up. I was doing faux Lamaze breathing on the car ride over.

Luckily, I'm not alone. My accomplices park behind me, and the three of us stroll up to the loading dock. I've never performed a scheme like this. I've never been out in the open. It's always letters and texts and pictures and whisper campaigns. But this time, it has to be me.

Val sits alone on a bench checking her phone, the cruise ship behind her making her look minuscule. She has on a simple black dress—no blazer tonight. She stands up as soon as she sees us.

"Becca? What are you doing here?" Val asks.

I'm flanked by Monica and Isabelle, Ezra's exes, the girls he suddenly decided to call it quits with one day.

"Mind if we join you?" I ask.

"Ezra's parking. He'll be here any minute." She says it like a warning, but I know Ezra can't hurt me. I'm not the one he's hurting.

Val holds her purse in front of her, as if shielding herself from us. I've never seen her so rigid, so prepared for a fight. I summon my courage and move on. "I'm quitting the breakup business, almost."

"Almost?"

"Before I retire, there's one couple I want to try to break up. You and Ezra."

"Goodbye, Becca," Val says sternly, but underneath, I see the real Val—my best friend—trying to climb out.

"Hear her out," Monica says. "Trust me. I wish I'd had a friend who'd done the same for me."

"Listen," Val says to me. "He told me what happened with you guys was a stupid mistake. He said his world wasn't in the same vicinity—"

"—of complete because he couldn't share it with you," Isabelle says. "Yeah, that one's from *Jerry Maguire.*"

"It's all just one big movie for him. Until one day the movie ends and suddenly the lights come up," Monica says. "Believe me. If you were given no warning, if everything seemed perfect until one day it was over, on to the next, you would've doused him in Diet Sprite, too."

"Becca wanted us to warn you, Val." Isabelle tries to put a comforting hand on her, but Val steps back.

She can't do stone-faced for too long, though. Her face is on the verge of crumbling into tears. And now I feel like an even worse friend. She's just trying to enjoy her evening. "I'm sorry, Val."

"Why are you doing this?" she squeaks out.

"Because if you get on that boat with Ezra, you're going to regret it. Maybe not today, or this week, but eventually, you'll see that this isn't it."

"Isn't what?"

"Love."

Val dabs at a tear before she lets it fall. "Becca Williamson talking about love?"

"It must be the apocalypse," I say. "It's like handbags. You would never buy a knockoff. Even if nobody could tell the difference. You would only get the real thing."

"Of course."

"So why aren't *you* holding out for the real thing?" I heave in and out. I feel like I'm fighting for my life, and in a way, I guess I am. "Because you deserve it."

Val sits down, her face frozen in solemnity. For the first time in our friendship, I can't read her expression.

I keep talking: "People always spout those ridiculous sayings about love. 'You can't control love' or 'they're meant to be.' I think that can also apply to friends." I dab at my eyes, but that doesn't stop the tears. "I don't know why or how you became my best friend, but I can't imagine anyone else in your place. And even if you never want to talk to me again, I want you to be happy above all."

The splashing of the water against the dock fills our silence. I think about all the eight million times Val and I have cracked up over the most random things, and how I don't want the last time we talk to be a downer like this.

"What's going on?" Ezra stands behind us in a blazer and gelled hair. Yes, he's still cute, objectively speaking. But there are lots of cute guys out there, and I have to hope that most of them aren't scumbags.

"Hey there, ex-lover," Monica says. "We were just having a chat with Val."

"About handbags," Isabelle says.

"If you'll excuse us, ladies," he says, voice cracking. I guess dumping girls via email leaves you ill-prepared for face-to-face confrontation. He takes Val's hand. "We have a date."

"Five minutes to departure! Last call for boarding!" a Starlight employee yells over a loudspeaker. Couples make their way aboard.

I gesture to the cruise ship, with Chinese lanterns strung around the deck and a pianist playing classical music in the main room. "It's just dinner on a boat," I say.

"It's a great date for my girlfriend," Ezra says. He spins Val to face him. "For the girl I love."

"You love me?"

"I love you, Valerie Hurst." He rubs her hand and smiles.

It's hard not to swoon when a guy says that to you. I get a little light-headed, and it wasn't even for me. When you hear those words, it's like being picked out from the crowd. That was his secret weapon, and he fired it. So I can't blame Val when she follows him onto the boat.

I have to sit down for a minute. Isabelle and Monica console me, which is nice but not at all helpful. My body feels hollow, and I recognize the hole in my heart. I've been ditched by my best friend. Again. Maybe this time I deserved it. I'm not just losing the person. I'm losing all our memories, this whole timeline. Memories are meant to be shared. And the worst part is—

"Hey."

I look up slowly, because I know that voice.

Val stands in front of me.

"Val?" My eyes dart to the ship. Ezra runs to the back deck and waves his hands frantically.

"Val! Val, what are you doing?" he yells. He grabs a crew member and points out his girlfriend ashore, presumably to get them to return to the dock. They pull him into the dining room.

Isabelle records his meltdown on her phone. "Love it."

I'm speechless. Val glances at the ship stoically. I'm reacting enough for the both of us. The ship gets smaller as it lunges farther into the Hudson.

"Are you hungry?" she asks me. I spot the beginnings of a trademark Val smile bubbling up on her face. "My dinner plans fell through."

# EPILOGUE, I.E. THIRTY MINUTES LATER

When we get back to town, I drive us over to the Queen Elizabeth Diner. I don't know how it got its name since I doubt the queen has ever been to New Jersey. And I doubt she would eat anything on the menu. Cigarette dispensers and a revolving case of layer cakes greet us upon entrance. I'll take it over Windows on the Water or a Starlight Cruise any day of the week.

Val scoots into a booth while I head to the bathroom. Pink tiles line the bathroom floor and walls. I check my makeup in the mirror, and I see Bari exit the stall behind me. I drop my Plumful lipstick into the pink sink.

She washes her hands in the neighboring sink, shooting me the look of death. "Don't you have some lives to ruin?"

"Not anymore." I try to out passive-aggressive her, but she's good.

"Thanks to you, I'm having dinner with *my parents* on a

Friday night." She shakes off excess water. "I can't believe this is my life now."

"I'm sorry." But when I think about, I'm not. Not anymore. I can't keep letting myself be the bad guy.

"You want to know why I did it?" I ask. I don't care who hears. I've had enough public scenes of humiliation that it's become old hat. "I broke you guys up because I'll never forget the look on Calista's face when she came to me. She wasn't angry. She was devastated."

"Devastated?"

"You made her feel like she was nothing."

Bari softens and unclenches herself. "I did?"

I use air quotes: "'You just don't understand because you're single.'"

Bari's stone-cold demeanor shrivels away.

"Sometimes, we take friends for granted," I say.

Bari leans against the wall and sinks down into a squat. She rests her chin on her knee, just like Calista. I exhale quietly.

"Call her," I tell Bari. "She misses her friend."

"She does? She told you?"

"Yes." What's one more lie?

"I didn't even like Derek that much. He was so pompous and controlling," Bari says.

He wasn't that into you either, I want to say.

"He's not like Jay," she says.

"Jay who?" I ask. I pick up my lipstick and reapply. (Don't give me that look. It fell unopened into the sink, and I wiped off the tube.)

"Wolpert. He's so hot. But I don't think he likes me like that."

Jay Wolpert... I rummage through my memory for some intel.

"Isn't Jay a huge Nets fan?" He sat behind me in bio class sophomore year. All he would talk about was basketball. It was like having your own personal ESPN. What little I know about sports, I eavesdropped from him.

"Yeah, he's big into sports."

"I think the NBA play-offs are coming up. You should just chat him up about that."

"I don't know. I can't just bring it up randomly."

"Guys love when girls talk about sports. It's like their fashion."

"I can't just walk up to him and start talking about point guards." Bari stands and checks out her hair in the mirror. Half is blond, the bottom half, brunette. Her head is a duplex. "I really need to get this fixed."

At least she knows it.

"He and his friends watch games at that bar and grill place the Hydrant. They always talked about it because the bartenders don't card." A plan forms in my head. Details sketch themselves out without trying. It's habit, like people who can't stop singing along to the radio. "They'll probably watch the play-offs there."

"So maybe I could watch the play-offs there, too?" Her face lights up with excitement, and I can't believe this was the girl who wanted to give me a swirlie a minute ago.

"No, no, no. That's too obvious. You need to build up to that. You need to bond with Jay about basketball first, then get him to invite you to watch with him." I gaze at both of us in the mirror, unsure what I'm getting into, but enjoying it.

"You think you can help me out?" Bari asks.

"For a hundred dollars via PayPal I can."

She shoots me a nasty look.

"Okay. Maybe this one's on the house."

* * * * *

# ACKNOWLEDGMENTS

This may be the closest I get to an Oscars acceptance speech, so I better make it count!

Thank you to Becky Vinter for believing in *The Break-Up Artist* from day one and getting it into the right hands. And thank you to my fantastic editor Annie Stone, whose excitement over Becca & co. never wavered and who took this story from good to great. Not bad for a couple of newbies.

I am so grateful that my book landed with the awesome Harlequin TEEN team. This has been a dream experience. Thank you to Kathleen Oudit and her team for designing such a striking, unique cover. And the marketing and PR team of Lisa Wray, Amy Jones, Mary Sheldon and Melissa Anthony for spreading the word. Also thank you to the sales team, who worked hard to get *The Break-Up Artist* onto shelves.

I couldn't have made it this far without the help and guidance of other writers. Thank you to my ragtag writer's group of poets, essayists and graphic novelists for whipping this book into shape and always being honest: Jen Daniels, Eric

Bjorlin, Sondra Morin, Matt Hieggelke, Jodie Aranas and Emily Johnson. Thank you to Brian Taylor for always believing in my writing, even when I didn't; to Michelle Krys and the OneFour KidLit group for connecting me with a rich network of other authors; and to the YA Valentines for the long, long email chains filled with virtual chocolate and words of semiwisdom.

I have to thank my family for always being in my corner; and Miss Julia, who's turned out to be my good-luck charm, oddly enough.

And finally, a special thank-you to Mike. You kept telling me I could do it, so I did it!

# QUESTIONS FOR DISCUSSION

1. Was Becca justified in her actions as the Break-Up Artist? She believed she was leveling the dating field at her school, but was she doing the right thing?

2. Do you think Huxley forgives Becca in the end? Does their reestablished friendship survive?

3. Out of Becca's many relationships—with friends, with her sister, with Ezra, with her mother—which one do you think developed the most in the novel, and why? Which one was the most important to her growth?

4. What if Becca truly were in love with Ezra? Would she have been justified in continuing to date him, despite Ezra's history with Val?

5. What is the author ultimately saying about the importance of trust in relationships? Does it differ in romantic relationships, friendships and family relationships?

6. Do you agree with Becca's mother when she explains that true love is simply being with "a person you still want to look at every day"? What do you think the role of romantic gestures should be in a healthy romantic relationship?

7. At the end of the novel, Becca wants to expose Coach Latham for hiring Becca to break up Steve and Huxley, but Coach Latham convinces her that going to the press would hurt her more than it would hurt him. Do you agree with this assessment? Why or why not?

8. Could your school use a Break-Up Artist? Why or why not?

9. Do you think Val should have forgiven Becca for kissing Ezra? Would you forgive your friend if he or she did the same thing?

# Q & A WITH PHILIP SIEGEL

**Q: What inspired you to write *The Break-Up Artist*?**

A: It's an idea that'd been rolling around in the back of my head for a while. I even wrote a play in college that was a much darker version of the story. One of my favorite movies is *My Best Friend's Wedding,* which I like to believe shares some DNA with *The Break-Up Artist.* I decided to revisit the idea after I watched a few friends wind up in unhealthy relationships, pairings that were a wrong fit from the start. It's a tough situation because many times, you can't be honest with them. They might ignore you or get offended or even stop talking to you. Some people are so desperate to be in a relationship that they won't listen to reason. (I had one friend who would repeatedly message me "I need a boy" and made charts about the best places to find potential boyfriends.) I learned that my situation wasn't unique; lots of people have friends stuck in bad relationships. Becca was born out of that frustration. Wouldn't it be nice if you could pay someone to break up terrible relationships?

**Q: This is your first novel. Was it hard to write it? What were some challenges of the writing process?**

A: The hardest part about writing this book was keeping Becca likable and making sure she didn't come off as a terrible person. Deep down, she's a good person and has good intentions, but she's still doing bad things. It took me a while to find that balance. I loved it, though. I get annoyed reading books where the main character never does or says a mean thing. People are gray. That's what makes characters like Becca and Huxley so fun to write. It was also difficult figuring out her break-up plans and making sure they seemed plausible. I had to keep asking myself what would make a couple break up out of the blue while keeping it realistic. That was a fun kind of difficult, like solving a puzzle.

**Q: What advice would you give to aspiring writers?**

A: If you want to get serious about writing, don't think of it as a fun hobby. Think of it as work. Many people want to be writers, and they expect it to be a blast whenever they sit at their computers. It's not. You're staring at the screen in frustration, trying to come up with the words. You're hating what you just wrote. You're dealing with a major plot hole that has no solution. It's not fun. I love having written, that sense of accomplishment, but actual writing can be tough. Don't get discouraged.

**Q: Tell us a little bit about where you're from. Was your high school like Ashland High School?**

A: There are definitely aspects of Ashland High that are based on my high school Wayne Hills in New Jersey. The

Student Dance Association is real and was a big deal at my school, for instance. There are a zillion pizza places, and they are all fantastic. I wrote what I knew. That made it easier to flesh out the setting and background details of the story. In the next book I write, I must include a scene with characters at a gas station. In NJ, it's illegal to pump your own gas, which is awesome in the wintertime.

**Q: You started out your career in L.A. How do you think the film and TV world has influenced your writing style?**

A: I studied screenwriting in college, and plot structure was ground into me. Movies and TV shows have clearly defined plots that as audiences we now expect. Inciting incident at the twenty-five-minute mark, the midpoint at the one-hour mark, et cetera. You can set your watch to it. I learned how to craft a story and keep it moving. You can have the most beautiful prose or sharpest dialogue, but if you have a boring story, nobody will read your book. That's especially true in YA. On some subconscious level, all the TV I watched growing up taught me how to write funny dialogue. I came of age during the reign of Must-See TV. Shows like *Friends, Seinfeld, Will & Grace, Frasier,* and *Just Shoot Me!* were filled with witty banter and hilarious one-liners, and I soaked it all in.

Also, working in the TV industry after college made me appreciate the hard work that comes with writing. You can't wait for inspiration to strike. Writers write. Imagine you're a writer on *CSI.* After fourteen years and 300-plus episodes, you have to keep coming up with fresh stories. You have to keep making DNA under a microscope exciting and entertaining. It doesn't matter if you have writer's block or if the muse hasn't spoken to you yet. You need to hit your deadlines. Because there must be twenty-two new episodes ready to air in a season—whether you're inspired or not.

**Q: I happen to know you're a bit of a movie buff. What are some of your all-time favorite movies?**
A: Um, how much time do you have? I'll try to narrow it down to a top ten: *American Beauty, Clueless, Election, Goodfellas, Independence Day, My Best Friend's Wedding, Pulp Fiction, Rushmore, Silence of the Lambs, Soapdish.* I'm probably leaving some out, but that's the gist. Those movies I can watch over and over and over. And in case you're wondering, yes, I do watch films from the twenty-first century, too.

**Q: Okay, let's talk a bit more about the book. Do you think if Becca hadn't been exposed as the Break-Up Artist, she would have stopped taking new jobs? Or would the lure of break-upping have been irresistible?**
A: I think she would have stopped no matter what. She saw firsthand how her schemes were affecting Huxley. She realized that the couples she broke up weren't filled with one-dimensional, evil people. They were just as swept up with romance and emotions as she was with Ezra.

**Q: Becca has learned the error of her vigilante ways. What's next for Becca? Are you writing another book about her adventures at Ashland High?**
A: I am! *The Break-Up Artist* tells a complete story, but I am

excited to revisit these characters and see how their lives have changed after everything that happened. Can Huxley and Becca reconcile? Will Diane stop spilling food on her sweatshirt? As you read in the epilogue, Becca is deciding to use her skills for good rather than evil. But we'll see if her scheming can make a smooth transition into matchmaking.